One for Sorrow
Two for Joy

One for Sorrow
Two for Joy

Clive Woodall

W F HOWES LTD

This large print edition published in 2004 by
W F Howes Ltd
Units 6/7, Victoria Mills, Fowke Street
Rothley, Leicester LE7 7PJ

1 3 5 7 9 10 8 6 4 2

First published in the United Kingdom in 2003
by Ziji Publishing

A CIP catalogue record for this book is available
from the British Library

ISBN 1 84505 703 1

Typeset by Palimpsest Book Production Limited,
Polmont, Stirlingshire
Printed and bound in Great Britain
by Antony Rowe Ltd, Chippenham, Wilts.

for Dad

BOOK ONE
ONE FOR SORROW

CHAPTER 1

Kirrick sat high in the ash tree, concealed from open view by the foliage and relatively safe. It was a glorious spring morning and he felt an almost uncontrollable urge to sing out, to celebrate the passing of a long and miserable winter. But Kirrick knew the dangers of such folly. The days of birdsong were long past. His very life depended on his silence.

Kirrick had been hunted for several months now. In the early days, the magpies weren't so persistent. They were naturally lazy and, as carrion eaters, could always find an easier meal. Things were different now, somehow. The latest hunt had been concerted, orchestrated and deadly. It had already claimed the life of Kirrick's mate, Celine. She had been worn down by the chase. Exhausted and terrified, she had finally broken cover. The end was swift and bloody. Kirrick had watched in horror, helpless, as his mate was torn apart.

Now, two weeks later, the grief had subsided – a robin is by nature an optimistic bird. But the memory would never leave him. As far as he knew, Kirrick was the only robin left in Birddom.

Certainly, in the months of his pursuit, he had seen no other, save Celine, nor any sign of their existence. The destruction of his species was all but complete. Indeed, many other familiar varieties of bird – sparrow, thrush, blackbird – were gone, living on only in the memory. Magpies were dominant throughout the land.

Their numbers had increased at a staggering rate. They had replaced the pigeon in the cities and the starling in the gardens. The unending supply of carrion by the roadside, a boon provided by Man's indifference to Nature, had been the trigger for their population explosion. But, as Kirrick had sensed, some force had begun to direct them. A malignant intelligence that had made possible their vanquishing of almost all other bird life.

As Kirrick sat hidden, he knew he was alone in the world. But loneliness gave him time to think. Whilst with Celine, the urge for survival had been total. But since her death, even in the heat of the chase, Kirrick was thinking constantly. He felt strongly that there must be a purpose to his survival. He knew that he had been spared, thus far, for a reason, and the memory of Celine's death drove him to seek for an answer.

Skulk and Skeet, two huge and menacing magpies, hopped across the newly-sprung fields, their eyes alert for any sign of movement in the wooded area to their right. The manner of their patrol was becoming increasingly desperate. They felt sure that the trail had gone cold, but fear of retribution had made them stay on for hours, in the forlorn hope that they might yet flush out the robin. They knew the price of failure. They had seen wings broken. Eyes pecked out. They were terrified to return without blood on their beaks. So they continued their methodical patrol. Watching. Always watching.

Kirrick's nerves were stretched to breaking point. He had sat motionless for hours, and almost a day of inactivity had made him feel faint with hunger and thirst. His toes cramped and his wings ached to be spread and flapped, to circulate the blood. Kirrick knew that the end was near. He would have to move soon, and feared that, whatever desperation drove him, it would not be enough to give him the speed to escape. His fate would be the mirror of Celine's. The cramps had worsened, becoming impossible to bear. He would have to move, voluntarily or otherwise.

Suddenly, a dreadful scream pierced the air. It came from the field over to his right. A luckless rabbit had become ensnared in a wire trap, and her agonising, tortured cries only speeded her fate. But those same cries saved Kirrick's life. For the magpies had flapped over to the stricken rabbit, eager for an easy meal. More importantly, they could now go back, with blood on their beaks, and bask in acclaim. So what if one robin escaped? Nature, they knew, needed two, and, anyway, he would probably fall foul of another scavenger before long. What difference could one single, small bird make?

★   ★   ★

5

Kirrick flew north. He travelled slowly and cautiously over several days and, as he flew, the countryside below him became more spartan and dramatic. The woodlands were replaced by steep, rolling upland pastures, with frequent rocky outcrops. He detected no sign of pursuit, but knew that this could only be a brief respite. The magpies' malignancy knew no bounds and their utter ruthlessness would never allow his escape.

So Kirrick flew on alone and as secretly as he could, shunning contact with other creatures who might later report his passing. He had no deliberate plan in choosing north as a direction for his escape. It just felt right. And as he flew, he thought. He needed help. There had to be an answer – a way out of the nightmare of his existence. But where to find it?

If Kirrick could have seen into the future, he would have been daunted indeed. This journey, arduous and fraught with danger, would be but a prelude to three more, covering the length and breadth of Birddom. A massive undertaking for one so small. But vital for the very existence of all that was good in the land.

After a few hours, Kirrick felt the need to rest and refresh himself. He had spotted the brook twinkling invitingly at him, some time ago, but had flown on, seeking the safest place to alight. He felt desperately lonely, but checked carefully to ensure that there were no other signs of life. Then he landed gracefully in a small hawthorn near the stream. As he closed his wings to his sides, he relaxed and rested gratefully for a few moments. But his need soon overcame him and he dropped down to the water's edge. He dipped his bright beak into the clear, rippling stream, and then tipped his head back, letting the cool water trickle down his throat.

It was an act of pure pleasure, and he took several more satisfying sips before getting down to the business of bathing. This he performed with the enthusiasm characteristic of his species, spraying water from the tips of his wings, the droplets catching the sunlight and sparkling like diamonds.

'You certainly seem to be enjoying that!'

Kirrick froze, terrified, his wings too wet to allow sudden flight.

'I said, you certainly seem to be to be enjoying your bath.'

It was a large bird who spoke. She had a long, sharp beak of jet black, a grey-tufted crest, and striking chestnut plumage on her cheeks. She was a grebe, and Kirrick had not seen her when he flew down, as she had been feeding below the surface.

'I've been flying a long way.'

Kirrick did not know why he spoke and was surprised at himself for doing so. But the need for companionship of any sort – for a kind of normality – kept him from retreat.

'My name is Anisse,' said the grebe. 'Where have you come from?'

'I'm Kirrick, and I've flown from far to the south. I've been flying since the dark of the moon.'

Anisse considered his words for a moment and then asked, 'But where are you going?'

'I don't know,' replied Kirrick. 'I've just been flying to get away from somewhere, not to get to somewhere, if you know what I mean.'

'Are you in some sort of trouble?'

Kirrick hopped back from the water's edge, and spread his wings to dry them as he considered his response. He instinctively felt safe enough with Anisse, large though she was. She was neither pursuer nor predator. And he wanted, so desperately, to tell her his story, to unburden himself after so long. But could he trust her? The caution that had been ingrained in him over the last months took centre-ground again.

'I am in great danger, Anisse, and I have no wish to bring that danger on to you. It is better that you should not become involved. Thank you for your kindness, but I really must go.'

Anisse looked at him sadly, and asked one more question.

'What are you looking for, Kirrick?'

'Wisdom,' the robin answered.

'Then maybe there is someone who can help you,' she ventured. 'There is an old owl who lives in the ancient forest of Tanglewood, not too far from here. He is deemed wise, even among his own kind, and might be able to give you the answers that you seek. Fly west, towards the setting sun. The owl is called Tomar and lives in the crooked fir. Tell him that I sent you. I am sure that he will treat you with kindness. He will help you, if he perceives, as I do, that your heart is true.'

'Goodbye, and thank you,' called Kirrick, as he flew up and away, with a direction now. A purpose to his journey.

In an abandoned and derelict warehouse in a city heartland, Skeet and Skulk were recounting their tale to the brothers of their coven. There were more than thirty magpies present, all eager to hear details of the massacre of yet another inferior species of bird.

Skeet and Skulk were basking in the admiration and attention of their peers. They recalled, in detail, their long hunt for the robin. They extolled their own patience, vigilance and cunning in stalking their prey. Finally, they told of how Kirrick broke cover, and went to ground amongst the low scrub and brambles, in the wooded area into which they had chased him.

Skeet had taken stance at a point close to where the robin had landed, whilst Skulk had flown further on and alighted to the rear. Skeet told of how he jeered at and taunted his enemy, as he drove him on through the undergrowth. Skulk regaled his excited audience with a vivid description of the robin's final moments when, confronted by the magpies, Kirrick had cowered and begged for mercy. They laughed wickedly as they portrayed his death to their friends, boasting of their cruelty and brutality as the robin was slaughtered.

'Now that's an interesting story.'

All eyes turned to the bird that perched on a rusty metal pole high to their left.

Traska would have seemed, to an outside observer, to be indistinguishable from the rest of the gathering. Like all magpies, his eyes and beak were jet black, as was most of his upper body. This contrasted strongly with the pure white of his belly and wing flashes. Maybe Traska's primaries were a more vivid oily blue than most, but this was only really apparent in open flight. At rest, as now, they lay along his back, crossing slightly above his rump and long black tail.

But this was no ordinary magpie. Traska was the most feared and reviled bird in the region. A vicious, sadistic leader, he had come to power in this particular coven only six months ago. He had arrived as a solitary, unannounced and unheralded. Usually, such birds are mobbed and driven off. But Traska had chosen well. He was a keenly intelligent magpie, and had not just arrived there at random. He had discovered that this particular coven was ripe for the plucking. Their leader was old and weak – no opposition at all to a bird of Traska's cunning and violent power. Typically, Traska's coup had been underhand. He had taken his opponent on his nest and had murdered him in his sleep. He had also despatched two other major domos in the coven, in similar fashion. They had been good strong magpies, whose only fault lay in their loyalty to their leader. They had been a loss, but Traska was determined, from the start, that his authority would be total and unquestioned.

Since that night, Traska had bullied and driven the coven, moulding them in his image. Any dissent had been murderously dealt with, often with sickening results. But Traska achieved his objective. His coven quickly became infamous among the corvidae. The rooks, crows, jackdaws and ravens, brothers all, knew of and feared them. Traska's own reputation was enhanced. He was certain that it would not go unnoticed.

His eyes stared down pitilessly at the two hapless magpies below him now.

'Interesting, but might I hazard to guess – not entirely accurate?' Traska went on in a soft, but menacing voice.

Immediately the mood of the magpies changed. The excitement became more feral and dangerous. Skeet and Skulk slumped uncomfortably whilst Traska continued.

'Correct me if I'm wrong.' No one dared. 'But I've had a few encounters with birds.'

This provoked harsh laughter. Traska was known to have murdered at least one of every known species of bird – those smaller than himself, of course.

'I have always found that robins go for height at the end. Height, and open spaces, in which to manoeuvre in a battle. Their speed and agility would be of no use to them on the ground.'

'But he was trying to hide, not fight,' replied Skulk, defiantly.

'True. As you tell your story, this is so. But surely, we've all heard about the courage of the robin. How one such bird even fought off an eagle who threatened his territory. And this Kirrick, being the last of the robins, must have been very brave and resourceful to survive for so long. Yet you tell us that he cowered and begged for mercy before the pair of you?'

These last words were spat out scornfully, as Traska fixed Skeet and Skulk with a steely glare, which chilled them to their tail-feathers. The other magpies in the coven closed in angrily around their two miserable brethren.

'Wait!' commanded Traska, continuing in a sweet, sarcastic voice. 'They may have another story to tell us . . .'

Skeet and Skulk knew then that they were dead.

Meanwhile, Kirrick had had no difficulty in finding Tanglewood. He had been a little apprehensive on seeing its size, the denseness of the trees, and the gloom within that seemed unaffected by changes in daylight in the world outside. Once he had ventured into its depths, Kirrick had also easily found the crooked fir tree. There were plenty of signs of recent occupancy. A littered nest in the bole of the tree. Scattered bones of small rodents at its foot. But of the owl himself, none.

Kirrick was suddenly at a loss as to what he should do. He was fairly sure that he hadn't been followed to the forest, but any comfort that he felt was counterbalanced by the ominous atmosphere of the place itself. It made him realise how small a creature he was, and how alone. Depression struck him hard and he wept, although he could not have told you why. Then weariness overtook him, and he slept.

He awoke to the softest of sounds – the slight ruffling of feathers, and a scratching of claws on a branch close by. Two large, unblinking eyes stared down at Kirrick, as the owl gently cleared his throat.

'I am surprised at you,' said Tomar. 'Sleeping out in open view in a perilous and unfamiliar place is not a wise thing to do, young fellow.' Tomar's voice was low and sonorous, but not unfriendly.

Kirrick plucked up his courage, and replied, 'Thank you, then, for not taking advantage of my folly. But forgive me my bad manners, intruding upon your territory uninvited and unannounced. My name is Kirrick, and I have flown such a long way to see you.'

'Indeed. Then tell me, Kirrick. Why have you come?'

'I need to know what is happening to the world. I seem to have spent most of my adult life fleeing from relentless pursuit. But it wasn't always like this. I can still remember happier times, although the memories become ever more difficult to recall. Why are the magpies doing this?'

Tomar looked at the robin thoughtfully. Was this the bird? He had known that someone would come. That he would be given a younger ally in this time of dire need. Kirrick had demonstrated his courage in coming so far. And, if he were not resourceful, would he still be alive? But was he the one to meet the challenges that lay ahead? The bird to carry out Tomar's plan, on which depended so much?

The old owl knew just how daunting a prospect the robin would face, and how important it was to the future of Birddom that Kirrick should succeed. Yet Tomar felt doubt. How could he ask so much of someone so small? Judge not a bird's heart by the span of his wings, he told himself. The robin would suffice. He had to. There was no choice, other than succumb to utter darkness, and that Tomar would never do. Kirrick felt the intensity of Tomar's appraisal. It was as if those great eyes were looking into his very soul and finding him wanting. He anxiously remained silent while the owl made up his mind.

At last, Tomar spoke. 'You ask what is happening in the world? Why the magpies have killed your loved ones? We will talk of that, Kirrick, and I will try to answer your questions. No doubt what I will have to say will provoke a dozen more, at least. Well, I will try to satisfy your curiosity as best as I can, although I do not have all the answers, for I am only one owl, and the enemy is powerful.'

Dawn saw an unappealing sight in the rafters of the derelict warehouse. Two carcasses hung pathetically from one of the beams. They had been stripped of their beautiful black and white plumage, and empty sockets remained, where once greed had glittered in their eyes. They had also been disembowelled. This was not usual treatment, but Traska had ordered it. He wanted to be sure about their stories and one certain way was to check the contents of their stomachs. The partially-digested rabbit confirmed his suspicions about the veracity of Skeet's and Skulk's tale.

So the robin was still alive. This was a job that could not be left unfinished. Traska's anger was terrible. He wreaked savage revenge on several more of his own coven, to appease his frustration and reinforce his leadership. Now, exhausted after his violent exertions, he rested and began to think. He knew that he would need help to find the robin. But he also knew that, in seeking support from other covens, he would intrinsically be admitting his own failure. He realised that it would not go unnoticed by his leader, Slyekin. Fear slithered into his stomach, and he defecated where he sat.

'Kirrick will pay for this!' he screeched. 'Kirrick must die!'

CHAPTER 2

Kirrick's first, overriding impression of
Tomar was one of great size and age. With
that age had come a certain infirmity.
Owls were renowned for silent flight, and Kirrick
would certainly never have heard any sound of
approach from Tomar in his youth. If he had been
a mouse, that may have made the difference
between silent death and an empty stomach for
the owl. Indeed, as Kirrick looked more closely
at the great bird, he could see that Tomar was thin
and scrawny. He had not been successful in the
hunt that evening. His vast experience, and the
quickness of his mind, ensured that he did not
starve. But now the hunt seemed longer and the
catches fewer. His best days were behind him in
that respect. But it was his mind that was needed,
not the strength of his body, and intelligence
gleamed in Tomar's eyes. So Tomar and Kirrick
settled down to talk.

'These are troublesome times, terrible times,
Kirrick. Birddom's very existence is threatened,
and it occurs to me that you may have a part to
play. But first, I want to know everything about

this bird who has so presumptuously perched himself on my nest-step.'

Tomar's eyes twinkled with merriment, and Kirrick could see that the old owl was teasing him. But the enquiry was a genuine one. Kirrick knew that he would have to win the old owl's trust before he could get the answers that he sought.

'You want to know my life's story? Are you prepared for a long evening?'

'Owls are known to be patient,' Tomar responded.

'Well then, I shall tell it, though maybe there is not too much worth the telling. I was hatched five summers ago, in June. I was one of three chicks in the second brood, but my brother died after only a few weeks. My mother's name was Elanor, and she was a truly beautiful bird. My father Halen loved her, and us, very much. And he was not afraid to show his affection. My time of fledging was very happy and secure, and I learned much from both my parents that has stood me in good stead in these less-than-happy times. My juvenile time was very much as for any other young robin. We fought and played, pretending to establish our territories. We flew without a care in the world, and our curiosity was limitless. I would often fly off alone and visit the human habitats, even though I had been warned to be wary of Man. But I never faced any dangers there, and the humans seemed to like my company. It was in one of their gardens that I met Celine, my mate.

She was a bright, vivacious young female, and

I loved her first for her adventurousness and spirit. She was often much bolder than I and would even take food from the hand of one of the younger humans. We were blissfully happy for a while. But then the murder started, and we knew real fear for the first time in our lives. Before the coming of the magpies, I must have known fifty robins in our area, outside of my own family. When Celine and I were finally forced to flee our home, we never encountered a single one.'

Tomar's eyes held true sadness in their gaze, as he listened to Kirrick's tale. Even with all that he had heard and seen, he was moved by the tragedy of the robin's story.

'My parents were among the last to be caught.' Kirrick continued. 'Their courage and resourcefulness had managed to protect us all for many months, whilst the holocaust was happening all around us. But finally they were trapped and killed by a large band of magpies. They fought magnificently, but had no chance against so many. We had been with them, but had departed just before the attack. We had flown only a short distance, and we could clearly hear the awful commotion. Celine and I both knew instantly what had happened, and we both realised that there was nothing that we could do to save them. It was the blackest day of my life. We flew on until we found a safe place to hide. There we let our grief overwhelm us. But we only had a short time of private sorrow before the pursuit became focused on us.

The following six weeks were the most terrifying that I have ever known. The days and nights blurred into one long and continuous nightmare. We rested little and slept even less. Our one hope was that the magpies who were hunting us would get bored or frustrated, and call off their pursuit. But they were relentless, and seemed driven to chase us, even to the ends of the world.'

As he relived the terror of those dark days, Kirrick found his heart racing. He opened and closed his beak several times, gulping in air to calm himself. Finally, he was able to speak again.

'Fatigue and hunger weakened us both, but it was the mental strain that took the greatest toll. Finally, it became too much for Celine. Her death was even worse than those of my parents. For I was witness to her end, and the feeling of utter helplessness was something that I have never been able to erase from my memory, nor ever will. I felt something else too. I felt ashamed. I thought of myself as a coward for not saving my Celine, although, once she had broken cover there was nothing that I could have done to help her. Part of me still feels that I should have sacrificed myself and died alongside my mate. But the other part of me believes that there is a reason for every action we take. That is why I am here.'

'Go on my friend,' Tomar urged gently, nodding as Kirrick's story confirmed his judgement about the robin.

'I was chased and harried constantly, even after

Celine was killed. It seems that the magpies' appetite for death is insatiable. Finally, I escaped by a stroke of sheer good fortune, when my hunters found another kill. I put as much distance as possible between us. I had no clear intentions – no idea, honestly, of what to do, beyond fleeing for my life. But then I met Anisse, the grebe, and it was she who suggested that I come to see you.'

'You were fortunate to have found Anisse to help you,' said Tomar, thoughtfully. 'But perhaps fortunate is not the right word, Kirrick. I believe that a far higher power than any of us understand controls our destiny. You were meant to find Anisse, just as she was meant to send you to me.'

Kirrick nodded his head in agreement.

'Yes. I've felt from the beginning that there had to be a purpose to it all. But there is just so much that I don't understand.'

Tomar hesitated initially about telling Kirrick everything, for fear of frightening the robin whose aid he needed so much. But the owl looked once more into Kirrick's eyes, and saw again the strength and resolve within the tiny frame. Tomar felt then that Kirrick had somehow been appointed for his quest, and sensed that the little robin would be equal to the challenges that lay ahead.

'Kirrick. There is much that you need to know. Time presses upon us, and our need is urgent. But you must understand fully the history behind our present troubles. Your courage will be tested to its very limits. You will face many dangers, and only the full knowledge of the importance of the quest that I will ask you to undertake will enable you to complete your tasks. It is a long story and, before we begin, I need to take you somewhere.'

With that, the old owl flapped his great wings, and took to the air, Kirrick following with a mounting curiosity. They breached the tree-tops, and headed north. The ground rose steadily beneath them and they used the thermal currents to rise higher with the land. After some time Kirrick spotted a copse of trees atop a rocky promentory.

Tomar dipped one wing and glided down, alighting on the tallest of a ring of massive oaks which encircled a lushly carpeted clearing. Even in the gloom of dusk, Kirrick could see many kinds of flowers, their soft petals closing as the light failed, and a profusion of vegetation. It was indeed a very beautiful place. But it was the feeling of utter serenity that was almost overwhelming.

'What is this place, Tomar?' Kirrick questioned, in hushed tones.

'Why do you ask? What do you feel?' Tomar's eyes shone as he looked at his small companion.

'That this is a holy place. There is such calm, and yet such power here.'

'You were well chosen, Kirrick. This was the site of the first Council of the Owls, many years ago. Birddom was in its infancy then, and all species lived together in harmony. The world was plentiful, and those enemies that we had were part of the natural order. Life was rich and good. It is hard to imagine such peace and happiness in these dark times. But then a danger appeared which threatened the innocence and beauty of that world. Man. This was the evil that first wrought chaos and disorder in the land. Man was the reason that the Council of the Owls was formed. A great unhappiness had descended upon the land. The peace and tranquillity of our world had been shattered by the intrusion of this new enemy. Habitats were destroyed and many individuals were killed. Fear of Man extinguished the joy in Birddom, and each species became insular, because of the threat to their survival. But one bird had the vision to see beyond petty interests. The birds needed to unite, if they were to survive in the face of such an enemy.

A barn owl, already advanced in years when the threat of man first arrived, was to become the first Great Owl. Her name was Praeda, and she was revered among her own kind for her compassion, strength and wisdom. She had voiced her concerns to her brethren, in an informal precursor to the official council, and had sent them out on a mission. A gathering was to be called and one representative of each species of bird was to attend. There had been some resistance initially, from birds concerned only with their own troubles. But the owls were held in high esteem throughout the land and the force of their argument prevailed. Every bird realised the threat that their enemy posed and all knew that they could not stand alone.'

Tomar's eyes glittered with pride in his ancestors and the years seemed to fall away from him as he continued.

'The gathering took place on Midsummer's Day, and to any eye it must have been an awesome and wondrous spectacle. Birds of all shapes and sizes filled the tree ring, or settled on the verdant grass beneath. No one species took pride of place. Chaffinch sat next to goshawk, and crossbill perched beside wood pigeon. On the ground, merganser grazed contentedly a few feet away from the raucous herring-gull. I can imagine that, to a bird, everyone would have been excited and full of expectancy. Every eye would have turned towards Praeda, as she flapped her wings, to quell her nerves, and cleared her throat before speaking.'

Kirrick was listening intently to every word of the old owl's story. 'What did she say? What did she say?' he cheeped, impatiently.

'Her words have gone down in history, my friend. Owls still remember everything that she said that day. The story has been passed down, unaltered, through the generations. Praeda spoke thus.

'Friends. Thank you all for coming here today. We have known times of great joy together, and we will know such times again! But be under no illusions. We face a terrible foe, at this moment in our lives and history. Future generations will judge us by what we decide today. We must not fail them! Man is, without doubt, the direst foe that we have ever had to face. Every bird here has lost loved

23

ones to a predator. But always we knew that he killed to live, and that our loss was part of the law of survival. Man, however, kills carelessly and to excess. He seems to take pleasure in the act alone. We must face the reality that Man will not go away. Nor will he change. So we must change.

We must plan our very existence – the way we live out our lives – to minimise the threat that he poses. Gone are the days when the whole world was ours. We must create a secret world, away from Man. To him, we must become as shadows, merest glimpses, seen and wondered at, but gone too soon for him to work his evil. For us to do this, we must have order. Every bird must think as much for the welfare of all birds as for that of his or her own family. And any threat to one, must be communicated to all. This is the only way that we can survive.'

It is a fine speech, is it not? And one which gave every bird there pause for thought. In the ensuing silence that followed her words, one bird spoke up. The goldcrest was the smallest bird among them, and many ears would have strained to hear his trembling voice.

'Praeda. Your words are very wise. We all know and fear Man. None among us is safe from his evil. We need to unite if we are to survive. But above all we need wisdom. Every bird in the land knows of the deep knowledge and sagacity of the owls. Your kind are respected and revered. We will put our trust in you to find a way to save us all.'

They say that the very ground shook with the noisy affirmation that emanated from the throat of every bird there that day, and that many an animal stirred in their burrow, frightened suddenly by the commotion.

So it was that the Council of the Owls came into being, and, for many years, Praeda led the Council, with wisdom and understanding. Birddom became unified under her beneficent leadership, and the Council drew up the rules, by which and through which all birds lived in relative safety. Man still made his malice, and many birds died as a result. But the flood had lessened to a trickle, and the crisis passed. Down the years, successive generations of Great Owls have protected Birddom from other dangers, natural and man-made. Their wisdom and common-sense have helped to overcome flood, famine, pollution and the remorseless destruction of our habitats. And each Great Owl took his or her office with gratitude, but also with solemnity, recognising the heritage that had been passed down from Praeda. The Council of the Owls was her legacy to the world and, throughout the ages, it was said that at Council meetings every member there could feel her presence. Our own Great Owl, Cerival, is a direct descendant from her line.'

Tomar was quiet for a long time, lost in memories that seemed to pain him deeply. Kirrick understood instinctively that there was sorrow aplenty in the tale still to come. But for now, he

25

mirrored the owl's silence and breathed deep the soft, fragrant evening air. Eventually, however, the questions that were tearing at his insides would not be denied. He cleared his beak, to gain Tomar's attention, and spoke.

'Great must Praeda have been to unite the whole of Birddom, and to guide it on a safe course. But surely the present Great Owl and the Council can do something about the terror that we face now. The magpies are killing my species!'

The face of the old owl turned towards him, showing not only his sorrow but concern at Kirrick's distress.

'The magpies are killing *every* species,' Tomar replied, gravely, and then told him of the wider picture, of the destruction that was happening the length and breadth of the country. He told him sorrowfully of the loss of the nightingale and the lark. He repeated tales, from far and wide, of planned and systematic genocide.

'But who is behind all this?' Kirrick questioned imploringly.

So it was, then, that Kirrick first heard tell of Slyekin. When Tomar spoke of him, the tone of his voice caught a harsher edge, and he had difficulty in controlling his bile. Slyekin was a magpie, unremarkable in appearance from others of his species. He was, in fact, rather on the small side, and had limped from an early age. But Slyekin was imbued with intelligence, cunning and, above all, evil. From birth he had demonstrated a terrible capacity for treachery, killing his siblings on the nest, within hours of hatching. Abandoned by his distraught parents, he had eaten his dead brothers and sisters to stay alive. Then, as a young adult, he had avenged himself on his mother and father by arranging for them to be murdered in a most sickening fashion and having their heads brought to him in his lair.

Sadistic and twisted though he was, it had been Slyekin's superiority of mind that had facilitated his rise through the ranks of the corvidae, overcoming his physical disability, which might in other circumstances have seen him ridiculed and rejected by his peers. But Slyekin quickly built his power-base on brute strength and savagery. He surrounded himself with dull-witted, but physically impressive 'friends', using them to subjugate others to his will. Few magpies, or any other bird for that matter, are genuinely evil. But they are easily led, especially when promised things beyond their own power to comprehend. While Slyekin's power grew, no magpie questioned the rightness of what they were doing, or even the benefits that they would accrue at the end of it all. For some, the power and dominance over other birdlife fed their egos. For others, the fear of murderous retribution prevented them from speaking out. It was as if no magpie had a single, independent thought, or held an opinion of his or her own. Their wills were bent, like slaves, to the service of their overlord and to his master-plan. However, to achieve his desired aim of the

27

annihilation of all other birdlife, Slyekin needed information, beyond his own acquisition among the corvidae. And so he turned to the Council of the Owls – the very essence of good and right in Birddom.

He befriended the present Great Owl, Cerival. Slyekin came as an acolyte, seeking wisdom, and his eagerness, fawning and flattery had deceived the wisest bird of his generation. The evil magpie became the Great Owl's pupil. He devoted his life, seemingly, to his Master's needs and, in return, was taught the lore of every bird in the land. Slyekin learnt their habitats, their song and their areas of weakness and vulnerability. He became such a common sight with Cerival that it seemed only natural that he should come with him to the Council of the Owls, which was his intention all along.

And all the while he listened and learned. Then, five years ago, when Slyekin felt that he had acquired all the knowledge that he needed, he disappeared without trace. Within a year, Slyekin had re-emerged, in all his dark glory and had taken control of the corvidae once more, but now with the tools that he needed to finish the job. The onslaught had started and birds began to die without number. The owls never held council again.

CHAPTER 3

It was nearly nightfall when Kirrick and Tomar flew back to Tanglewood. Yet Kirrick was too excited to be tired. There was so much that he wanted to know. The stories that Tomar had told him about the Council of the Owls in the olden days had fired his imagination. He had heard little mention of them during his short life, but their power and influence had obviously been diminished by Slyekin's treachery. However, in Tomar, Kirrick felt that he could sense the strength and wisdom that conveyed the very essence of everything that the Council had stood for. He wanted to know more about the old owl, but already felt that he could trust him.

When the pair alighted near the crooked fir tree, Tomar had barely folded his wings before Kirrick began bombarding him with questions. What had happened to the other members of the Council of the Owls since it had been disbanded? What had happened to the Great Owl, Cerival? Was he still alive? And would Tomar be the next Great Owl? Tomar explained, with great patience, that the members of the Council, numbering twelve in all, had returned to their homes over the length and breadth of Birddom, and had not met since that day of betrayal. As for the Great Owl, Cerival was still alive, as far as Tomar knew. He had taken it very badly, and Birddom had lost a lot of its light and might when that wonderful bird had closed his mind to its need.

'But how is the Great Owl chosen?' asked Kirrick. 'Birddom needs strong leadership now, like never before.'

'It is usual for the Great Owl to serve in that role, once chosen, until the end of his days. But the members of the Council have the power, if they are united, to overthrow the Great Owl and banish him from the Council. This is recognised as good control on the supremacy of the leader, but it needs all eleven other members of the Council to invoke it.'

Tomar spoke with solemnity, remembering the bitter altercations that he had faced with one or two of the more junior members of the Council of the Owls in the aftermath of Slyekin's betrayal. They had wanted to depose Cerival. They had felt strongly that his position had been irredeemably weakened. But Tomar had argued that haste made for bad decisions and that the Great Owl was not the enemy. He had counselled that they should go back to their homes and reflect on their own failures in allowing Slyekin's rise to power. Their minds should be turned towards finding a solution. Their wisdom would serve the Council better than their anger. Tomar admitted to Kirrick that he held little hope that those particular Council members would have yet arrived at a solution to their present problems.

'Then why were they chosen? How does an owl become a member of the Council?' Kirrick made no attempt to conceal his fascination, and Tomar felt an inner glow of contentment as he looked at the robin's eager face. This was the bird he needed.

'The Council elect a new member from time to time. Usually this is to replace an owl who has died. But, as I have mentioned, disgraced owls can be and have been banished, although the same rules apply as for the leader himself. Eleven owls against one is the creed. However, an owl must first be chosen by his peers, family and friends, and deemed suitable for the solemnity of the office. And he or she must be willing to serve, for there are great sacrifices to be made when becoming a member of the Council. No owl chosen is allowed to take a mate. This had been the lore of the Council for many generations now. It was deemed wise, because the Council members needed to serve the whole of Birddom. And to do so often would mean taking decisions which affected all birds' lives – owls included. So, if a conflict of interest was to be avoided, it was decided that those sitting on the Council of the Owls would be better able to make dispassionate and wise decisions and laws, if they had no loved ones to consider.

So, my young friend, you see now, I hope, that there were never too many owls clamouring to become new members of the Council! But I jest.

It is a high honour indeed to be chosen and to serve Birddom as one of its leaders. I like to think that, over the years, I have been able to make a contribution to its welfare, through my actions on the Council of the Owls. It has been rather a long tenure, and many faces have changed over the years. But Cerival, my true friend, has been there always, leading us all with great strength and wisdom. His present fall into despair, haunted by the enormity of his betrayal, has saddened me beyond bearing, and that is why I am so determined to find a solution, to defeat Slyekin's evil plans and to bring peace back to Birddom and peace of mind back to my friend.'

So now it fell to Tomar to match his mind to the evil genius of Slyekin. Tomar knew that he had learnt well, and did not underestimate the task of defeating him. His own age had cast him in the role of general in the war against the magpies. The strength that he could best offer would be the brilliance of his mind. He had devised a plan to end the corvidae's dominance of Birddom. If successful, it would deliver a hammer-blow to Slyekin's ambition. In Kirrick, he at last had someone young, brave and fit for the labours that he would need to undertake. For Tomar's plan needed the robin. As a messenger. A herald. An ambassador. Kirrick would have to undertake three journeys, more dangerous than anything that he had experienced in his short life.

★　★　★

Whilst Kirrick and Tomar had been talking through the night about Slyekin, the magpie himself was doing some strong talking. Or screaming to be more precise. He had summoned Traska, his deputy, to his refuge – a dark and desolate place, swampy and chill. The summoning had been accompanied by Slyekin's two largest henchmen, a pair of crows with dull, expressionless black eyes and wickedly sharp beaks. It was not wise to refuse such an invitation.

At the beginning, the conversation had been general and polite, which had made Traska even more ill at ease. He knew and used such techniques himself. Then, abruptly, Slyekin had asked for an account of the progress of his coven in eliminating the species which they had been designated.

It was no use lying. Traska knew too well that Slyekin had ears everywhere and would know already of his failure with the robin. So he told it straight, blaming the failings of others, but, ultimately, shouldering the responsibility himself. For a while Slyekin ranted spectacularly and hysterically, and Traska prepared for the worst, when suddenly, the mood changed again and Slyekin began to discuss quite calmly what needed to be done. Traska was to be given the task of personally dealing with the problem of eliminating Kirrick. He was to be the hunter. Traska's own lieutenant could look after the coven whilst he was away. They would be given something else to do.

Traska could see his power being whittled away, and yet he felt elated. Firstly because he was being given the chance for revenge – killing the robin would be so sweet – and, more importantly, because he realised that Slyekin needed him. Needed him enough to choke back his desire for vengeance. Traska felt powerful. In his own cruel mind, Slyekin's restraint showed weakness, and Traska began, for the first time, to have doubts about his leader. In time these doubts would grow disproportionate to fact, and he would envisage a different future for the magpie kingdom – and a new leader.

However, for now, such dreams were cut short by his curt dismissal from Slyekin's presence, with the parting message, spoken softly, but with menace,

'I'd rather you didn't fail me again!'

As evening approached, Kirrick awoke from a deep, dreamless sleep. He had pondered long over Tomar's plan and had doubted his own ability to bring about all that the owl had spoken of. But his resolve and courage carried the day and, once decided on his set course, he had been eager to talk again to his wise companion about Darreal, the first of the mighty birds that he had to journey so far to see.

As the old owl had emerged from his tree hole, blinking in the gentle, late-afternoon sunlight, Kirrick fell upon him with questions.

'Whoa! Slow down! My brain is still on the nest!' muttered Tomar.

But he too felt the eagerness and excitement of impending action, of the fruition of all his weeks and months of planning. Kirrick was crucial to those plans. His strength would be tested to its limits by three such arduous journeys, with little opportunity for respite. Time was pressing upon them and Tomar could brook no further delay. The little robin had to have completed his appointed task in time for the Great Feast. But Tomar had faith that Kirrick would not fail. Indeed both robin and owl knew that the plan could succeed.

So many variables still needed to fall into place. They would need a tremendous amount of good fortune and, all the while, terrible dangers lay ahead, both from the enemy and from the task itself. Kirrick's conviction heartened and encouraged the owl, however, while the robin felt an implicit faith in Tomar's strategy. The old owl answered Kirrick's questions about Darreal, and the two birds then discussed the entire plan over and over again. Sometimes, something that Kirrick said made Tomar revise an idea, to improve on a particular part of the venture. Both felt the need for urgency and yet knew that, to be successful, they needed to be absolutely certain of every step along this perilous path that they were plotting.

However, shortly before nightfall, a deep and comfortable silence fell over them both. They perched close together, an incongruous looking pair – owl and robin, side by side. They knew that the preparation was over and that the die was cast irrevocably. The future of all bird life lay in their hearts and heads. Kirrick would carry the hope of generations on his back and wings. The great adventure was about to begin.

Traska's skills as a hunter were renowned and feared by his peers in the magpie kingdom. When he left the lair of Slyekin, he knew that he would have to follow a trail gone cold and he cursed Skeet and Skulk for their ineptitude. But he did not doubt himself. He would find the robin and, when he found him, he would kill him. He looked forward to the solitude of the chase. As a leader, he had had to rely on the efficiency of others. As a predator, he need only trust in himself. He knew which he preferred.

Traska had always been alone, for as long as he could remember. His mother had told him how she had been made an outcast, though through no fault of her own, when disease had struck her, disfiguring her countenance, and the other magpies had driven her away. She had only recently mated then and the shock of her suitor's rejection of her, once the illness took hold, had torn her heart apart. So had the cruelty of those that she had thought of as her friends. She had admitted to her infant son that, as one of the crowd, she had joined in their taunting of others, and had thought nothing of it. But when she herself had become the focus of such unwelcome attention, she had realised how vicious and hurtful it was. Alone, she had had no strength to retaliate, and no one to appeal to for help. Her own family had turned against her, just as vehemently as the rest. Not a single bird had showed her any mercy at all, and she had been forced to flee from the only home that she had ever known, terrified and confused. Traska could picture her clearly in his mind, flying for many miles, frantically searching for a safe place to lay her egg, and his anger boiled at the injustice. Several times she had met other magpies, but their reactions had mirrored those of her own coven. Finally she had collapsed, exhausted, and had dragged herself into a dense thicket, where she laid her single egg on a sparse bed of moss, that she had pulled together from beak's reach around her.

It was a poor nest into which to bring a new life, but she had tried, as best she could, to provide enough warmth to incubate her egg. Her body heat had been quite low due to her exhaustion and the disease had weakened her still further. Shorn of the strength to feed, she had been unable to forage anyway, as she could not have left her egg exposed. Under normal circumstances, it would have been her mate's task to find food for her, whilst she sat on the nest. But there had been no one to help her. Helpless, she had starved, while sitting there waiting for her chick to hatch.

His mother had told him that her relief and joy at his birth had been immediately stifled by her anxiety over what to do now that he was there, beak already open, and demanding food. She had known that she had to feed Traska, and equally she had known the dangers inherent in so doing.

She would have had to leave him, vulnerable and cold in the nest, whilst she foraged desperately for life-giving nourishment.

She had managed to find sufficient food for her baby, but with no time to feed herself, anxious as she had been to return to the nest, and to provide the food and warmth that Traska had needed to survive. Each trip had used up more of her limited reserves of energy and she must have known then that she was dying. Only her determination that Traska must live had kept her going. But, finally, the day had come when she knew that she had done all that she could for him.

Traska would survive. As she had lain dying on the nest next to him, Traska's mother had told him about all that she had experienced at the wings of the other magpies and, looking back now, he knew that this was when the first seed of hatred had been planted inside his tiny heart. When Traska had awakened the next morning she was dead. Her body had been stiff and cold, overcome at last by starvation and the effects of her illness.

She had lived barely long enough to fledge her young son, and her one satisfaction must have been that the crippling disease had not affected Traska. To the extent that he was a fine physical specimen, this had been so. But the infection had damaged and warped his brain, and the hardship of his young life, alone and afraid, had, over time, moulded Traska's character.

His every thought and action, from that time

on, had been the epitome of evil. He admitted this to himself and revelled in the fact. Cruelty had become his trademark, and it had been natural, therefore, that, as a juvenile, he should have come under the influence of Slyekin. Traska thought back to their time together with a perverse pleasure. Theirs had been an unholy collaboration. Each had rejoiced in the wickedness of the other, and both magpies had learnt much which had further blackened their souls.

To Traska, Slyekin had been everything that he had aspired to. For Slyekin had power, and it had attracted his young companion, in the way that a flame attracts a moth. Traska had watched and learned, as his leader had gone about his dealings with his minions. Slyekin's utter ruthlessness had thrilled him, as had his callous use of violence to reinforce his authority. Slyekin too, Traska was sure, had gained great satisfaction, as the pupil had tried to emulate and sometimes even outdo his master. Slyekin had chosen well. For, in Traska, he must have seen a magpie ideally suited to furthering his plan for eradicating all other birdlife. He had known how much Traska would have relished the prospect of murder and that he would have had the authority to dominate other magpies, forcing them to do likewise, until his aim was achieved.

Traska knew, in his black heart, that Slyekin must have had times of doubt, fearing that his pupil might grow too powerful and try to usurp his own position as leader of all the corvidae. But

Slyekin's supreme vanity and belief in his invulnerability would soon have overcome this. Besides, they had been having too much fun together. Traska remembered that he had stayed with him for many more months, as companion and pupil, and admitted to himself that his evil mind had undoubtedly been bent to Slyekin's designs.

Traska thought of the time when he had left Slyekin's lair, and had made his way back to his home territory. There, he had wreaked his vengeance upon those birds who had so cruelly rejected his mother. Indeed, their heartlessness, in their dealings with her, had become, for many, a physical reality, as Traska had ripped out their pulsing hearts, gorging himself, and bathing in their blood. The evil magpie's beak parted, as he panted in excitement at the memory. Not a single bird, save Traska himself, had lived to tell the tale of this atrocity, and Traska had never once, in the times to come, given it a second thought, but had moved on to find his own coven. Now, that too had been taken away from him, and he realised that it was time to move on again. He had his appointed task, and knew that he dared not fail.

Traska flew to the wooded area where Kirrick had last been seen. Taking his time, he methodically searched the copse where Skeet and Skulk had cornered the robin. He was looking for droppings, and loose feathers. He knew that Kirrick must have been greatly frightened during the chase, and that fear may have led him to leave tell-tale signs. Many a bird in great danger had been known to pull out their own feathers, in their anxiety. But Kirrick was no ordinary bird, and Traska's frustration and anger increased as he searched fruitlessly.

When he was sure that he had covered the ground thoroughly, and had seen no sign, Traska knew that he would need luck to find the robin. He stopped his frantic activity, and settled down to think. Where would Kirrick go? He was a lone robin. His species had been decimated by the magpies, and no other robin was known to exist the length and breadth of Birddom. So what would he do if he were in Kirrick's position? Where would he flee to?

Traska knew that Kirrick and Celine had been pursued into his territory from the east. He had no doubt also that Kirrick would know the strength of the presence of magpies in the south. All birdlife, or what was left of it, knew that this was the heart of the magpie kingdom. So, would Kirrick have flown west or north? The robin had attained a brief respite in his pursuit, when Skeet and Skulk had taken the easy option with the rabbit. But he would have had no time to plan his escape. Fear and panic would have driven him to flee, to get as far away as possible from the greatest source of his peril. Traska took to the air, flapped his wings, and headed north.

CHAPTER 4

Now that the time for parting had come, Kirrick felt sad to be leaving the old owl. He had very quickly grown fond of Tomar, and had cherished the companionship and the comfort it gave, after such a long period of terror. Kirrick felt daunted by what lay ahead of him, and, not for the last time in his journeying, began to consider himself inadequate to the task. But he knew that, once he started, the adventure itself would carry him on, and would give him little time for such doubts. Survival itself would be enough to think about. His journey to find Darreal would be long and arduous, through unfamiliar territory, and Kirrick wondered what sort of reception he would get at the end of it all.

'Well, you will never know if you don't get going,' said Tomar briskly, adding more gently, 'Time is pressing, and I fear increasingly for your safety here.'

'I wish you were going with me!' replied Kirrick.

'So do I,' muttered the owl wearily.

'Don't worry, Tomar. I will not fail you!' said Kirrick bravely, and, in that instant, the robin took to the sky, paused in mid-air as if in salute, and flew away.

As he watched Kirrick go, Tomar spoke a blessing for the robin's departure, and for his safe journey. Then he settled down into his tree hole for an anxious and troubled sleep.

Kirrick headed west, towards the far-distant mountains that Tomar had told him about – the destination of his first journey. As he left Tanglewood, his keen sight picked out his likeliest route. He decided to avoid the dense conurbation of human habitation, which lay slightly to the south. Tomar's warnings, and historical references to Man, persuaded Kirrick to steer well clear of them. Also, he knew that the magpies were very prevalent in such urban areas nowadays, scavenging on the detritus left by Man, as well as feasting on the carcasses of creatures killed by his machines.

Kirrick's chosen route would take him over lonely, barren land, granite-hard and unyielding, even in this the softest of seasons. Worms would be scarce for many long miles, and Kirrick would not be able to utilise the food sources set out by humans in their gardens. But he knew that Nature would provide for him. And, more importantly, Kirrick reasoned that his choice of direction would give him the greatest chance of avoiding contact with his enemies. For, having talked at such length with Tomar, the little robin was more afraid than ever of the magpies. Now that he comprehended the magnitude of their male-volence, Kirrick knew that much more than his own survival rested on his succeeding in his mission. So he flew steadily, and with vigilance, alert to any possible danger. He knew that he had a long way to go, and that caution, rather than speed, would be his best ally. However, he had barely flown a few miles when ill-fortune struck.

Kirrick was flying over a small copse, when he heard a high-pitched shriek of terror. Before he knew what was happening, he had to take desperate avoiding action as a blue tit emerged from the trees in a headlong flight of blind panic, pursued by a pair of magpies. The two blue-winged assassins were laughing, calling to each other, and taunting the blue tit as they chased her.

Kirrick could see how exhausted the little bird was, and knew with familiar certainty that her end was near. Her only hope lay in his being able to draw off the pursuit. He knew that the magpies must have seen him. He'd had no time to find cover. So, boldly and recklessly, he flew in an angled path, flashing across the very beaks of the two hunters. One magpie peeled off, and began to come after Kirrick – but only briefly. He then circled back, and rejoined his companion in pursuit of the blue tit. They had their orders. In that moment, Kirrick knew that the little bird, like so many others, was doomed. He knew also that he had increased the danger of his own position tenfold. He might as well have shouted from the treetop: 'This way! This way!'

Kirrick flew on with a heavy heart.

Traska had decided to make full use of the corvidae network, in his pursuit of Kirrick. The rooks and jackdaws, crows and jays hated and feared the magpies for what they were doing. But, as cousins, they had been pretty much left alone, whilst the destruction of other species had been unrelenting. So, although they took no active part in the genocide, they offered help and information, in return for their own safety and peace. The magpies had seldom had need to use this spying network, but they had never been faced with any prey who was proving to be as brave and resourceful as this robin. So Traska flew far and wide, seeking out his brethren, questioning and probing. When he received less than helpful replies, he was quite savage in his retribution, and word soon got around among the corvidae that this was one magpie that you didn't mess with.

Unfortunately, this violence backfired on Traska, as helpful cousins sent him off on false trails in their eagerness to tell him what they thought he wanted to hear. But these birds too paid dearly for their folly. Traska's frustration increased. The trail had indeed gone cold. He flew on to the north, uncertain of what to do next. He knew that he could not fail – the consequences were too appalling to contemplate. Yet he could not see a way to succeed. He continued the hunt on instinct alone, sure that Kirrick had chosen this way. His pursuit was urgent, unlike the robin's cautious retreat from his encounter with Skeet and Skulk. Unknowingly, Traska was closing the gap on his quarry.

As he travelled, he continued to interrogate the local corvidae, and so, at last, he got the news that he was waiting for. A rook had not long returned to the coven from a foraging expedition down by the very brook that had been the scene of Kirrick's encounter with Anisse, the grebe. He had overheard Anisse discussing the young robin with her mate. Kirrick had obviously made a strong impression on her, however brief their encounter.

Traska knew that he had found a way to influence events in his favour. From what the rook told him, Anisse had not known about Kirrick's pursuit by the magpies. She only knew that he was in some sort of danger. Traska would go and see this grebe. But first he found out from the rook the whereabouts of the local magpie coven, then flew there to consult with its leader. Mere mention of Slyekin enabled Traska to obtain the help that he needed, and soon five magpies were flying off in unison towards the brook where Anisse lived.

A rain storm had caused Kirrick to find shelter in a pretty, wooded vale. Electricity crackled overhead and Kirrick cowered, as the claps of thunder boomed close by. He had journeyed for more than two weeks since his encounter with the blue tit and her pursuers, and in that time he had pushed himself to the limit, travelling fast and resting little. Yet he was still barely halfway towards his first destination, with two more such journeys to undertake.

Kirrick shivered with the wet and cold, and began to doubt himself, when faced with the enormity of what he had begun. Still, he knew that he must do whatever he could. Perhaps Tomar would find another lieutenant to carry out the other journeys? He must go on regardless, and succeed on this one. But, for now, he had little option, other than remaining where he was and waiting out the storm. Tired and miserable, Kirrick dozed.

He dreamed of Celine, and of his home. Their nest had been a hole in a roadside bank, at the edge of a woodland, but close to human habitation. The pair of robins had often interacted with Man, and had benefited from kindness shown to them. But, in his dream, Tomar's words about Praeda and the Council, and the evil that Man had wrought, produced confusing and frightening images in Kirrick's mind. The friendly humans of his experience became sinister and dangerous. Smiles revealed sharp fangs ready to tear and rend. Eyes that, in reality, had shown only pleasure at their presence, were hooded and full of menace. Kirrick's dreaming soon turned to nightmare, as the humans turned into huge magpies, and he and Celine were forced to flee in terror. He roused himself, and sat trembling, until the effects of the nightmare slowly passed. Then, still exhausted,

Kirrick fell once more into a deep, and this time, dreamless sleep.

When Kirrick woke, it was to the sudden knowledge that the storm had passed. The air was fresh and clear, and the light much brighter, even though no sun yet broke through the cloud cover. However, it was the silence, after the wild music of the storm, that Kirrick noticed most. And yet, not all was silent. A buzzing nearby signalled activity which quickened Kirrick's pulse, and made him realise just how hungry he was. He flew down from his perch to a low bush, which was showing the first signs of bearing blossom. A few insects busied themselves here, collecting nectar, but more hovered above the carpet of celandines and bluebells, which covered the woodland floor. Kirrick darted here and there, setting about the task of feeding with relish. On the underside of some leaves he found several juicy grubs, which he pecked from their insecure perches, and devoured greedily. So intent was Kirrick on his feast that he became careless.

For other creatures were looking for a meal. Other creatures were hungry. With snake-like movements, a small but vicious hunter stalked the robin. The eyes that fixed upon him were black and shining, and the reddish-brown pelt was sleek and wet from the undergrowth. The weasel edged closer to where Kirrick was feeding, and then struck with lightening speed.

The rain, which had so dispirited Kirrick, now

became his saviour. For the robin had seen a movement, reflected in the droplets of water hanging pendulously from the leaves where he was feasting. Instinctively he took flight, and his speed and agility just enabled him to avoid the weasel's attack. The weasel cursed, and spat two feathers from his mouth. Then he slunk off in search of an easier meal. Badly shaken, Kirrick flew back to his perch in the tree where he had rested earlier, his heart pounding.

'Foolish bird!' he berated himself. 'What were you thinking of? You weren't thinking at all – unless it was of your stomach!'

And with that, the relief of his narrow escape overtook Kirrick. He began to laugh, cheeping with merriment, until the tears fell from his shining eyes and his scarlet chest feathers became wet.

Anisse was alone when she spotted the magpie. She, like all birdlife, knew of, and loathed the activities of these evil creatures against the small bird population. But she felt no fear or danger from a solitary magpie, such as this one who was hopping boldly towards her. Her size advantage, and the sharpness of her beak, gave her confidence.

'What do you want?' she called out, when she felt that the magpie had come close enough.

'Oh. I just want to have a talk with you,' replied Traska.

'What about?' Anisse asked, cautiously. 'I have little to do with your kind.'

'I'm looking for the robin. Do you know where he may have gone?' Traska enquired menacingly.

'I don't know anything about a robin. Now don't bother me any more!' snapped the grebe, and took a step forward.

At that moment, the four other magpies descended on Anisse from all sides, attacking her savagely and causing her grievous injuries to the head and neck. Blood streamed from the lacerations and, although Anisse got in a few, telling blows herself, she was soon cowed. At a sharp signal from Traska, the other magpies fell back, and he peered angrily down at the stricken grebe.

'I don't like repeating myself!' he shouted in her face. 'Where did the robin go to?'

Anisse glanced around desperately, but could see the hopelessness of her position. She would have to tell. And so, Traska learnt of Kirrick's visit to Tanglewood, and to Tomar, the owl. The magpie nodded thoughtfully. He had learnt much about Tomar from Slyekin, and knew that the owl would be a worthy adversary. But he soon shook off any premonition of troubles ahead, as he looked at the abject bird before him.

'Thank you.' said Traska, wickedly. 'That wasn't too painful now, was it?'

Then he turned to the other magpies.

'Kill her!' he said, and flew off.

Kirrick journeyed on, flying high and swiftly, over the changing landscape below. He crossed the gently-moving, mirrored waters of a large river and headed further west, towards the dark and impressive peaks of the looming mountain range. The mountain air was cold and crisp. Snow still laid a thick coating on most of the high peaks, its hold not yet diminished by the spring sunshine.

Tomar had told Kirrick that he would find Darreal in the mountains bordering a great lake. Darreal was a red kite, an extremely rare species of bird, found only in these harsh mountains. They had been hunted almost to extinction, by Man this time, rather than magpie. Darreal's clan was the last of its kind and relied, for its continued survival, on the wisdom of its leader. For Darreal was respected, far and wide, for his courage and his intellect, and had, for many years, led the Gathering of the Falcons. Tomar had known that this bird held great sway, and could, if persuaded by Kirrick, give consider-able aid to the cause of defeating the magpies, once and for all.

The owl and the robin had discussed this at length, but now, as Kirrick approached his dark, forbidding destination, his one thought was how easy it would be for Darreal to eat him!

As Traska flew towards Tanglewood, he thought about his next plan of action. He had no wish, at present, to confront Tomar. That would impinge upon Slyekin's wider plan for the owl's kind and, although he would have very much enjoyed persuading Tomar to reveal the robin's whereabouts, Traska knew that now was not the time to anger his master. He must first succeed in his quest, and find the robin without the owl's 'help'.

So Traska followed the consistent pattern of hunting that he had used so far, and sought the local magpie coven and its leader. Traska had arrived during a celebration and was welcomed with open wings, and invited to join in the feasting. Despite his impatience, Traska controlled himself and settled to listen as the local magpies bragged and boasted about the successful completion of their task. No blue tits now flew in their skies. Traska praised them for their thoroughness, and then began to ask for news of the robin.

The magpie leader showed little interest in Traska's enquiries, being too intent on his own achievements. Traska was sorely tempted to rip out this bird's bragging tongue, but he knew that numbers were against him. He had all but given up, when he finally got a positive response from one of the pair of magpies who were the focus of attention, having been the killers of the last blue tit.

'Yeah. I remember now. We saw a robin a while back. Bleedin' mad he was. Nearly took my beak off!'

'Why didn't you kill him?' Traska asked venomously.

'Not our job, mate. Our orders is to kill blue tits, and we done that all right!'

Loud and raucous cheers greeted this, and the magpie puffed up with pride.

'What happened to the robin?' cajoled Traska, in a conciliatory tone.

'Oh, he gave up and flew off, he did, real sharpish like,' replied the proud bird.

'What direction?' queried Traska.

But it was the other of the pair of killers who replied.

'He went off straight as an arrow. I watched him for a while, see, but then I got sort of distracted.'

With that, he laughed cruelly to himself, remembering how sweet and violent that 'distraction' had been.

'Which way?' Traska repeated impatiently.

'Oh, sorry mate. Didn't I say? He went west.'

Traska stayed barely long enough to show courtesy to his hosts, then slipped away. He was tempted to stay, as the celebrations had sunk into debauchery, but his desire for glory in his quest was stronger. When Traska was alone once more, he alighted atop a tall tree and stared westwards. From what he had learnt, Kirrick had been gone on his journey for several days. Traska did not know where the robin's destination lay, or his purpose in going there. He considered once more going back and interrogating the old owl, but rejected the idea. He was too far behind already. Traska knew that he had to trust to his luck and ingenuity to succeed.

He gazed into the far distance, as if willing his

sight to exceed its natural boundaries, and seek out the cursed robin. Then he focused sharply. A thin line ran straight for miles in the direction that he knew he must take. Along the motorway thundered many heavy vehicles. The speed and endurance of these monstrous machines impressed Traska, and he knew, in that instant, what he must do. But how?

As Traska pondered on the difficulty of his choice, it was made immeasurably easier for him. An old, open truck had parked at a service station, less than a mile away. The back of the vehicle was laden with straw. Without hesitation, Traska flew down, landed in the soft straw and buried himself in its warmth, until only his eyes and beak showed. He felt strangely excited. All wild creatures had a loathing for mankind, and his casual cruelty, although, at times, this same behaviour caused Traska to feel admiration. He, too, was of that nature. A minute or two later, Traska felt a deep rumble as the engine started. Then the truck set off, heading west along the motorway.

Kirrick felt absolutely exhausted, but relieved now that he had finally reached his destination. He knew that his mission was an urgent one, but his body cried out for rest. It was approaching late afternoon, and Kirrick decided to leave his daunting meeting with Darreal until the next day, when he would be fresher, and more alert.

Looking for a place to alight, Kirrick suddenly spotted a bright scarlet patch, which made the juices in his beak flood. He hadn't realised how hungry he was, and could scarcely believe his good fortune in finding a patch of wild strawberries at this altitude, and this early in the year. He flew down and began to peck hungrily at the succulent young fruit. Kirrick knew that he had to be careful after his near miss with the weasel, but the temptation of the fruit proved too much, and he set about gorging himself.

So it was that he nearly jumped out of his feathers, when a rustle, in the undergrowth nearby, announced that he was not alone. However, this time, no predator appeared to threaten life and limb. Instead, a small, brown mouse peered out of the long grass and then edged shyly forward to share in Kirrick's meal. Animal and bird settled comfortably, side by side, concentrating on the pleasure of that sweet and juicy repast.

A speck in the sky high overhead hovered with deadly purpose. Darreal's keen sight had picked out the mouse and the robin way below. He waited, adjusting his wingtips, as a cross-wind buffeted him at this high altitude. Then, as the wind died, he folded his wings and fell into a stoop, his speed increasing to an incredible velocity, as he dived down upon his hapless prey. Darreal could not tell you why he changed his mind. But, at the last split second, he made the necessary adjustment, and took the mouse in his wickedly curved talons. Kirrick was frozen to the spot with the shock of seeing the mouse killed before his eyes. Darreal circled low, with the mouse held firmly in his claws, and, seeing that the robin had made no move, he swung back towards Kirrick, as if to attack again. But he could not complete another kill with his talons still full of mouse, and he had no intention of dropping one meal for just the promise of another.

Darreal's frustration, however, changed to amazement when Kirrick recovered his senses, and spoke his name.

'I'm looking for one of your kind named Darreal. Do you know him?'

'Better than any other, I should say,' replied the kite. 'I *am* Darreal. And who may you be?'

'I'm Kirrick, and I've flown such a long way to see you.'

As he said this, the robin's whole body slumped, as exhaustion took him again.

'Can you fly a little further?' asked Darreal, more kindly. 'I can show you a safe place where you can rest. We can talk more in the morning.'

So, in yet another unusual collaboration, kite and robin flew off together to Darreal's home.

The warmth of the straw, and the motion and deep hum of the truck, lulled Traska into a profound sleep. Many miles passed beneath the wheels of the vehicle while he slept, and Traska woke only when the truck pulled to a halt, and he heard voices. A female hitch-hiker was being offered a lift, and, as she climbed up into the cabin next to the driver,

Traska took the opportunity to shake off his covering of straw, and hop down from the rear of the truck.

As luck would have it, a meal presented itself almost immediately, in the form of a dead hedgehog by the roadside. Traska's sharp beak soon tore at it, and devoured the rent flesh of the unfortunate animal. When he was sated, Traska flew up into a nearby tree and rested while considering his position. He did not know where he was. He did not know, furthermore, where Kirrick was. He was hunting blind, relying only on his instinct. Still, it had served him well in the past. He pondered again on why Kirrick had come on such a perilous journey.

'Consider the facts,' Traska asked himself. 'The robin was sent to see Tomar the owl. Then he flew off over hundreds of miles, to a land entirely strange to him. Why?'

Traska flapped his wings, to shake off a loose piece of straw that was annoying him.

'He could be searching for another robin. But why would Tomar know of such things? Or he could have been sent, by the old owl, with a message for another owl. But why so far, and why here?'

Traska's anger built as he realised the enormity of his task, in finding Kirrick in this unfamiliar land. An opportunity to vent his rage, in savage violence, presented itself, in the form of a juvenile jackdaw, who had the misfortune to be flying in the locality. Traska took wing, and proceeded to pursue, harass, and finally ground the young bird. A few minutes later, Traska returned to his tree with a bloodied beak, feeling much better, and able again to focus on the task ahead. The jackdaw, on the other hand, could no longer fly anywhere. He lay, broken and bleeding, awaiting his inevitable fate at the jaws of some fortunate predator.

Traska decided to seek for news of the owls in this region, and, to that end, he contacted the local magpies. He felt sure that this all had something to do with the Council of the Owls. So, Traska asked his brethren about the wisest and most revered owl to live hereabouts. The magpies spoke, with superstitious awe, about an ancient, snowy owl called Isidris. The more melodramatic amongst them called him the Ghost Owl, for, as a silent, white spectre in flight, he had killed many of their kind. Traska derided such fancifulness and learned, from the more pragmatic of his hosts, that Isidris' home could be found in the mountains to the west, barely a day's flight away.

Then, he proceeded to organise the local magpies. Their leader was weak and ineffective, and Traska had no difficulty in dominating him. The magpies were sent out to other covens, and to all the local corvidae groupings. Traska wanted the skies to be watched night and day, and set about establishing a cordon of his brethren from north to south in the region. He wanted news the minute Kirrick flew back east. For fly back he must, if Traska's growing feeling about Tomar's plans were correct.

'He *must* be planning to reconvene the Council of the Owls,' Traska told himself again and again. He felt uneasy at the thought, for he knew that he was up against something far more daunting than a resilient, but ultimately insignificant, small bird.

So Traska started out to visit Isidris, leaving behind a network of watchers, who would report back at the first sight of Kirrick. No piece of the sky would go unmonitored. Kirrick was trapped. He had him at last.

CHAPTER 5

Kirrick slept until the sun was high in the sky. When he finally woke, he found that ample food and water had been provided for him. He ate and drank his fill, then looked around for Darreal. As if in answer to the call of the robin's subconscious, the kite dropped out of the sky, and took a stance nearby.

'I'm glad to see you are well,' said Darreal. 'Do you feel rested?'

'Thank you, yes,' replied Kirrick courteously.

'You have been very brave,' said the kite. 'Brave but foolish. You could so easily have been killed.'

'Oh, not so easily, as others have found!' cheeped the robin, his chest feathers puffing up ever so slightly with pride. 'A formidable foe, I see.' responded Darreal, chuckling 'I'd better keep you as a friend then. But, tell me, why have you come here on so perilous a journey?'

Then Kirrick proceeded to tell him of his flight from the pursuit of the magpies, of Tomar, and of the plan to defeat the enemy. Darreal knew of the Council of the Owls, of course. His falcons had modelled their own Gathering on the owls' example.

And, in days gone by, they had often sought each other's wisdom and support, in times of need or danger. Darreal was sad at the passing of so potent a force for good in the land. He also knew Tomar well, and had a high regard for the old owl. But even he was impressed by his breadth of vision. Darreal probed and questioned, seeking for weak areas in the plan, and clarifying a point here and there. Kirrick explained the purpose of his other journeys, and the role that would need to be played by Darreal and his comrades on the Gathering of the Falcons.

'When would you need our aid?' Darreal queried, with a definite trace of eagerness, and Kirrick's heart leapt with joy. He had achieved the first task set for him – winning the support of this great bird. He told Darreal of the time and the place, and the kite nodded approvingly at the audacity of the plan.

'Yes, that is good, Kirrick. I will call a meeting of all the falcon leaders for tomorrow night. You must be there, of course. But I will be alongside you, have no fear. And I give you my word, Kirrick. We will not be found wanting. The falcons will be there in your hour of need – and triumph!'

Kirrick was thrilled that his quest had been met with such positive support. He knew that the full Gathering of the Falcons would need to be won over, but, in Darreal, he had found a dynamic and decisive ally who, he sensed, would deliver what he had promised. Kirrick's thoughts turned to Tomar, and how pleased the old owl would be, but Darreal's words cut into his reverie.

'You should go and see Isidris – you who like owls so much!' chuckled the kite. 'Besides, he is an important ally.'

'I have heard of Isidris. Tomar spoke of him. He said that he was a wise member of the Council of the Owls, and a trusted friend. Where can I find him?' asked Kirrick.

So Darreal began to tell Kirrick a little more about the snowy owl. Isidris lived in a cave, high on the side of the steepest mountain in the region, less than an hour's journey away. Isidris was of venerable age, but his eye was still bright, and his mind quick. He lived a solitary existence, for, as with all other members of the Council of the Owls, Isidris had never taken a mate. His mastery of the art of totally silent flight was legendary, and Darreal's description of his ability in the hunt matched that given by the magpies to Traska.

'I agree with Tomar. Isidris is wise, and I have often sought his advice when I was troubled. You can trust him,' promised the kite. 'Would that the Council of the Owls were reformed once more. All of Birddom misses their wisdom.'

Vowing to return on the morrow, Kirrick set out to seek the cave home of Isidris, little knowing of the terrible danger that lay ahead.

When Traska arrived at Isidris' cave, he announced his presence with a loud, raucous caw, calling the owl out of his home as if summoning a servant. He waited and waited, but nothing happened. So Traska began to hop imperiously towards the mouth of the cave. The next instant he felt a sharp tug of pain, as a single feather was ripped from behind his ear. He spun round but saw nothing. Then he turned to face the cave again as Isidris emerged, blinking. In his mouth he held the solitary feather.

'That's a very poor way to treat a guest,' thundered Traska.

'A guest is someone who is invited,' replied Isidris, 'and someone who shows a little manners!'

'Forgive me,' cajoled the magpie, 'I only wanted to talk to you. My need is a pressing one, but now I am ashamed of my rudeness.'

'Perfumed words on a poisoned tongue!' thought the owl, but he stepped forward and faced Traska.

'What is it you want of me?' asked Isidris.

'It is said that you are the wisest and most esteemed bird in these parts,' said Traska, continuing the flattery, which he mistakenly believed would win Isidris over.

'Then it is wisely said!' exclaimed Isidris, in an amused tone.

Traska mistook this self-mockery for conceit, and continued to feed the owl with praise.

'Such a wise and knowledgeable owl would know of all things, large and small, that went on in his domain. Such a great bird would be aware of any stranger who might enter his territory.'

'I am aware of *you*! But then again, you've made yourself fairly obvious,' teased Isidris. 'But, presumably, it is of another that you speak?'

'I am looking for a robin, who is named Kirrick. I am sure that he has been sent here to see you, Isidris.'

'Why should he come to see me, and what is your interest in him?'

'He brings a message from Tomar, the tawny owl from Tanglewood, near where I live,' Traska lied. 'And, if he has delivered that message, then I am to accompany him, on Tomar's instructions, to see that he gets safe passage back. The world is a dangerous place for a small robin.'

'So it would seem,' replied Isidris, with a trace of irony. 'But, as it is, I fear that you have wasted your journey. For your friend is not here, nor has he been. I know Tomar well enough, but nothing of a robin called Kirrick. Good day to you.'

And with that, Isidris dismissed Traska, as curtly as the magpie had initially summoned him. Traska was left open-beaked, as the owl turned, and disappeared into the gloom of his cave.

Could he have been wrong? And if so, where did he go now? No. Traska was certain that, somehow, the Council of the Owls was bound up in all this. Isidris must be lying. Emboldened, Traska hopped forward into the mouth of the cave. The fetid smell of bones, and long-dead carcasses assailed his nostrils. He shook himself, and continued brazenly into the depths of the cave, calling out as he did so.

'Isidris, I have other questions to ask. Can you spare me a little more of your time?'

* * *

Just as Traska disappeared into the blackness of the cave, Kirrick flew into the clearing in front of Isidris' home. He alighted on a small tree stump, a few feet from the entrance, and paused to compose himself.

'How do you greet an owl?' Kirrick wondered to himself, for when he had come face to face with Tomar, it had been the owl who had spoken first. Now, he felt daunted at disturbing Isidris, and framed his words courteously in his mind before he spoke.

But, just as he felt he had them right, and opened his beak to call out his greeting, he stopped himself. For, from within the cave, there came noises. Noises of raised voices, harsh and angry, and then of a deep rumbling. Kirrick instinctively looked for cover, and, seeing a small crevice at the mouth of the cave, squeezed himself into the gap. A second later he stared, in astonishment, as a ball of black and white was bowled past him out of the entrance.

Traska picked himself up, and shook his feathers to rid himself of the dust and cobwebs. His face was a mask of fury.

'You have made a big mistake!' he screamed into the cave.

'Begone, before I correct my latest mistake,' replied Isidris ominously, and Traska flapped hurriedly away.

Isidris hopped slowly to the mouth of the cave and watched the magpie recede into the distance. Kirrick remained very still in his hiding place. He had no wish to further anger an owl who had dealt so summarily with his last guest! But Isidris seemed aware of his presence.

'You must be very uncomfortable in there,' he stated.

Kirrick emerged cautiously, prepared for flight, but Isidris continued kindly,

'It's Kirrick, isn't it? Do not be afraid, I only deal with unwelcome visitors like that.'

'How do you know my name?' asked Kirrick.

'Oh, I heard it mentioned only recently,' replied the owl, then proceeded to tell Kirrick about Traska's visit.

'He's lying, of course,' said the robin. 'At least in part. I *have* come from Tomar of Tanglewood. Do you know him?'

'Tomar and I are well aquainted. He has been a true friend to me on many occasions. But what of this magpie?' queried Isidris.

'I thought that I had escaped from their pursuit,' answered Kirrick. 'But it seems that the magpies will not be satisfied until we are all dead. That is why my mission is so important.'

So saying, Kirrick spoke then, at length, of his experiences, and of the plan which Tomar had devised. Isidris listened intently, nodding from time to time, but saying nothing. After Kirrick had finished talking, the owl remained deep in thought. Finally he spoke.

'Kirrick. You are a very important little bird. These magpies do not yet know the extent of your mission, but they will stop at nothing to kill you.

Your luck has held so far. However, spies are everywhere. This magpie will expect you to return east to Tomar. You will be in great danger if you do so.'

The owl paused for a moment, preening a few of his white feathers.

'Wait here while I take a look around. Keep yourself hidden, Kirrick. I will return shortly.'

Without further ado, Isidris flapped his great wings and took to the sky, circling far out to the north. Kirrick returned to the rock crevice, and settled down to wait on Isidris' return. Then he listened gravely as the white owl reported on the cordon set up to watch for him. Together, they discussed Kirrick's predicament, and devised a plan for his escape. But they would need the help of the falcons.

'I will come with you,' Isidris said. 'I have many friends on the Gathering, and my word is not without influence there.'

So robin and owl set off, choosing a secret way to avoid prying eyes, and made their way to Darreal's home, where the Gathering of the Falcons would be held.

Kirrick stood resolutely before the steely gaze of the collected leadership of the falcons and told his tale. His courage nearly failed him in the face of such a formidable array of sharp beaks and talons. His voice faltered at the beginning, but, once he began to explain to the assembly about the grave danger faced by every small bird, his words gained in strength and power with the passion of his convictions. His eyes sparked with the anger that he felt at the massacre of so many innocents, and his chest swelled with pride, puffing out his glorious red feathers, at the role that he had been chosen to play. The Gathering of the Falcons listened intently to the robin's story. As predators themselves, they were not unaware of the increasing scarcity of the small bird population in their own region. But their very role as hunters meant that few other species were brave enough to confront them, and thereby impart the knowledge about the magpies' violent depredations. To a bird, they were impressed by Kirrick's courage in travelling such a distance, and into such possible danger. This added much credence to his words.

Kirrick then spoke, with affection, of Tomar, and dared any there, by his defiant posture, to question the wisdom of the old owl's plan. He related much of what the two of them had discussed together, and so the falcons learned the truth about Slyekin, and the downfall of the Council of the Owls. Isidris, though a council member, and a good friend to the falcons, had spoken little of the disbanding, or of the reasons behind it. He had also kept himself to himself, to a large extent, preferring solitude to company. And this reclusive behaviour meant that rumour, rather than fact, was the only source of information open to the other birds thereabouts. It was unusual, therefore, for him to be present at this meeting, and added further weight to the importance of Kirrick's mission, and of Tomar's plan.

Darreal then spoke in support of the little robin,

and embellished that plan with promises of glory and honour for the assembled company. Finally, Isidris told of his encounter with Traska, and of his strategy for helping Kirrick escape. He called for their support for the robin and, almost with one voice, they assented immediately.

Only one young falcon voiced his disapproval. The surly-looking peregrine sat apart from the others, and expressed his doubts at interfering in something that did not concern them.

'We have no quarrel with the magpies. They cause us no harm.'

'Not now, maybe,' replied Isidris. 'But do you think they will stop with the destruction of the smaller birds? They want total dominance. Your turn will come. For, though you are strong individually, you are few in numbers.'

'Isidris speaks wisely,' said Darreal. 'We must do whatever we can to help eradicate this evil.'

'I still feel that we should mind our own business,' retorted the peregrine defiantly. 'I have a young family to look after.'

'It is the future of your children that is at stake!' cried Kirrick.

'No more of this,' pronounced Darreal firmly. 'Kirrick, you have our total support. We will come to your aid when you need us.'

Loud cheers greeted Darreal's words. Then the Gathering gradually broke up and the falcons returned to their homes. The few that remained began to discuss the diversion needed to help Kirrick escape. The magpies and the other corvidae were watching the skies. Well, they'd give them something to watch. Meanwhile, Darreal called over the peregrine who had opposed the majority in the meeting.

'I understand your concern, Jespar. We do not choose such a course of action lightly. But Kirrick speaks the truth. Consider the many species of bird whose song no longer graces our countryside.'

'I don't care,' responded Jespar, petulantly. 'Don't you see, Darreal? We can live with the corvidae in peace. They mean no harm to us.'

'Tell that to Kirrick's mate!' snapped Darreal sharply. 'The smaller birds posed no threat to the magpies. They were just wiped out on a leader's whim. Who is to say what a mentality like that might or might not do? We must defend ourselves.'

'Defend ourselves, yes,' pleaded the peregrine. 'But do so here at home, where we know the ground and have the advantage.'

'Where do you draw the line, Jespar? At the river? At the end of this valley? At the edge of your nest?'

Darreal turned away and went to join Kirrick and Isidris, who were going over the details of the robin's passage to freedom. Jespar was left alone and, brooding, he slipped quietly away.

Isidris voiced a worry, which both Darreal and Kirrick also shared.

'I do not trust that one,' he said. 'I think we had better revise our plan for your escape, Kirrick. The diversion should go ahead, to avoid any suspicion. But I think we should choose another way for you to depart. Leave it to me, both of you. I'll be back in a little while. I've just got to go and see an old friend.'

With that, the snowy owl flew off on his own private mission. Darreal was sore at heart at the thought that one of his own Gathering might betray them all. He had known Jespar a long time, ever since he had been a fledgling. The peregrine's father had been a loyal friend, and had shown his bravery on many occasions. It was hard, therefore, to see his offspring in such a harsh light. But Darreal could take no chances. He excused himself from Kirrick's company, and flew off to search for Jespar.

It was late at night when Darreal returned to his home. Kirrick and Isidris were in high spirits, laughing at the brilliance of the owl's daring plan for the robin's escape. The laughter died in their beaks when they saw the blackness of the look in the kite's eyes. Darreal spoke in sombre and halting tones, as he described trailing Jespar to the magpies' coven. He told of his helplessness and desolation, as the peregrine had performed his traitorous act. Darreal had waited until Jespar had left the coven, and then had confronted him.

Jespar confessed that he had told Traska and the other magpies about Kirrick's imminent departure. But he had not revealed the details of Tomar's plan. His honour had held to that degree. He said he had felt that, if Kirrick was captured, there would be no need for the falcons to fly east in answer to Tomar's call, that the life of one bird would be a price worth paying, for continued peace with the corvidae.

Darreal had executed the peregrine without hesitation, and the awfulness of that act had been tempered only slightly with relief that Kirrick's mission had not been jeopardised.

The next day was glorious. The sky was cloudless, and a breathtaking blue in colour. Kirrick would have wished it otherwise, for an overcast day might have provided more favourable conditions for his escape. The robin felt a curious mixture of emotions. He was restless with the knowledge that the next great journey was about to begin. He felt excited and frightened at the same time, and in about equal measures. He trusted Isidris' plan, but knew the deadly consequences if he was caught by Traska. Finally, Kirrick felt sadness. He had made good friends here, and felt safe. A part of him desired to lay aside his burden and remain in the company of Darreal and his family. But the robin knew that the safety was an illusion. The only hope for the long-term survival of any of them was to succeed in the task Tomar had given him.

Darreal's arrival interrupted Kirrick's thoughts. The kite saw to it that practical considerations were put to the fore.

'You have a long and dangerous journey ahead of you,' counselled Darreal. 'You should spend your time feeding, not dreaming. Build up your strength, Kirrick. You are going to need it.'

So Kirrick spent the remainder of the morning foraging and, in doing so, forgot for a while the onerous nature of the task ahead. Isidris found the robin just before noon. 'Are you ready for your journey, Kirrick?' asked the owl.

'I am ready,' replied the robin in a brave voice.

'Then it is time for you to meet my friend, Estelle. I have told her all about you, and she is eager to meet you,' said Isidris. 'She is nearby and waiting for you. But we must hurry, Kirrick, for time is short. The falcons are almost ready for their diversion.'

When the sun stood at its highest point, Darreal and another falcon took flight and began a spiralling dance against the blue of the sky. They swooped and dived in unison, then climbed again and began the same ritualistic movements once more. This time they were joined by two more of their brethren. The symmetry of their dance was truly beautiful to see and many creatures stopped and stared in awe at the falcons, as they completed their sequence.

As if from nowhere, four smaller, darker birds of prey came into view. This time, however, they brought discord, not harmony, into the choreography of the birds' flight. They swooped, screaming, upon Darreal and his companions, talons raised. Only split second reactions allowed the falcons to avoid the attack. Darreal's quartet then turned on their assailants and the sky was filled with the spectacular sights of a battle-royal.

Only the watching magpies were unimpressed by the spectacle presented before them. Thanks to Jespar, they were well aware of what the falcons were doing. Traska had instructed all of them to remain vigilant in watching for the robin. Still, it was very difficult not to be drawn to the drama being presented for them. Certainly, the battle seemed real enough for those watching. The agility and timing of the falcons' challenges made them extremely convincing and, just when the battle seemed to be flagging, more falcons would join the fray. At its height, twenty of these noble birds fought for supremacy of the skies.

Then, at a signal from Darreal, all the falcons disengaged from their mock combat. Each bird had, in the midst of their performance, picked out an individual from the watching cordon of corvidae. Now, without hesitation, they swooped upon their hapless prey, their challenges suddenly lethal. Several hit their targets on the first pass, and the magpies exploded with the impact of their talons. Blood and feathers covered the ground below.

Traska cursed violently. This was not supposed to happen. Jespar had told him nothing of this. The falcons seemed intent on punching a hole through his watchers. Traska retreated to a safe distance as the mayhem continued, his eyes ever-watchful for the solitary robin. He marshalled his forces and began to set up another cordon. Now that the initial element of surprise was lost, Traska knew that he had superior numbers, and the falcons seemed to realise this too, for, after a few sporadic attacks, they broke off the engagement and, to a bird, disappeared from whence they had come.

Traska was triumphant. The falcons had failed. Of course, he had lost a few of his number. But they were expendable. And, anyway, they would be avenged. An attack like this could not go unanswered. However, that would have to wait. It was not Traska's concern. The local corvidae would be able to exact revenge for this outrage. The most important thing to Traska was that Kirrick had not escaped.

Gliding along the tranquil waters of the river, the swan had watched the affray in the skies overhead. She seemed only mildly interested in the battle raging above her and sailed on, intent on her own journey. Her wings were held high, in an arc, to protect her brood of young cygnets, who rode in safety on her back. The swan swam on. Occasionally she twisted her long and graceful neck, and laid her head along her flanks, as if to give one of her youngsters a caress. Actually, she was turning like this to talk.

'Are you all right, Kirrick?' asked Estelle.

'I'm fine, thank you,' replied the robin courteously, moving position slightly to avoid a cygnet's webbed foot.

'Keep yourself well hidden,' the swan advised.

'The danger is not yet past. I will tell you when I feel that we are safe.'

So the robin nestled into the soft, warm down of the swan and her brood, and Estelle sailed majestically on, unobserved – save by one pair of eyes. From his vantage point, a hundred feet above, Isidris kept watch over Kirrick's departure. He hovered patiently overhead, alert for any sign of interference by the magpies. But there was none. Traska's cordon showed no interest in the slow passage of the swan along the river.

And so it was that Kirrick passed out of the clutches of the evil magpie. He stayed snug on Estelle's back for many miles, and only showed himself when the swan reached the estuary.

'I think it's time for you to go, Kirrick,' Estelle called softly. 'From here our paths are very different. I have seen no sign of any corvidae for a while. You should be safe now.'

'How can I ever repay you?' asked Kirrick.

'Succeed in your task. You will be the saviour of us all,' replied the swan. 'Go quickly now, and may the Creator speed your wings!'

CHAPTER 6

Tomar had been sick for several days now and was feeling very weak. He had not eaten for sometime, as the illness had made him too slow to catch any worthwhile prey. Now hunger forced him out of his natural haunts and took him to the edge of some farmland. He knew that many animals died here, caught in the farmer's traps. Tomar was not proud of himself for taking such a meal. He knew also that the traps represented danger, for he would be forced to eat his meal on the ground, rather than be able to carry it to the safety of the trees.

He glided silently along the treeline, keeping low to avoid being silhouetted against the evening sky. A farmer's gun would not be the instrument of Tomar's demise. His eyes searched the ground below, and the old owl could scarcely believe his luck when he spotted a rabbit lying prone, but still alive, in a small gully at the edge of a field. Tomar could see no sign of a trap, but the animal was clearly in agony, and, as the owl watched, the rabbit began to convulse, arching his back to an almost impossible angle, as the pain took him.

Tomar flew down and landed next to the stricken creature. As the convulsion receded, the rabbit turned, and his gaze met the owl's stare.

'Beware!' choked the rabbit. 'Do not eat me, or your life will be forfeit too!'

His words were stopped, as another spasm of pain shook him.

'For pity's sake, kill me,' he begged. 'But do not eat me.'

Tomar understood. With a swift blow of his mighty beak, he broke the rabbit's neck, and stood broodingly over the poisoned carcass. His hunger forgotten for the moment, Tomar let his mind concentrate on the chance that had presented itself to him. The possibilities it offered were amazing and it fitted in so neatly with his existing plan. Poison!

As the old owl lost himself in thought, a veritable army of insects began to invade the body of the recently-deceased rabbit. Every orifice was assailed with vigour as the ants and roaches began their feast. The presence of the owl ensured that other carrion eaters kept well away and the insects took full advantage, devouring the rabbit from within. At length, Tomar shook himself from his dreaming and focused on the tiny creatures, busy on the body of the rabbit.

He almost laughed. It was all so perfect. In a rush of pure elation, Tomar took off, and performed a cartwheel in the sky, looping round, and then landing, exhausted in a nearby tree.

'You foolish old bird!' he admonished himself. 'You've got little enough energy as it is, without wasting it in such an exhibition.'

But try as he might, he could not but feel exhilarated at this new turn of events. He would need time to formulate his plan fully. But, what an opportunity! It doubled their chances of success against the magpies.

As night fell, Traska began to suspect that something had gone wrong. He had held all the aces, but someone had slipped a wild card into the pack. He felt increasingly sure that Kirrick had gone. Traska could not see how the damned robin could have escaped, but his sixth sense told him that it was so.

As usual, he vented his anger on those around him and then settled down to think. He would have to begin the hunt all over again and he knew he must not delay. The local magpie leader was summoned and Traska instructed him to maintain the cordon for five full days more. The corvidae were angered by this. They wanted immediate retribution against the falcons. But no one dared to argue with Traska. So they agreed to continue their vigil. Satisfied, Traska looked at the options open to him.

He could return to Tanglewood, far to the east, in the hope that Kirrick would report back to Tomar. But, somehow, Traska knew that the robin would not take this course of action. Jespar had said that the plan had been for the falcons to create a diversion, whilst Kirrick slipped away to the north. After the dramatic and bloody change to the original script, Traska was uncertain as to whether he could trust any detail of what the peregrine had reported. Certainly, he had set a strong watch to the north of the region, and nothing had been seen of the robin. In addition, the falcons had tried to break through his cordon at its heart, which, if successful, would have allowed Kirrick egress in the direction of Tomar's home, to the east.

But Traska was beginning to understand the mind of his enemy. He sensed that the robin, forewarned of his presence, would be bold enough to strike out alone once more, following whatever mission it was that Tomar had given him. When Jespar had said that Kirrick would leave by a northerly route, Traska had believed that the robin would then double back, and return east to Tanglewood. But now, the more he thought about it, the more the magpie realised that it had been Kirrick's intention to fly north. That could only mean that there was more at stake than he had thought. The more complicated that the plot became – and Kirrick's second journey seemed to confirm this – the more threatened Traska felt. Tomar's plan could only mean danger for the corvidae, and the only magpie who could prevent the plan's success was Traska.

'Kirrick must be stopped!'

*   *   *

Tomar knew that he must now risk considerable danger. The old owl knew more about humans than just about any other bird still living, and he knew that he would have his best chance with the juvenile of the species. Tomar stayed close to the farmland for many hours, resting and watching. Hunger gnawed at his insides, but he remained at his post. The opportunity was too important to miss. Suddenly, Tomar's body tensed, and he quivered with a mixture of fear and excitement. A young boy was coming across the field to check on the traps.

The old owl glided down to the ground, at the very edge of the tilled land and, as the child approached, he began to hop painfully and slowly towards the woodland, dragging his wing as he did so. He fluttered and stumbled feebly, and the boy's attention was caught. As he came closer, Tomar turned his head to look at the boy. His large, limpid eyes displayed his pain and fear.

The child spoke soothingly to him. 'You look just about done in, old fella. There, there. Don't be frightened. I won't hurt you.'

With a gentleness that belied his heritage, the farmer's son picked up the owl, grunting with surprise at the weight of the bird. Tomar held himself still in the boy's arms, ready at any moment to flap his huge wings and escape, should danger present itself. But he sensed no threat from the child.

The boy carried the owl back across the open

field and towards some outbuildings, his traps momentarily forgotten. He stopped at the door of a small shed. It was slightly ajar and the boy forced it open with his foot. Then, shouldering the door aside, he moved into the gloomy interior, and deposited the old owl on a large bench.

'I'll get you something to eat. You just stay there. Don't move,' the boy commanded in a kindly voice.

Tomar had no intention of moving. His plan had succeeded beyond his wildest expectations. The boy soon returned, carrying a small, wriggling creature which he held up before Tomar's eyes, as if for inspection. The owl snatched greedily at the young rodent, and swallowed it down with immense satisfaction. The boy seemed pleased by this and produced another tempting morsel from his pocket, holding it by the tail. Tomar held his beak wide as the child fed him. Then he squawked his thanks.

'Had enough? Well, you just rest here for a while until you're better. That wing of yours'll heal in no time.'

As soon as the boy had left, Tomar took the opportunity to look around the wooden building. As usual with such storage facilities, it was full of all sorts of implements necessary, at one time of the year or another, on a working farm. Tomar hopped along the bench, inspecting a set of crudely made shelves, nailed massively to the rear wall of the shed. They had rows of containers of varying shapes and sizes – jars, tins, and bottles

– all displaying bright and colourful labels, clearly stating their contents and its purpose. On some of the older containers, where the labels had faded or peeled, the farmer had affixed his own, so that no mistakes could be made in their usage.

All of this was of absolutely no use to the old owl, who could not read. He was even unaware of the significance of the black cross on orange background, or of the skull and crossbones displayed, as a warning, on many of the bottles and cans. Tomar looked crestfallen as he stared helplessly at the array before him. Then he shook his head and muttered to himself.

'So, Mister Clever, it's not going to be so easy, after all. Think hard, old bird. There must be a way!'

As Tomar pondered over his problem, the boy was in the farmer's kitchen, being fed himself. When he had sated his appetite, typically huge for a child growing up in the countryside, he slipped from the table and made his way quickly outside, eager to see the owl again. But as he crossed the farmyard, he stopped suddenly, remembering his unfinished task with the traps.

The boy returned to the shed where he had left Tomar and, on entering, was greeted with a shriek from the old owl. He reached his hand out carefully, and ruffled Tomar's feathers. Then, he turned his mind to practical considerations and began to collect the items he would need to reset and replenish the traps. He selected a few nooses and wires, and then moved over to a small refrigerator, from which he withdrew several pieces of offal and a variety of vegetables for bait. Standing straight once again, he turned, and came over to where Tomar sat. Reaching behind the owl, the boy stood on tiptoe to take down a small phial from the shelves. Tomar knew that he had to act quickly, whilst the boy was close, for his subterfuge to be maintained. Without hesitation, he hopped onto the boy's shoulder, and pecked gently at his ear.

'Want to come with me, eh?' said the child. 'Yes, I suppose it must be pretty boring cooped up in this place. OK. Off we go then.'

And, with that, the boy strode manfully out of the shed and off across the fields. He was a strong lad, but the heavy owl weighed cruelly on his shoulder. Tomar sensed this and shifted his position, flapping his wings to ease the pressure from his talons.

Boy and owl progressed happily in this fashion, to the far edge of the farm's perimeter. Then Tomar was set down on a tree stump to watch, as the child prepared one of the traps. First he removed a dead squirrel and placed the prone body into his sack. Then he baited the trap once again with a small, enticing piece of turnip. Finally, he uncorked the bottle and carefully spread a few drops of the poison over the bait.

Tomar watched intently, and noticed how little force the boy needed to remove and replace the stopper in the phial. The child came back to the tree stump, picked the owl up, and deposited him on his shoulder. Then they set off towards the next trap, the boy whistling happily. When they reached the site, they found no sign of bait or animal. Obviously, some unfortunate creature had evaded the trap, but was somewhere in the undergrowth, having suffered a lingering death from the effects of the poison.

The boy cursed softly. He was a practical child and knew the necessity of protecting the crops and livestock. But he was also kindhearted, and hated the idea of the agony his traps sometimes caused. He far preferred the quick, clean kill. The boy got out the phial and placed it on the ground beside him, as he reached into the bag to select some fresh bait.

Feeling an instant of regret, Tomar stirred himself into action. He swooped down, seized the phial in his talons and, flapping his great wings, miraculously now free of any injury, flew off and disappeared over the tree line. As he did so, he turned to look back and saw the boy standing, wide-eyed and open-mouthed, staring in astonishment at the receding image of the owl. Then Tomar lost sight of the child and, looking ahead once more, set his course for home.

Many days and nights passed, as Kirrick travelled north, towards his next destination, and an encounter that he feared even more than the last. A falcon was intimidating enough, but an eagle? . . . Still, Kirrick knew that he had no choice. The future of Birddom was in his wings alone. This second journey was long and arduous, and took the little robin to the very limits of his strength. He had already flown so far, and the need for escape from Traska's trap had meant that Kirrick had found scant time for rest and recovery. Only his strength of purpose kept him going. That, and the knowledge that his first quest had been successful. Kirrick faced many hazards and dangers (the tales of which would, in times to come, add to the near legendary stature of this brave bird). Suffice for now to say that the robin triumphed in the face of adversity on several, life-threatening occasions.

Kirrick's second journey was almost fatally delayed when he became seriously ill, less than halfway to his destination. The infection was virulent and immediate, affecting his breathing and making flight impossible. He first realised that something was wrong after a short stop for food and water. On taking to the air once more, he felt leaden-winged and struggled to gain any height. His vision swam and a pain stabbed across his chest. Kirrick bravely tried to ignore the discomfort, but soon realised that he could not go on.

Fortunately, he was, at that time, flying over a heavily-wooded area, and quickly found a place to alight and rest. His intention, on landing, was just to get his breath back and then to find somewhere safe to sleep off the sickness that he felt. But the swiftness of the infection would allow no such luxury. In a matter of minutes, it had him in its grip, and he had no choice but to go to ground and lay there, in surrender to the raging, wracking agonies of the illness. For two days, Kirrick was in delirium, his mind racing and swirling, nightmare images tormenting him as he lay utterly helpless.

He was very vulnerable then and could easily have fallen prey to a predator, exposed as he was, with only a small covering of leaf debris which he had gathered around him before the sickness had swallowed him up entirely. But the very illness which was trying to destroy him from the inside became his saviour. For, in his delirium, Kirrick began to make noises. Loud, clear and haunting, his voice rose and fell, echoing around the woodland. It was an eerie, unnatural sound, unlike the call of any bird, and it made the hairs rise on the back of the necks of animals which ventured nearby. Each and every animal turned away and circumvented the area, giving this strange-sounding creature a very wide berth.

Kirrick's recovery was slow, but gradually he emerged from the nightmare world into which the sickness had plunged him. In his weakened state, he had no idea of how much time he had lost, but he made sure that he foraged and fed well, knowing the need to replenish his reserves of strength, for the journey still to come. He was worried that the delay would prove costly to Tomar's plan, but knew also that he could not afford to launch into a head-long flight into possible danger. Certain now of pursuit, Kirrick journeyed cautiously and avoided any deliberate contact with other wildlife, who might pass on knowledge of his whereabouts. Kirrick had seen his enemy once and had no wish to be so close to the evil magpie again. But no bird can be made invisible, and Kirrick had left enough clues and signs to allow successful pursuit by a determined hunter. And Traska was very determined.

Traska had not gone off immediately after the robin, but had isolated himself from all company for a while, giving himself time to think clearly. He knew the direction that Kirrick had taken and, knowing that, for some purpose, the robin had made contact with the falcons, he felt it safe to assume that Kirrick's second mission must be along similar lines. So, who was the robin journeying to visit? Tomar was clearly seeking allies, and such ones that were amongst the largest and most powerful in the land. The falcons were, individually, as perfect a killing machine as the Creator had devised in Birddom. Their lack of numbers meant that they posed little threat to the corvidae. But what if . . .?

Traska's mind took the next logical step and he gasped, stunned by where it took him. The robin was going to the eagles! If that was true, then everything that the magpies had worked to achieve could be lost. But only if Kirrick succeeded. Logic told him to report back at once to Slyekin and warn

88

him of the danger that lay ahead. But, in doing so, he knew that his position would remain diminished, and he was by no means certain that, in this case, forewarned would necessarily be forearmed.

Anyway, his vanity dictated that he would not be outwitted and defeated by a *mere* robin. No, now that Traska knew where Kirrick was going and why, he could finally end this. The magpie knew that, in open flight, over such a distance, he could overhaul the robin, but catching up with Kirrick, in terms of time, was very different to finding him in the vastness of the landscape ahead. So Traska decided that his best chance lay in outdistancing the robin and, once ahead, in choosing a suitable place of ambush. Knowing, with a certainty, what he must do, Traska took a hasty meal, and then set off in pursuit of the robin.

Tomar sat contented in his nest hole. He was proud of himself and of what he had achieved. If only Kirrick were here to hear about his exploits. Tomar wondered about the little robin and the adventures that he must be having. It was hard to have no word of Kirrick, but Tomar had every faith in the bird he had chosen. Kirrick would not fail him.

Nor must he fail the robin. This new idea of his improved their overall chance of success, but it needed careful planning. He must allow himself time to do what he did best – using his mind to think things through, to evaluate and then to decide. Tomar knew that he had to make an alliance unlike any known before and to do so he needed to find a suitable inducement, to make such strange bedfellows fall in with his plan.

So the old owl spent a long night pondering on just what he could offer in return for their aid in his quest. Just before dawn, a look of satisfaction came over the owl's face and, smiling to himself, he closed his eyes for sleep. He knew what he could offer the insects.

CHAPTER 7

K irrick flew on, over a landscape of increasing beauty. Deeply-forested glens gave way to rocky, mountainous outcrops. Heather covered the hillside with rich, purple and brown hues and everywhere water was in abundance. Sunlight shimmered in reflection from mirrored lochs, and waterfalls cascaded down steep inclines, as rivers fed into their unfathomable depths.

Kirrick knew that he had nearly reached his destination and, now that he was close, his earlier feeling of fear was replaced by an eagerness and excitement, born of anticipation for what lay ahead. Eagles! Kirrick had been impressed and even somewhat in awe of Darreal, Tomar and Isidris. But now he was going to meet one who could justifiably claim the title of king of all bird life. Kirrick felt daunted by his task of persuading such a majestic bird that he must do the bidding of so lowly a robin. But he had total faith in Tomar's master plan. It had been vindicated already in his dealings with the falcons and he knew that he would, with luck, find a favourable reception once more.

Suddenly, a flash of scarlet in the distance caught Kirrick's eye. He stopped in mid-air, his pulse racing and his eyes swivelling frantically round for another tantalising glimpse. He had seen her, he knew he had! It couldn't have just been his imagination.

Yes, there, over in the gorse, down to his right. A beautiful female robin. It was beyond all hope. Kirrick had been so sure that he was the last. He had travelled so far and had seen no sign. But there she was, and she hadn't seen him. His heart leapt with joy and he swooped down towards her, opening his beak to sing out his greeting. At that instant, a stinging, searing pain exploded into his leg, as the pellet hit him. His swoop turned into a freefall and blackness took him as he tumbled earthwards.

When he awoke, the first thing that Kirrick saw was his reflection, his image superimposed upon a lustrous black. Focusing with difficulty, because of the pain, he looked into the beautiful face of the female robin. Her features changed, from a show of concern and anxiety into one of delight that he had regained consciousness. When she spoke, the gentleness in her voice enhanced Kirrick's first impression of her, and his heart turned over with an immediate feeling of love for this pretty young robin.

'Ah! You're awake then. You've been unconscious for a long time. I thought I'd lost you more than once. But you're a fighter, aren't you?'

'What is your name?' asked Kirrick, in a weak voice.

'I'm called Portia, and until now I thought I was the only robin left alive. Indeed, if that young boy had had his way, I might have been. Honestly, I could peck his eyes out!'

Kirrick laughed. 'Well, I'm Kirrick, and, as for taking revenge on my behalf, please be my guest!'

Portia looked tenderly at the injured robin.

'You're accent is strange. You're not from around here. What brings you to these parts?'

'I'd heard of your loveliness!' Kirrick teased, and Portia blushed to match her chest feathers. 'But seriously, it's a very long story.'

'Well, you'll not be going anywhere for a while, with that leg of yours all shot up,' replied Portia. 'Besides, I've always enjoyed a good tale.'

She put her head on one side and listened as Kirrick began. She was, in turn, fascinated and appalled as she heard of his adventures. Kirrick, for his part, ceased to feel the pain of his leg, as he stared into the beautiful eyes of this wonderful bird, and time seemed to fly by. There were tears in Portia's eyes as Kirrick came to the end of his tale, and she said simply,

'What can I do to help you, Kirrick?'

'Well, you could get me something to eat!'

Portia scratched him playfully with her claws and then flew off in search of a meal. The pain returned with a vengeance and Kirrick's head swam, as he looked at the damage to his leg. He tried to rise. The agony was excruciating and took his breath away, but he steeled himself against it. Heavily favouring his good leg, he stood and swiftly launched himself into an experimental flight. The leg felt strange and ungainly, but presented no problem when flying. However, Kirrick realised that another difficulty would have to be overcome. How could he land on one leg?

'Oh well,' he said. 'What flies up, must come down!'

So, he slowly glided back to the spot where Portia had found him. His landing was, to say the least, undignified, but he managed it without further damage to his injured leg, and looked up, proudly, as Portia reappeared with a beak full of worms. But her eyes flashed angrily and, depositing the worms on the ground, holding them securely in her claws, she admonished Kirrick severely.

'What do you think you're playing at, you stupid robin? Do you think I'm going to waste my time caring for you, only to see you break your good leg in such a display of madness? Your injury needs time to heal!'

'But that's just the point,' Kirrick responded vehemently. 'We have no time. We must go on and finish this mission. There is so much still to do and so many other lives are dependant on our success!'

Portia quietened at Kirrick's reply. 'You really are an extraordinary bird, Kirrick,' she stated gently. 'Forgive my anger. It was born out of concern and love.'

She moved close to Kirrick and they sat together in a wonderful silence, their bodies softly touching and their heads held close. Portia began to tell Kirrick of her own life and of the dangers that had beset her. The depredations of the magpies, in this part of the land, had been just as devastating as in the south. The linnet, wren, siskin and brambling had been eradicated entirely, and very few other species of small bird could boast more than a handful of surviving individuals at best. Portia had seen her family wiped out and had known of dozens of other robins massacred by the brutal magpies. These evil birds were not indigenous to the highlands, but had moved in with a purpose, marauding into the mountains, to murder and destroy.

Portia herself had faced terrible danger on several occasions and had escaped more than once by the breadth of her tail-feathers. Her family had been more resilient than most. But then, they were amongst the robin elite. However, the advent of such evil had destroyed the social distinctions. Every robin died just the same. Her mother and father were no exceptions.

It had taken a dozen of the large corvidae to down the plucky pair, and her father had put up a spectacular show of defiance, fighting bravely against the odds before he was mobbed and torn apart. Portia's mother died protecting her daughter and only great fortune saved the beautiful robin herself. But before she could tell Kirrick of her own escape, Portia was overcome with a resurgence of grief.

Kirrick wrapped her in his wings and held her tightly while she cried. In this position, exhausted, they slept. As they did so, the worms, which Portia had so painstakingly collected, wriggled silently away, disbelieving their good fortune.

Traska had flown hard and with very little rest and, on arriving in the highlands, he had bullied and badgered the magpies of the local corvidae covens, bending them to his will. One headstrong local leader had challenged Traska, resenting his demands, and the evil magpie had taken the opportunity to show the local birds his power and ruthlessness. Traska had left the other magpie torn and bloody, with broken wings and both eyes pecked from his head. That particular coven got the message and word soon spread that this was a magpie that you did not cross.

Traska sought news of any sightings of robins in the area and asked about the eagles and their leader. All the magpies spat out one name: Storne, the great golden eagle. Their hatred of him knew no bounds, for, under his leadership, the eagles had persecuted the local corvidae, disdainful of their habits as carrion-eaters, and in retribution for their attacks on other bird life. Here was an ally indeed for Kirrick and Traska was now more desperate and determined than ever that the robin should not make it through to the eagle's lair.

Traska posted watchers over several miles, to the south of the valley in which Storne's eyrie was sited. They were to report back immediately if the robin was spotted. The nature of the terrain made it almost certain that Kirrick would have to come this way, and Traska selected the fastest and fiercest of the local magpies to help him ambush the robin. Other magpies and local corvidae were arranged as a rearguard, to protect the main party from attack by the eagles. The trap was set. All they had to do now was wait – wait for that accursed robin.

Traska's old coven had been especially chosen by Slyekin to help organise the Great Feast. This was an annual event, held in the autumn, when the humans celebrated their harvest and before many animals began their long winter hibernation. This time of year had been chosen for the abundance of food that it provided for the magpies. Each feast had succeeded in outdoing its predecessor and now the annual event attracted corvidae from covens all over the country. It was a gathering in celebration of the magpies' increasing dominance over Birddom. Slyekin always enjoyed the Great Feast because, as leader, he was fawned over and adulated, which fed his enormous vanity. It also gave him the opportunity to provide spectacular entertainment for the delectation of his followers.

Last year's 'Thrush Thrash' had gone down very well. The cruel visual pageant had been a fitting climax to the feasting and fornication. It had also served the purpose of wiping out the last of that particular species of songbird.

This year, though, Slyekin felt that he had devised the ultimate titillation for his massed ranks, and one that would give him a definite personal satisfaction. Using the lesser minions in Traska's old coven, Slyekin had sent word across the land about the Great Feast, and he guaranteed that the turnout would be unparalleled, especially once everyone knew about this year's planned entertainment.

The same messengers had summoned the blackest, vilest and most brutal magpies from each coven to Slyekin's lair, and the refuge was now fast filling up with savage, violent and downright malevolent birds. Slyekin kept them waiting, unknowing of the plan, awaiting the last arrivals. Fights broke out with increasing frequency and one or two lesser magpies did not survive to carry out their task.

Finally, however, Slyekin was ready. He called all the gathered flock together and outlined his plan. His aim was to capture all the members of the Council of the Owls, starting with the Great Owl, Cerival himself. They would have one final council meeting, after all. He would humiliate them and destroy them. It would be entertainment fitting for the magpies, a tribute to this year in which they had finally all but wiped out the country's small bird population. It would also give his magpies a taste for greater prey, when they saw how easy it was to defeat the oh-so-wise and wonderful owls.

The Council's twelve owls were regarded by all birds as the Law. The disbanding of the Council had been essential for Slyekin to succeed in his plans for total dominance. But Slyekin had seen them in action. He knew of their strength and their power. Only in destroying them utterly would he be able to feel safe. Once the owls were truly defeated, there would be nothing to stop him.

So, like a farmer set on an early harvest, Slyekin sent out his battalions to reap a fine crop. The first six owls of the Council would soon be in his clutches.

Kirrick and Portia awoke together at sunrise. At first, neither showed any inclination to move from the mutual warmth and comfort of their position, but then both robins realised how hungry they were. Portia flew off in search of a mouth-watering breakfast. Kirrick foraged nearby, and found a few choice berries and grubs to add to the meal.

On her return, they set about satisfying their hunger, and then, encouraged by Portia, Kirrick made his way gingerly to the brook, to drink and bathe in its cool, clear waters. The pair of them frolicked and splashed about in the waters, and Portia trilled with laughter when Kirrick showed off once too often for his injurious condition and toppled over backwards into the water with an undignified splash.

The warm rays of the sun soon dried the robins and they sat down once more to talk, each eager to know every little thing about the other. Indeed, so engrossed were they that it was evening before they realised it and, a little guiltily, but with pleasurable expectation, they decided to remain where they were for one more night, before beginning their journey to see the leader of the eagles.

As they settled down close together, Kirrick asked Portia what she knew about the eagles.

'They have been our protectors and our lords for some time now, since the magpies began their evil work. If it weren't for them, we'd have all been dead long ago. Storne is their leader. He is a fine bird, a golden eagle of great size and power. But he is also kind and wise.'

'You know him?' gasped Kirrick incredulously.

'Oh, yes. It was Storne who saved me when my parents were killed,' Portia replied, smiling. 'Would that he had come sooner, but fate would not have it so. He had been patrolling in this area to deter the corvidae. All the eagles do this, under his instruction. Few magpies would ever dare risk engaging in battle with an eagle and their very presence became our protection. Of course, the magpies had already reaped a bloody harvest before Storne realised their intentions, and he carries that sorrow very heavily in his heart. My family were just unlucky to have fallen foul of a raiding party after Storne had circled out to the north, drawn off by a sighting of magpies attacking a defenceless pair of goldfinches. For all that I feel my loss keenly, I would not have wished for their deaths, even at the expense of my own family. But for Storne, there might indeed have been no robins left, in this part of Birddom at least.'

'But why didn't you tell me sooner?' Kirrick asked.

'I didn't want you to be too eager to set off,' she answered mischievously. 'Besides, I thought it might be a nice surprise.'

'A wonderful surprise,' said Kirrick. 'With you by my side, I'll have no trouble in winning over the eagles to my cause.'

'You would have had no trouble in winning over Storne, mighty as he is. After all, you won me over.'

Portia giggled and kissed Kirrick, with a peck to his cheek. Then the two robins snuggled close and talked long into the night, their need for sleep put aside as they planned what they would have to do next. They both knew that the danger was far from over.

Cerival, the Great Owl, was the first to be taken. He showed little surprise at this latest act of treachery by his former pupil, and offered scant resistance to the twenty or so corvidae who had been sent to capture him. This disappointed the magpies, who were spoiling for a battle, and they had to content themselves with vicious pecks and raucous taunts, as they drove the old owl on towards Slyekin's lair.

Once the shock of his entrapment had worn off, Cerival had quickly divined the intentions of Slyekin. He wondered how many of the Council of the Owls would make it back alive, to face whatever humiliations Slyekin had in store for them. Probably all of them, he decided. He knew Slyekin too well to believe that any of his followers would disobey him. And Slyekin would want all of the owls brought to him alive, of that he was sure.

The journey back to Slyekin's lair was laborious, and the magpies would indeed have dearly enjoyed murdering the old owl when he stopped in weariness. But they had their instructions and all knew the penalty of failure. Finally, the magpies brought the Great Owl to the retreat in the dark, wet marsh, and he came face to face again with his former pupil, now his greatest foe.

'So, old bird! I hear you didn't put up much of a fight,' sneered Slyekin.

'It wasn't a very fair fight,' replied the owl. 'Not one against one, like you and me.'

At his comment, Slyekin's henchmen crowded forward to protect their leader.

'Too important to do your own dirty work?' Cerival provoked. 'Or too cowardly?'

'Take him away and guard him well. I don't want a feather on his head touched, until I'm ready for him. Then, old one, you will pay a high price for those words!'

It was Portia whose sense of danger saved the pair of robins. Kirrick had been flying at her side, without a care in the world, head in the clouds and dreaming. They had set off that morning, eager to continue the journey and to meet with Storne. Kirrick bubbled over with optimism. Now that he had Portia, nothing could go wrong. And, for a long while, her mood matched his. The weather was glorious, the scenery breathtaking, and both birds were full to the brim with love.

Portia spotted the first magpie at a distance and reacted immediately. She tucked in her wings and fell, like a stone, to the ground. Kirrick instinctively followed suit, although he had been unaware of the cause of Portia's actions. The landing jarred his injured leg badly, but he hobbled quickly after his partner as Portia ran for the dense cover of the heather. All the while she never took her eyes from the menacing image of the airborne magpie, hoping against hope that she had been in time.

But the danger had not passed. A second black and white shape joined the first and they began to fly unerringly towards the very spot where Kirrick and Portia had alighted with such urgency. The two magpies circled overhead for what seemed like an age, and Kirrick held Portia motionless in his wings. Then, with a harsh cry, the first of the corvidae peeled off and, followed soon after by the second, disappeared in the direction of Storne's valley.

'That was close,' said Kirrick. 'Oh what a fool I am! Putting us in danger like that, with my head full of cotton wool. We were lucky.'

'Oh, they saw us all right,' replied Portia, in a matter of fact tone. 'What I cannot understand is why they didn't attack us. They were marking our position. They had us trapped. To fly off like that just doesn't make sense.'

'Oh yes it does,' exclaimed Kirrick. 'Traska!'

Portia shuddered at the mention of that name. Kirrick, remembering the cordon set up for him in Darreal's homeland, realised that Traska had somehow overtaken him and was, even now, laying in wait for them. He cried out in dismay, but Portia stilled him and looked deep into his eyes.

'We're not done yet,' she coaxed. 'But it will be so hard, Kirrick. They'll be watching the skies for us.'

'I know,' replied the brave robin. 'We have no choice. We walk.'

'But your leg,' said Portia, great concern in her voice.

'It will follow where I lead,' joked Kirrick, lightly. 'Come on now. We must get moving. I fear to delay any longer.'

Slyekin's sense of triumph increased with each capture of the high-and-mighty owls. He exulted in their humiliation and crowed, in derision, as they were brought, one by one, to stand impotently before him. Soon the first six were in his grasp. He had planned with great care. He feared the Council of the Owls more than anything else. But, without the Great Owl himself, it could not reconvene.

Slyekin had also chosen the other owls with a plan in mind. Of the twelve, he had picked out the strongest and youngest. The warriors. He needed time to take away their spirit, to subdue them completely. They had stood no chance against his cohorts anyway. Sheer weight of numbers had seen to that, although several had resisted bravely. No, with these owls in captivity, Slyekin was sure that he had negated any possible threat from that source. The remaining owls were old, weak specimens. They would present no problem. He would have his victory. His moment of glory.

CHAPTER 8

It wasn't long before Traska began to close the net. Kirrick and Portia looked on in desperation, as a flight of magpies flew overhead and alighted to the rear of them. Then, the pursuers spread out in search formation and began the sweep back towards the valley where Traska waited, like a spider at the centre of his web. A pair of magpies also took station aloft, watching and waiting, should the robins break cover.

Kirrick's leg became increasingly troublesome the further he and Portia journeyed by foot. The pain was constant now, but Kirrick forced it down and gave his fullest attention to their desperate plight. Even allowing for the care that the magpies were taking, in ensuring that neither bird escaped from the trap, they would, at this rate, close with the robins in very little time.

'I will not let it end here!' exclaimed Kirrick, in defiance of their predicament. 'We must not fail.'

'We will find a way, my love,' answered Portia, attempting to reassure her partner.

'But we'd need to be invisible to get out of this

one,' Kirrick said. 'Or else we need another bit of trickery, like my escape with Estelle.'

At this Portia looked up sharply at Kirrick. His mood had changed noticeably. 'You've thought of something?' she queried, hopefully.

'It's just an idea,' he replied. 'Portia, my darling. Are you afraid of the dark?'

When she replied bravely in the negative, Kirrick went on:

'Then everything depends on luck. That, and rabbit droppings.'

Portia and Kirrick hurried on as best they could, searching frantically for the tell-tale signs that would signal their salvation. With every minute that passed the magpies got closer and Portia showed increasing signs of panic.

'Just hold it together,' begged Kirrick. 'Trust me, and we'll get out of this alive.'

But Portia wasn't looking at Kirrick. Her eyes sparkled with excitement. 'Over there!' she cried, and Kirrick hushed her quickly, lest their pursuers should hear.

'Look, Kirrick,' she continued in a soft, but still excited voice, 'I think we may have found our miracle.'

Sure enough, just as Kirrick had hoped, they had found a cluster of the unmistakable purple-coloured, oval droppings of the rabbit.

'Now, find the entrance to his warren. We have no time to lose.'

Both robins devoured the surrounding scenery

with their eyes, looking for the rabbit hole that would lead to safety, and it was Portia's sharp eyesight that spotted it first. She had nearly missed it, taking it for a shadow on the hill slope ahead, but, at the very moment that her gaze passed, it was drawn back by the emerging head of a dun-coloured rabbit, his ears pricked up for any sound that might indicate danger. Then the rabbit relaxed and hopped slowly out of the burrow towards a nearby, tasty clump of dandelions. Controlling their sense of urgency and desperation, Kirrick and Portia crept cautiously nearer to the feeding rabbit. Suddenly his ears pricked up and he sat upright on his hind legs.

'Please!' cheeped Portia. 'Please don't give us away!'

The rabbit looked questioningly at the pair of robins, and then his eyes took in the scene behind them. Four of the magpie hunters had reached the edge of the thicket, where Kirrick and Portia had been only minutes before, and they were coming on remorselessly.

'Quick. Follow me,' the rabbit instructed. 'But mind you keep under cover. It'll be easier if I hop back through the longer grass over there. They won't see you that way.' So saying, the kindly animal moved off at a leisurely pace, so as not to hold the attention of the pursuing magpies, and the two robins followed as carefully as they could. Their nerves were stretched to breaking point, but they finally reached the entrance to the rabbit's home. Just then, one of the magpies let out a loud squawk. Kirrick and Portia froze for a moment, sure that they had been spotted. But their luck had held. The unfortunate magpie had blundered into a nest of stinging ants and was, even now, flapping and screeching in pain and annoyance, trying to peck and shake the little insects from his feathers.

Taking advantage of the commotion, Kirrick and Portia plunged into the darkness of the burrow, the rabbit following and then turning to block the entrance. But there was no need. They had not been seen. The rabbit followed the pair down the long tunnel, to a point where it opened out into a wide underground hall. The space within surprised Kirrick, and helped to lessen his feeling of claustrophobia. He turned to face his new-found ally. Neither of the robins had had first-hand experience of rabbits. They had seen them often enough, hopping in leisurely fashion across the hillsides, or scurrying swiftly back to their burrows at any sign of danger. But this was the first time that either Kirrick or Portia had found themselves in the presence of one. Kirrick looked at the rabbit, who was returning his gaze with an amused smile playing across his whiskers. And my, but they were fine whiskers! And such long ears! But it was the rabbit's teeth that fascinated Kirrick most of all. They were fine and strong, protruding prominently from his upper jaw, and were almost unnaturally white, with just the sheen of staining from the juices of the plants that he had so recently nibbled. Kirrick found himself staring and then remembered his manners.

'Thank you so much for your help,' he said. 'I'm Kirrick and this is Portia. We owe you our lives.'

'I never thought of robins as a subterranean species of bird,' joked the rabbit. 'I'm Oliver, and I'm glad to have been of service. But tell me, what have you two hardened criminals done to deserve such a posse?'

Kirrick related the bare facts of the tale and Oliver greeted each twist of the plot with equanimity. He was of a cheerful disposition and a smile never seemed far from his lips. However, his visage took on a darker tone, with Kirrick's mention of the purpose of his visit to Storne.

'It is rare that that name is mentioned in this warren. The eagles are no friends to our folk!' proclaimed Oliver.

'Do not speak ill of such fine birds,' answered Portia, defiantly.

'Obviously the eagles do not eat robins,' said Oliver, with a wry grin.

'What do you mean, you've lost them?'

Traska interrogated the hapless pair of magpies cowering in front of him, and his anger mounted as he was told of the robins' miraculous disappearance.

'We can't understand it. We know they went to ground and we felt sure we had them. There's no way they could have got through. We had them surrounded. But then . . . nothing! They suddenly just weren't there!'

The magpie blustered desperately, hoping against hope that Traska would accept his excuses. But a single look at the viciousness glaring from his interrogator's eyes, showed the reality of the magpie's position. Traska would not tolerate failure, and his frustration at being thwarted yet again needed an urgent outlet. It was to the gathering corvidae's total amazement, therefore, when Traska turned and took to the air without a further word or action. Everyone gave an audible squawk of relief, and the tension evaporated as Traska's silhouette disappeared over the horizon.

As Traska flew away, he was seething inside. Anger, frustration, bitterness and rage churned in his stomach, mixing with a baser emotion. This time the outlet of simple violence was not sufficient. Traska's eyes scoured the scenery below, alert and eager in his lust, for the first glimpse of his victim. The frisson of excitement built and built, until his mind was crazed with desire.

And then he saw her. She was alone and happily oblivious to all around her. Bathing, the young magpie sang softly to herself – a child of Nature, in harmony with her surroundings. Traska thought he had never seen anyone so beautiful, but this only fuelled his passion. For this pair there would be no courtship or ceremonious display. For this female, barely out of adolescence, there would be no nest, no mate.

Traska fell upon her and took her, with a savagery born of his need. Her shocked cries, her tears at the pain, goaded him still further. His physical size meant that she was no match and she was soon cowed, weeping silently, as his violence upon her continued. The swirl of emotions raced and boiled inside him, finally exploding, leaving him drained, physically and mentally, as he slumped over her, pinning her still beneath him. And, as the rage and frustration washed away, they were replaced by an inrushing tide of guilt and remorse for what he had done. The pain this caused him astonished Traska in its intensity and, in his twisted mind, it focused his anger, once again, on its source. Why should he feel pity for her? She was weak and he strong. She was his, to do with as he pleased She was nothing!

As these thoughts filled his mind with hate, Traska began to beat the young magpie as he took her again, until she fainted from the pain and violence perpetrated upon her.

When she regained consciousness, Katya was alone. Her bruises and physical injuries, whilst horrific, gave her no pain. She was numbed. Her brain could not cope with the outrage perpetrated upon her. All joy and happiness in her were extinguished, like a snuffed candle, and the husk of her body was filled with desolation. She, who until

112

that time had only known good, had been ruined forever by evil. The father of her unborn child had never even known her name, nor she his. But she would not forget him, and the thought of revenge planted a small seed in her shattered mind, a crumb of comfort and a purpose to sustain her. For now, as she lay broken and bleeding, it was the only thing that kept her alive.

The robins had foraged successfully, the underground dwellings providing an ample supply of juicy worms. When they rejoined Oliver, Kirrick impressed upon him their need for urgency, and the rabbit offered to act as a guide through the myriad of warrens and tunnels that honeycombed the hillsides, bordering Storne's valley.

'You can travel right to the eagle's nest site, without ever going above ground,' Oliver boasted. 'Not that any of us have ventured there. That would be like committing suicide. The eagles have even sharper eyes than they have beaks!'

'We must go there without delay. Our cause will not succeed without the eagles,' said Kirrick simply.

Their journey, through the underground labyrinth, took less time than they had expected, although the robins would have been hopelessly lost without the expertise of their guide. Several times they had faced a choice of ways, but Oliver had barely paused and Kirrick and Portia had followed gratefully.

'Here we are,' announced Oliver, as they arrived

in a narrow, sloping tunnel, at the end of which gleamed a welcoming light. Kirrick and Portia gazed longingly at the end of the passage, eager to be out in the open air, after the claustrophobia of the tunnels.

'Go with care, or you may go to your deaths!' warned the rabbit.

'Don't worry,' answered Portia, 'We've been through too much to end up as a meal for a hungry eagle.'

CHAPTER 9

When Kirrick was brought before the great golden eagle, he was immediately overawed by Storne's sheer physical presence. The eagle was a magnificent example of his species. He measured a full three feet in length, from beak to tail. His plumage was a lustrous brown, with lighter golden colouring on the head and neck. His beak seemed particularly frightening to Kirrick: wickedly hooked and powerful. Yet his eyes shone with kindness and welcome, and he greeted Portia like an honoured guest.

Portia introduced Kirrick with pride and Storne settled down to listen. Kirrick told him about their journey, and their purpose in coming so far. Storne was impressed at Kirrick's accomplishments and laughed out loud, squawking merrily, at the daring escapes from his magpie hunters. On learning that Traska had pursued them to the very gates of his own fortress stronghold, Storne mused as to how he could best welcome his other 'guest'. But, listening to the council of the smaller bird, Storne accepted that his best course of action for now would be inaction. The time was not yet right for full-blown confrontation with this particular enemy and there would be ample opportunity for battle, if Tomar's plan came to fruition.

Storne was cautious initially. He was lord of his domain, and supremely confident of his own dominance in his homeland. But he had never once ventured beyond the highlands, although his searches for food and patrolling of the skies in protection of the smaller birds had carried him over many square miles. But it was all familiar territory. Storne marvelled at Kirrick. This tiny little bird had already made journeys far beyond Storne's own experience and the eagle envied this brave robin his adventurousness.

His fears were twofold. He did not like leaving his own home unguarded, and he felt a slight trepidation at travelling to a strange region, where he and his eagles would not be able to use the terrain to their own advantage. Storne experienced a queasy feeling in his craw. He was afraid of no other bird, and would match any in single combat. But the sheer malevolence of the creature who could plan such genocide – Storne could not call him a bird – was undoubtedly intimidating.

However, right was right, and Storne felt such a rage and hatred for the magpies, for their murderous activities on his own doorstep, that he could not help but feel it even more keenly, when told of the wider picture of Birddom-wide destruction and despair. He could not fault Tomar's plan, and realised the crucial importance of the role that he and his legions would have to play. He resolved that he would not be found wanting. So, he forced his misgivings way down into the pit of his stomach and gave a positive and vibrant affirmation of support to the robin's proposals.

Once again, Kirrick was overwhelmed with gratitude. Dame Fortune was favouring his mission. He had succeeded twice in gaining vital support for Tomar's plan. If anything, the great eagle was even more enthusiastic than Darreal. Kirrick now had won over two formidable allies and, with one more great journey to undertake, he felt confident that he could deliver a triumvirate of overpowering proportions, to meet Tomar's needs at the appointed time.

The eagle and the two robins talked through the long, hot day, comfortable in each other's company. The great eagle was an autocrat. He would need no council to ratify his decision. The eagles would fly, when the time came.

Whilst Portia and Storne exchanged more local news, Kirrick reflected on his next course of action. Time was at a premium and he still had far to go. The third journey would be the longest, but at least he would have the companionship of his mate. Then a sudden doubt assailed him. Would Portia come with him?

Back in Tanglewood, Tomar was thinking about Kirrick. It had been such a long time with no news of the robin. Could one small bird survive, let alone achieve the tasks given him? With a shrug of his massive wings, he let it go. Tomar had other things to worry about. He had succeeded at the farm, and now he had the poison.

However, what had seemed like a brilliant idea at the time, now presented intractable difficulties. Just how did an owl go about communicating with insects? Of course, birds and mammals shared a common language, as well as their own individual tongues. This was a necessity born of a common foe – Man. The ability to communicate, to warn of impending danger, was mutually beneficial to all creatures. But insects did not face the same threats from mankind, and there had been little need for interaction with them until now.

Tomar's thoughts went back to the golden days, when the Council of the Owls had presided over the lore of Birddom. Each member of the council had been chosen for their special skills, contributing to the whole. The Great Owl, Cerival, leader of the Council, was the wisest of all. But another was chosen for her knowledge of other wildlife. Her name was Caitlin. She was a little owl, and her diminutive stature used to seem incongruous at the Council. However, it belied her value. As a communicator, she had spread the word of the Council to many of their animal neighbours, and her contacts had enabled her to receive much useful information. Tomar knew that Caitlin would be able to find a translator for him. Suddenly, the old owl's enthusiasm evaporated.

'Face reality,' he told himself. 'There's no way of getting in touch with Caitlin.'

The little owl lived in woodland, high on the rolling downs, hundreds of miles to the south. Tomar cursed his advancing age and infirmity. His mind could encompass the whole of the world, but he was too old to travel beyond the confines of his own forest home. Caitlin, whose help Tomar needed so badly, might just as well not have existed. The old owl would have to think of another way.

Weary once more, Tomar settled down to rest and sleep. Perhaps a new day would bring fresh hope, fresh ideas. So much depended upon the success of his plans.

Each of the six owls, in turn, were brought before Slyekin. The evil magpie had kept them isolated since their capture. They had been ill-treated by their jailers and were weak with hunger and abuse. Slyekin derided them, making fun of their predicament, and belittling the strength of the Council of the Owls. He called them fools, whose do-gooder activities had left them wide open to a genius like himself. What answer had they had to his brilliance? What protection had the lore of the Council been able to provide Birddom, when he had put his master-plan into action?

Each owl stood before him. Some abject, some

defiant, all impotent in the face of such evil. It was this thought that tortured the owls, as much as any physical harm that was done to them. They had failed when they had been most needed. Indeed, they had, by their instruction of Slyekin, provided the tools to do the job.

So, in this way, the magpie weakened their spirit, whilst captivity weakened their bodies. Slyekin was content. His plans were working. Like clockwork. Not that he, for one moment, entertained a single doubt. He was infallible. A genius. A god!

When Kirrick and Portia took their leave of Storne, they stuck to their decision to go back through the rabbit tunnels. The robins were both eager to tell Oliver of the agreement made with Storne. When he had heard of the help given to the two robins, the great eagle had vowed that he would ensure that the rabbits would no longer be hunted by his kind. In future, they would search farther afield for their food. Kirrick and Portia were sure that the rabbits would be delighted with the news of their future safety from talons of the eagles, and were very pleased to be able to do a favour for Oliver, in return for his kindness towards them.

The rabbit had promised to return the following day, to guide the pair through the maze of warrens. Kirrick knew that Portia had been right to suggest this. The tunnels would provide their safest route away from Storne's eyrie, and Oliver would easily be able to find them a suitable alternative exit, if Traska and his cohorts were persistent enough to still be searching the area where they had entered the warren. However, Kirrick viewed the prospect of another subterranean journey with some trepidation, and was thankful that they would not have to make the journey unguided. No sooner had Kirrick and Portia started into the tunnels, when Oliver appeared. Their cries of greeting died on their beaks, when they saw how distressed the rabbit seemed. And when he spoke, they could hear the anguish in his voice.

'The magpies are in the tunnels!'

The robins listened, aghast, as Oliver told of how the magpies had continued to search the area where Kirrick and Portia had disappeared so effectively. The rabbits had watched, with amusement, as scores of the black and white birds had joined in, combing the countryside for clues.

But then one magpie had arrived, and the stakes had suddenly been raised. Oliver had known, from Kirrick's story, that this must be the one who had been pursuing the robin all over Birddom. Perhaps Traska had guessed how the robins had disappeared, or perhaps he had just been lucky. Whichever it was, he had turned the attention of his hordes upon the rabbits themselves. They had chased, harried, and isolated a young doe rabbit. Several of the large birds had gathered around her menacingly. Then, without warning, they had attacked. The other rabbits had tried to rush to

121

her aid, but had been beaten back by the sheer numbers of the magpie hunters.

The young doe, badly wounded, had been in no state to resist when Traska began his interrogation. He had quickly learnt of the robins' method of escape, also gaining confirmation that it was now a pair for which he was hunting. Traska had reacted swiftly. Reinforcing his commands with brutal severity at the slightest dissent, he had ordered his troops into the rabbit warrens. However, Oliver had also been quick-thinking. He had organised several of the younger, stronger bucks to fight a rearguard action, whilst a team of rabbits were sent to block up the tunnels that provided the most direct passage through the warren. Oliver had left his companions at this point, and had used all speed to come and warn Kirrick and Portia of the new menace awaiting them.

Kirrick and Portia returned at once to Storne's eyrie. The great eagle listened with concern as the tale of the rabbits' peril was unfolded.

'This cannot go unpunished. Besides, it will be a good rehearsal for what is to come.'

So, with these words, the eagle flew off, to gather a strike-force to more than match the power of the magpie coven. Kirrick knew that he really ought to take the opportunity to leave, with or without Portia, and begin his arduous flight south on the final journey that would, hopefully, bring Tomar's plan to fruition. But, for now, both of the robins had to stay to see the outcome of the battle. Perhaps, in some small way, they could help. In any case, they could not leave the area with the magpies in such numbers. They took to the air in unison, and followed the flight of deadly predators, as they headed, straight as an arrow, for their battle ground.

The magpies had made little progress through the tunnels, and had turned to squabbling amongst each other in their frustration. Several of the rabbits had been killed, some savagely tortured. But they were on home territory, and the magpies were in an entirely alien world. Their fear of Traska decreased with time spent in the tunnels, and soon their forward advance ground to a halt.

'I've had enough of this,' voiced one disgruntled bird, 'I'm gonna get back out in the fresh air where I belong!'

Most of the other magpies murmured their assent at this comment, and soon all the attackers were in retreat. However, Traska was waiting at the entrance to the tunnels, and fell upon the first couple of magpies who tried to leave. But the remainder of his force spilled out of the rabbits' warrens, and took to the skies gratefully, enjoying their freedom after the constraints of their underground sojourn.

Thus it was that the magpies were in no position to repel the sudden, swift and merciless attack from the eagles who appeared out of nowhere, but who were now very much amongst them. Individually the magpies were no match for their superior foes. The ensuing battle fast became a rout, which soon turned into a massacre.

It was Traska's cunning sense of self-preservation that saved him from the eagles' attack. He could see the hunter quickly becoming the hunted, and had dodged into the rabbits' tunnels to avoid the talons of a swooping attacker. Once inside, he had no option but to career at random through numerous passageways, terrified of pursuit, uncaring of his destination. He was no longer concerned about the robins. He was fleeing for his life.

Indeed, it was some time before he allowed himself to slow down, and take stock of his situation. He could hear no sound of pursuit, and he rested for a while, chest heaving with the exertions of his escape, and with the lack of air in the confines of the tunnels. Traska was hopelessly lost, but knew he had to continue on blindly, in the hope of finding another way out of this maze. He knew that he could not go back. That would be a fatal mistake.

Kirrick and Portia had seen Traska disappear into the very tunnels that had proved their escape route from the magpies. Storne disengaged from the battle, and took stance at the entrance, surveying his victory. The magpies were decimated and the few remaining survivors fled in desperation. At a signal from Storne, the eagles ceased their pursuit of the rabble, and the proud birds returned to their mountain home.

Storne, however, lingered for a while, reluctant in the aftermath of victory to experience the sadness of a parting. But Kirrick's relief at the outcome of the battle was tempered by the resurgence of his fears about losing his precious love, Portia. So far, everything that she had said and done proved her love for him. But would she be prepared to leave her homeland and face unknown perils by his side?

Portia sensed that Kirrick was troubled, and intuitively knew the reason.

'I never want to be apart from you again, my love.'

Kirrick and Portia were anxious now to be on their way, and so took their leave for a second time. Kirrick was relieved that they could journey now in open flight, rather than travel below ground. Accompanied by Storne, the pair of robins flew down to say their farewells to Oliver. The rabbit hopped nervously from one foot to the other at the arrival of the massive eagle, but stopped just short of fleeing for the safety of his tunnels. Portia introduced Storne to the rabbit, and told Oliver of the agreement that the eagles had made, regarding the safety of his own folk. This Storne affirmed, with a nod of his mighty head, and then turned to Kirrick.

'Journey safely, my little friend, and don't worry!' exclaimed Storne. 'I'll have a watch kept on both ends of the warren. And if that damned bird is foolish enough to venture out on my territory, he will find a warm reception awaiting him!'

'Goodbye then,' said Kirrick. 'And thank you for all your help. Until we meet again!'

'We know the time and the place,' replied the great eagle. 'We will be there, never fear!'

Kirrick and Portia turned then, and, gauging their heading by the position of the sun, set off on their long flight south.

Slyekin felt that he had waited long enough. Although the feast was still some weeks away, he was eager to bring the remainder of the Council of the Owls under his control. Only by the capture of the final six owls could he bring his plan to absolute fruition. But he wanted to increase the agony of the Great Owl, to maximise the hurt done to his pride and honour.

Slyekin had decided to capture the remaining owls one by one. In this way he sought to extinguish any flicker of hope in Cerival's heart, but to do so with exquisite slowness. Slyekin sent for his henchmen, and gave instructions for a quintet of magpies to set off immediately. Theirs was the longest journey. They were being sent to capture the snowy owl, Isidris. To see him humbled would wound the Great Owl sorely. That would be fine, but Slyekin did not wish to delay his personal pleasure by waiting for their return from such a distance. So he decided that a second party should be sent out to capture one of the owls somewhere nearer.

Slyekin laughed as he realised how little force would be needed this time. He would only need to send three of his elite magpies to capture Caitlin. The little owl would provide scant resistance, but might give them a lot of amusement when they had her in their grasp. Slyekin grinned with cruel satisfaction. Each owl on the Council in some way represented some thing he could never do, could never be. His hatred for them all burned deeply inside him. But they would bow down before him, spreading their wings in self-abasement. Yes. He would make them grovel. And then he would kill them!

CHAPTER 10

While Kirrick and Portia were in the early stages of their long flight south, and Traska meandered, helpless and lost, in the labyrinthine rabbit warren, Tomar had a visit from a rather unexpected guest. He had made a rare and very welcome catch, and was settling down to his meal, when a familiar face peered into his nest hole.

'Well, well! I haven't seen you in ages,' said the old owl. 'You look as if you've been in the wars.'

This was rather an understatement. His visitor's face and body were a mass of cuts and bruises, and the owl's admiration for his guest increased as the story unfolded. It was a tale of amazing courage in the face of extreme brutality, and Tomar's expression showed his anger and his concern at his friend's treatment.

Anisse stayed for the remainder of the day and Tomar filled his companion with renewed hope when he told of the plan that he and Kirrick had worked so hard on.

'It will be so fitting. No tyranny such as theirs

should be allowed to continue,' stated Anisse vehemently.

'But I am grieved that you should have suffered so painfully for your small part in this adventure,' said Tomar, pityingly.

'Don't worry about me. I'll survive,' replied the grebe. 'Anyway, I'm proud that I have been of some help to Birddom. I feared that I might have been its betrayer, when I was forced to tell that evil magpie about yourself and Kirrick. I am glad that everything has turned out for the best.'

'It is far too soon to say that,' Tomar responded, gravely. 'I've still had no news about Kirrick. We can only hope, almost against hope, that one small, young bird can achieve the enormous tasks that have been set for him. It is a great burden to place on so slight a pair of wings! And yet I feel, in my aching old bones, that Kirrick will not fail. He is an extraordinary bird, that one!'

'I felt that too, however brief our acquaintance. But it is all beyond our control now. For the moment it is good just to rest, and talk with a friend.'

And so the owl and grebe passed an evening in comfortable companionship, and, when it came time for sleeping, the grebe chose to stay close by. She found a suitable nesting site in the adjacent undergrowth and made herself a makeshift home to provide her with a basic comfort.

'It's good to see you, my friend,' said the old

owl, as they bade each other goodnight. 'Good to see you alive!'

The very next day, Tomar received another guest, whose arrival delighted him even more than that of Anisse. A broad smile spread across his beak and the warmth of his welcome was mirrored in the eyes of Caitlin, who quickly settled down on a perch beside her friend. Tomar made the introductions between his two visitors and then asked the first of many questions, which crowded into his mind.

'How did you know that I needed you?'

'I had absolutely no idea, my dear,' replied the little owl. 'Pure coincidence, I assure you. And yet . . . perhaps it was meant to be.'

'Then what brings you here? It's been such a long time since I've seen you, or any of the Council.' Tomar's face was a mask of regret.

'Too long, my friend, too long,' reiterated Caitlin. 'But I have been keeping in touch with one of our fellow Council members. Do you remember young Tarquin?'

'Very well. A most capable young owl, though a bit short of temper, if my memory serves me well,' replied Tomar.

'Yes. Well, he and I were near neighbours, when you consider how wide-spread the council members are. So, after we disbanded, I used to go and visit him every few weeks, just to keep in touch. Purely sociable, though I suspect that he thinks of me as a bit of an old fusspot.'

Caitlin paused, and Tomar proffered the appropriate demural. Satisfied, the little owl continued.

'Well. I went to visit him two weeks ago, but he wasn't there. This surprised me, as he knew I'd be coming. But what worried me more was the state of his home. His nest was very nearly destroyed, and there were signs of a struggle everywhere. I asked around among the small mammals who live nearby. There was no great love lost there, I can tell you. Tarquin must have had a voracious appetite. But they finally told me of his capture by a large band of magpies. They didn't know where he had been taken, or why. And neither do I. So I decided to go and visit the Great Owl, but the story was the same there. I just can't understand it!'

'I can,' answered Tomar. 'So Cerival himself has fallen. It is even more vital that we succeed now.'

Then, Tomar went on to explain everything to Caitlin. The actions of Slyekin, Kirrick's mission, his pursuit by Traska and the plan for the defeat of the evil magpies. Caitlin listened attentively, often clapping her wings in delight at the various details and intricacies of Tomar's masterful ideas. In reply to Tomar's enquiry, Caitlin quickly affirmed that she would be able to find a suitable intermediary for the talks with the insects. But Tomar still looked troubled.

'Your news is grave to me,' he said to his friend. 'It looks as though Slyekin plans to capture all of us.'

'But we are forewarned,' replied Caitlin. 'We must hide. I know of many places where they would never find us.'

'We must make all speed to advance our plans,' stated Tomar. 'Anisse can see that they are followed through. But, when they come for us, I am of a mind that we should offer no resistance, nor show any spirit. We must allow ourselves to be taken meekly.' Enlightenment dawned on the little owl's face.

'Why, you crafty . . . genius. You already have a plan to rescue the Council!'

'A plan, no. But an idea, well maybe. I'll need to think it through. But for now, we have little time to waste. Caitlin, my friend. Can you fetch your interpreter for me? We must begin our part of the plan.'

Traska had long since lost all sense of direction. He also had no idea how long he had been wandering along these damned tunnels. He felt disoriented, confused and angry. There were sufficient worms to keep him adequately fed, although he had soon grown tired of this particular cuisine. He had also quickly discovered that, by using his cruelly sharp beak, he could peck holes in the roots which infested many of the passageways, thereby gaining access to precious water.

He had thought once or twice of going back the way he came. In his tortured mind, even facing an eagle would be better than continuing on in this nightmare. But the many twists and turns that he had taken precluded this. There was no way that he could find his way back. He had to go on.

So he continued, staggering and stumbling, as the oppressive weight of his failure bore down upon him. Depression seeped insidiously into his brain, and he felt near to giving up. How easy it would be just to lay down and not get up again. All he had to do was stop walking along these infernal tunnels.

The tunnels! Something registered in his be-fuddled brain. The tunnel along which he was travelling was definitely rising, which must mean that it would lead to a way out! Hope surged renewed through Traska's weary body, and he quickened his pace. The path was indeed climbing towards the surface, the plant roots were younger and less gnarled here, and the soil more friable. Traska exulted. He would soon be free!

He strode boldly round a bend in the tunnel and stopped, thunderstruck. There was no way ahead. The passage was blocked and the blockage was old and hard-packed, like concrete. Traska stared in despair at the earth which barred his way, then spun round frantically, as if fearful that some vengeful demon would magically seal the warren behind him, entombing him.

A worm fell at his feet, and then another. He looked up at the ceiling of the tunnel. More worms were wriggling half in, half out of the earth above his head and, where one fell from his entry hole, a thin bead of light showed through.

Traska almost cried in relief, and then set about excavating himself from this hell-hole. The roof of the passage was very thin and fragile at this point and the soil was easy to dig through. Traska's eyes were constantly and painfully blinded by falling earth, as he hacked away with his beak. Soon, however, he made a hole through to the surface and gulped, as the deliciously cool and fresh air hit his face. Working frantically, he widened the hole, and soon was able to squeeze himself through.

Free!

Kirrick and Portia had decided, almost at once, that they should go to see Tomar before embarking on the third and final journey. Now that Traska was no longer a threat, Kirrick felt safer in returning to his friend. There was so much to tell the old owl. Portia was eager to meet Tomar, after all that Kirrick had told her about this wonderful, wise old bird.

So on they flew, over many nights and days, as fast as their wings could carry them. And while they flew, they talked about something that had scarcely seemed possible to either of them when the year had begun. They talked about the future – their future after the magpies' defeat.

'It has been such a long time since we dared to hope for an end to this nightmare. But every part of Tomar's plan seems to be turning out just as he envisaged it. I really believe, for the first time if I am honest, that we might succeed. That Birddom just might have a future.'

The future was very much on the mind of the young female magpie, as she brooded on her nest. Katya's whole being was focused on the egg upon which she sat. Here was the implement of her redemption. Her physical injuries had healed. After all, she had been young and healthy. But the mental scars remained, their damage irreversible. Katya had retreated into a small and comfortable place inside her mind. And it was from there that she looked out at the world, unseeing. Her mind was wholly intent on the birth of her offspring, and the commencement of his indoctrination. Her son would be her avenger.

He would grow big and strong. She would see that no harm came to him. And she would teach him. Not the joyous, natural things that her parents had taught her. But hatred. Hatred and vengeance.

It was an astonishing sight that met Tomar's eyes when he looked out over the clearing. This part of Tanglewood had traditionally been a meeting place, once, memorably for the Council of the Owls itself. It was the perfect natural design, a mini amphitheatre. The trees surrounding the clearing reflected the sound inwards, so no nuance or inflection was lost to the audience. It was also a setting of great beauty, verdant and tranquil.

But what Tomar saw was a living cloak, covering every patch of green, every twig and leaf. It was unchanging in size, but constantly shifting before his gaze. It was a carpet of insects, which smothered the clearing.

Tomar turned to talk to Caitlin, who was sitting, similarly awestruck, beside him.

'We face a dangerous foe in the magpies. But if these were ever arrayed against us . . .' Tomar left the sentence unfinished. Hopefully, this vast army would be on his side.

Caitlin's interpreter was a star-nosed mole. He was exceedingly old, and looked as though he wore a coat of dust, his fur being softest grey in colour. He was totally blind, but his hearing was exceptionally acute. Above all, he was a learned mole, who had spent his whole life mastering the myriad dialects and languages of insects. Caitlin had known him a great many years and a friendship of sorts had grown between them based on academic interest. But until now, Caitlin had had little use for his special skills.

The mole was called Jonathan, an unusually simple name for one so venerable and learned. When he spoke, Tomar had to chuckle inside. Caitlin had made herself indispensable. The rounded and flowery language used by the mole made him every bit as indecipherable as the insects themselves. Caitlin would have to translate for the translator!

Ever since the insects had moved en masse into

the clearing, there had been a constant low hum of noise. Now, as Tomar rose up to address his audience, a stillness and absolute silence descended upon the gathering. Tomar began to speak.

'My friends. We live in a troubled world. We all have many natural enemies, and face many dangers. It is a sadness to me that we come together as strangers, and only in a time of dire need. But that is the way of things. I wish it were otherwise. I have asked for this meeting because we face an unnatural enemy, and we need your help in defeating him and returning to the natural order of things.'

As Tomar spoke, his deep, rich voice was matched by the sonorous, guttural tones of Jonathan, as the mole translated for him. Each sentence had to be translated three different ways for the waiting audience, so the process was slow and painstaking. But this could not detract from the power and fervour of Tomar's message, as he continued.

'Ever since Slyekin turned Birddom upside down with his evil, we have concentrated – species and individual – on survival. We have hoped against hope that somehow things would change. We have been living in a fool's paradise. Slyekin is bent on the total destruction of all bird life, save his own race. He will not be happy until he has destroyed us all. We must fight back. Our greatest strength is one that is an alien concept to him. Unity. Our plan is to unite all that remains of

Birddom in a war against the magpies. Slyekin will not expect us to have the courage to take sides against him. He believes he has broken our spirit. He will find out that he is wrong. But we must take our chance. We must utterly defeat the magpies. There will be no second opportunity. Slyekin is too clever for that.'

Tomar paused, momentarily uncertain as to how he should continue. Then, boldly, he plunged on.

'We will put forward a mighty army against the corvidae. But they have extinguished many species and, at best, we can hope only to match their strength in battle. We need a surprise element to defeat them. We need your help.'

Having said this, Tomar went on to detail his plans to his captivated audience. He produced and set down before them the phial of poison. Whereas it had been small in his talons, it now stood like a great monolith, in front of the thousands of tiny insects.

'Man has always been our common enemy. Yet now he has come to our aid, albeit inadvertently. A brave, but doomed creature showed me the way. Poison will be our surprise weapon. But I need your help in setting the trap. Your kind alone are immune to this type of poison. What would be lethal to any of us will not harm you in any way. If you choose to help us, your task will be to poison all the carrion and carcasses, for a radius of a mile around Slyekin's lair. The magpies are lazy birds. They will gather as local a harvest as possible to provide their feast. You can help us deliver a decisive blow, a blow for freedom and justice. Will you help us?'

Slyekin was furious at this first setback to his plans. Where could that confounded owl be? He had no fears that Caitlin could be a threat in any way. She was the least of the owls, and yet, in a way, the most important for Slyekin to capture. Being the weakest link in the Council, she would provide the fulcrum point for his humiliation of the owls. Slyekin, like all bullies, had chosen to pick on the smallest and most vulnerable of his enemies. He needed Caitlin. He had to have her found.

Slyekin rounded on his lieutenants and, screaming in his rage, exhorted them to new efforts in finding the missing bird. Then, having issued these orders, he calmed himself and thought for a while. Isidris would soon be in his grasp. Caitlin was but a troublesome, temporary problem. She would be found and captured. It was time for Tomar.

Pain, like a knife, twisted in Slyekin's guts, as he remembered the old owl. Of all the owls, Tomar was the one that he hated the most. The Great Owl had been a trusting fool. Others of the Council had been susceptible to manipulation and coercion. But Tomar stood, in Slyekin's memory, like an ancient rock, solid as granite. The owl was wise, just and honourable. Everything which

Slyekin stood against. He must be defeated. But first, he must be caught. Slyekin summoned his most trusted henchman and bade him select a particularly vicious band of magpies. Then he sent them after Tomar.

Kirrick and Portia were resting, exhausted at the end of a long day's flight. The moon was bright in the summer night sky and they gazed at it in silence. Each was lost in their own separate thoughts. Kirrick was thinking back to his childhood. His relationship with Portia had deepened beyond their initial attraction and affection. It had moved towards a more lasting commitment and now looked to have a permanency, awaiting only the consummation of their physical love.

So Kirrick was thinking back to his father, and their brief relationship, before he became another victim of the magpies' oppression. His memories were fond ones. His father had been loving, kind and a wise teacher. Kirrick hoped his own children would be able to say the same of him. His father had also taught him courage, and had embued him with a sense of fun in all things. This combination of a brave heart and high spirits had served Kirrick well in the subsequent years.

Portia, too, was thinking of parenthood. She was ready to mate. Her very own nest. A clutch of eggs to warm and hatch. Young to feed. The season was right . . . and she wanted him so badly. A smile played across her beak, as she thought, 'Why wait?'

It had been a hard day and Tomar was drained. Long hours had been spent in persuasion, and negotiation. The insects were hard bargainers. They were, of necessity, practical creatures, and, whilst they felt sympathy for the plight of Birddom, they wanted a more tangible reward than just the gratitude of the owls. Tomar had pointed out that they would benefit materially by the greater availability of carrion when the corvidae were defeated and banished. The king of insects held out for something more concrete and guaranteed. Finally Tomar suggested something that had been his intention all along.

'When the magpies have been defeated, and order is restored to Birddom, we will reconvene the Council of the Owls. Many things will have changed forever. There will be chances to start afresh. Birds are, by nature, omnivorous. We will pass a law that no bird shall take an insect for food. Your kind shall be safe, in perpetuity, as a show of gratitude for the aid which we seek now.'

Their leaders had gone away into the vast throng, and Tomar and Caitlin had suffered an agonising wait, while their proposals were discussed. Then, finally, a decision was reached, and now the eyes of the owls were focused on the phial of poison, carried on the willing backs of hundreds of tiny creatures, as the insects left the clearing. The plan had worked. Everything would be in place, as Tomar had envisaged it. Now it all depended upon Kirrick. Tomar's thoughts turned again to the brave little robin, on whom all their hopes were pinned. He could not know that reality had exceeded his wildest dreams, and that, even now, Kirrick was but a few miles away. Tomorrow should see their reunion. But what else would the day bring?

CHAPTER 11

Kirrick and Portia awoke, eager to be off. It was like coming home, and both robins were looking forward to reaching Tanglewood and seeing Tomar. Their flight south had been unerring in its accuracy. All birds are expert navigators and the pair of robins were no exception. They seemed to have an inbuilt compass which guided them over unknown territory to their destination.

After an hour of flying, Kirrick espied the familiar and impressive spread of Tanglewood itself. He turned to Portia and, following his gaze, she too viewed, for the first time in her case, the dark and imposing woodland ahead of them.

'It'll be good to see Tomar,' exclaimed Kirrick. 'I've got so much to tell him.'

The pair dipped their wings and flew down to the canopy of the forest.

Kirrick's reactions were quickest and his heart stilled as Portia hesitated, before joining him in a headlong flight for cover when a large band of magpies and crows rose out of the treetops. Kirrick's relief at not being seen soon turned to dismay as he saw Tomar in their midst, abject and meek, obviously captive. There was another owl also, whom Kirrick did not know, and they were being taken away south, he realised, as the corvidae wheeled in formation and set off.

Kirrick's impulsive, but impractical, reaction was to somehow rescue his friend. But Portia stilled his impetuosity.

'Don't be a fool, Kirrick. You can't help him now, and it's more important than ever that you finish your task!'

It had been first light when they had come for the owls. They had come in numbers and Tomar had been surprised by the suddenness of their arrival. He was only thankful that he had been able to conclude his business with the insects. He had known that they would come for him, of course, although their surprise and glee, at finding not one, but two owls, caused him quiet amusement.

It probably turned to the owls' advantage, as the corvidae were less brutal when facing a pair of owls, however disparate in size. Indeed, there was a measure of relief in the magpies' reactions when Tomar and Caitlin submitted so docilely to their demands. They had expected much more of a fight. But Caitlin had accepted Tomar's advice to offer no resistance and, in any case, her size was hardly conducive to a battle royal with such a mob of huge and menacing birds. The corvidae mocked the pair of owls, deriding their lack of courage and pouring scorn upon their much-vaunted wisdom, in letting themselves be taken so easily. But Tomar and Caitlin refused to rise to the bait and maintained a dignified silence in the face of this barrage of insults. The leader of this band of corvidae, a bulky, but battle-hardened crow with a bloodstained beak, was particularly vitriolic in his abuse of the two owls.

'You two miserable specimens can't possibly be members of the great Council of the Owls. Look at the pair of you. You wouldn't make a decent owl between you! There you stand, trembling with fear. And you were supposed to be the Law Makers, the highest in the land. You're not fit to brush the dust off a magpie's tail! Slyekin won't have any trouble with you two, that's for sure. Come on then. We'd best be off. You've got an appointment to keep!'

The crow chuckled cruelly and, with the help of his cohorts, jostled and harried the owls into flight. And so it was that, by the time Kirrick and Portia reached Tanglewood, the owls had allowed themselves to be captured and flown off to Slyekin's lair.

Kirrick felt totally distraught and dejected. In spite of Portia's pleadings, he did not know what to do. What would be the point of going on with the plan without Tomar? They had made no firm battle-plans for the day itself and now the general had been captured. Kirrick was a messenger, not a leader of armies. He felt helpless in the face of the old owl's capture.

The robin sat, motionless as stone, for a long time. Each thought raised fresh doubts, each hope was dashed by reason. He had never felt more inadequate to the task. Finally, though, one thing shone clear, through all the chaos in his mind. To fail would be to subject all Birddom to a never-ending blackness. There would be no future for anyone. Kirrick could think of no revision to Tomar's plan that could improve their chances. As for the battle itself, greater birds than he would be on the side of right. They would know what to do when the time came. His priority must be to provide them with sufficient forces to finish the job.

Kirrick looked up at Portia, and touched her face tenderly with his wing.

'I'm sorry,' he said. 'I felt so lost seeing Tomar defeated like that. But you are right. We must carry on with the plan, and without delay. The journey that remains is shorter than our last one, my love. But we must fly fast and hard. Time will not wait for us. Do you feel fit enough to leave so soon?'

'I could fly twice around the world with you by my side,' answered his beautiful companion.

'What are we waiting for, then?'

And so it was that the robins' choice of immediate departure meant that they neglected to fly on to Tomar's home, where Anisse waited, charged with passing on a message of hope to Kirrick.

News that everything that was happening was according to Tomar's plan.

But perhaps Fate had again stepped in with a guiding hand, because, as Kirrick and Portia embarked on their final journey, another far less welcome visitor arrived at Tomar's crooked tree. He was tired and dishevelled, for he had been flying for days without rest. Urgency, and an increasing sense of recklessness, had driven him here. Traska had chosen to confront the owl, whose machinations were driving him to distraction. Even the caution he felt, following his last encounter with one of Tomar's brethren, could not halt his headlong charge south to Tanglewood. He had to know why that dratted little robin had been giving him the run-around, all over the country.

So Traska's immediate frustration was enormous when, on arriving at Tomar's home, he found the place deserted. It was indeed fortunate for Anisse that she was away finding food, for when Traska saw that the nest site was empty his rage was frightening. As usual, he sought an immediate violent outlet for his anger and this time the unfortunate recipients of his wrath were a pair of young gulls, who had the misfortune to be travelling in the wrong piece of sky that day. When Traska had returned to Tomar's favourite perch on the crooked tree, only one young seagull continued on his journey. His sister lay, dead and mutilated, on the forest floor.

As his rage calmed, Traska pondered on the situation which now faced him, and the decisions that he must take. His first course of action had to be to find out where Tomar had gone. Why had the owl left Tanglewood? Was Kirrick with him? Was this an escalation, or even the culmination of their plans? Fear rose into his throat and he spat it out, along with a few remaining seagull feathers.

He chose, first, to revisit the local coven of the corvidae, whose help he had sought when he first began hunting the robin. Traska was pleased to find that their braggart leader had been replaced with a magpie, whose no nonsense and concise responses to Traska's enquiries were a refreshingly welcome change. The evil magpie quickly learnt, to his great satisfaction, of Tomar's capture. He was also fascinated to be given news of the Great Feast, which this year promised to be unsurpassed. Rumours were already circulating wildly about the festivities to come, and the special entertainments that Slyekin had planned.

Traska's enquiries about Kirrick elicited no response, and the magpie retreated into himself as he considered the implications of the news he had received. So Kirrick had not returned to see his friend, or, if he had, had been and gone. Where? Traska had no idea. And Tomar had been taken to Slyekin's lair, along with the rest of the Council of the Owls. He almost felt pity for them. Slyekin would see to it that they got no enjoyment from the entertainment.

Tomar's plan must now have gone awry. The magpies were surely safe. The robin alone would not be able to finish whatever complex design had been in the old owl's mind. The fortunate intervention by Slyekin, to satisfy his own devious plans, must surely now have ended once and for all the threat that Kirrick posed. Besides, Traska was not about to go off on another wild goose chase after that foolhardy bird. Slyekin would be not a little interested to hear of Tomar's schemes against him. Perhaps he might even invite Traska to participate in the entertainment. How he would relish destroying that owl! Traska, his mind made up, took to the air and, following the route of the band of corvidae who had trapped Tomar, headed south to Slyekin's lair.

Kirrick and Portia flew as they had never flown before. The Great Feast was little more than a week away, and Kirrick knew how vital this third and final mission was. The eagles and the falcons were mighty and noble warriors, but, for Tomar's plan to succeed, they needed others, who were more streetwise in the ways of fighting. Kirrick's last mission was to journey to the eastern shores, to seek the aid of the sea birds. Cormorant and shag, petrel and skua, gannet and seagull. Each one honed and hardened in their constant battles for food and territory. And in their wars against their raging, elemental enemy – the sea. So the pair of robins flew fast and hard. They passed over Kirrick's former home, but he hardly paused. There was nothing but sorrow there for him now. His future was elsewhere. He glanced over at Portia.

'Come on, slowcoach!' she chided lovingly. 'You must be getting old!'

They journeyed for two days and nights before they saw the sea. Just as they reached the coast, they cut across an estuary. Both birds had flown without rest and were tired and thirsty. But, as Kirrick began to dip his wing and turn in descent towards the river, Portia gasped. The sun had caught the mass of blue water and reflected in sparkles off its mirrored surface. Portia had never seen the sea before, and its beautiful colour and sheer vast expanse entranced her. By comparison, the muddy brown waters of the estuary seemed very uninviting. Without warning she banked and sped off to the shore line. Kirrick realised her intentions too late to stop her, and his warning was whipped away on the sea breeze.

At the first taste of the brackish fluid Portia gagged, choked and swallowed. By the time Kirrick reached her, she had begun to retch. She was dizzy and disorientated. Kirrick looked into her eyes and was alarmed at the dull sheen which returned his gaze. Portia slumped to the ground and lay still on her side. Kirrick stared around him in distress. What could he do?

His attention was grasped by an explosive commotion ahead of him. A hissing and snarling turned his insides to jelly. A large, ginger cat, lean and viscious, had caught a plump, male bullfinch and was taunting him, and toying with him. The bullfinch was standing his ground bravely, and responding with obscenities and taunts of his own.

'Call yourself a cat? I've seen more frightening guinea pigs. Bloody stupid moggy. You couldn't catch a soddin' cold!'

The cat spat venomously and crouched, flattening his ears before the pounce. Kirrick was torn between his real concern for Portia and the horror of the scene being played out before him. But only momentarily. He just *had* to help that brave bullfinch. Without hesitation, he dive-bombed the unfortunate feline, catching it in a fleshy part of the neck. The cat yelped, and spun round to face its unlikely assailant. But Kirrick had retreated to the skies, well out of reach. And the diversion had been enough for the bullfinch to scramble to safety. The cat swung round and screamed in frustration at the realisation of a lost meal. Then it slunk off into the bushes. When he was sure that it was safe, Kirrick flew down and called out to the bullfinch. A black head and a chest of purest pink came into view, as he emerged from his hiding place.

'Phew, thanks ever so much. That was really brave of you, that was. How can I ever repay you?'

'You must help me,' replied the robin desperately. 'My mate is sick. She drank sea water, and I'm afraid she may be . . .'

Kirrick gasped in agony, as the thought of losing his beloved Portia hit him.

'How much did she drink?' asked the bullfinch.

'Not much, I think,' Kirrick answered hesitantly.

'What she needs is water, and lots of it,' the finch stated determinedly. 'Where is she?'

'Over by the shoreline,' responded Kirrick.

'Well, we'd better help her quick then. She's in danger there, all right. Too exposed, see. She'd make a much easier meal for that flippin' cat!'

'But what can we do?' asked the robin in exasperation.

'Fetch me a leaf, a strong one, mind. Good. Now, catch hold of that end and help me drag it over here.'

So saying, the bullfinch proceeded to pull the leaf over to the river's edge. Kirrick quickly divined his intentions, but was still troubled.

'Won't that water be just as bad as the sea water?'

'No, mate. The tide's going out, see. So the river's emptying into the sea. That's why it looks so mucky. You don't drink it when the water looks clear, because that's when the tide's coming in, and washing the estuary clean of silt and mud and such.'

And, having had the final, authoritative say in the matter, the bullfinch dragged his end of the leaf into the water. When it was half-filled, the pair tested it for weight and, finding that they could manage it, flew slowly and in cumbersome fashion to where Portia lay.

Kirrick tipped her head back and the bullfinch forced the tip of the leaf into her beak. The inrushing water made her gasp and choke, bringing up the vile sea water from her stomach. They repeated the process, twice refilling the leaf, until they had purged her completely. She huddled exhausted and shivering, but Kirrick's heart leapt for joy, as he saw the spark return to her eyes.

'How can I ever thank you?' Kirrick asked gratefully.

'Oh, you know, one good turn 'n all that,' replied the bullfinch. 'My name's Mickey, by the way.'

'I'm Kirrick, and this is Portia. We're on our way to see the leader of the sea birds.'

'What, old Kraken? What you wanna go and see him for?'

In answer to Mickey's question, Kirrick gave him a brief summary of his quest and adventures. The bullfinch's eyes widened in amazement as the tale unfolded.

'Right. There's no time to lose then,' he stated boldly when Kirrick had finished. 'I can take you both to where Kraken lives. I don't fancy getting too close myself, mind. He gets a bit cranky and he is a fair powerful bird.'

If Traska had thought that his arrival at Slyekin's lair would be triumphal, he could not have been more mistaken. He had so much news to impart, so much that was vital to the magpies' continued dominance of Birddom. But Slyekin was in no mood for long discussions. Traska had timed his entrance poorly. Slyekin had just learned from his minions that one member of the Council of the Owls had been over-enthusiastically persuaded by his captors, and had not survived the journey. Whilst Slyekin wanted the Council members dead, he had also wanted to choose the time and place, and so he felt thwarted. It lessened his upcoming triumph at the Great Feast. Slyekin was swift in his vengeance and the offending magpies were, even now, hanging by their necks and watching their lives slip away through the slit in their bellies.

Traska had presented himself before Slyekin, full of his own self-importance, and had failed to see the warning signs in his leader's bearing and manner. He had opened his beak to begin his long, prepared speech, but had been silenced by a single question.

'Have you managed to kill the robin?'

Traska's anxiety and hesitancy, as he desperately framed an answer to appease, was pitiful to see. Slyekin's immediate thirst for violence had been slaked, but his anger was real as he summoned his huge side kicks.

'Take him away. Just get him out of my sight!'

And, to Traska, 'I'll deal with you later!'

The clifftop where Kraken lived was precipitous and covered with a slime of droppings from hundreds of seabirds. The colony was strictly hierarchical and Kraken rested, in pride of place, on a promentory overlooking the whole of his domain. Kraken was a huge, black-backed gull, certainly the largest seagull seen in these parts for many a generation. His beak was almost as long as Kirrick's body and, when he stretched and yawned, his wings measured fully four feet.

Kraken was a proud and fearsome leader of his own kind. But he was also very wise in the lore of sea and air, and was generally recognised as the head bird among all the seabirds in this region. When Mickey had taken Kirrick and Portia to see the great gull, the clamorous noise coming from the cliff top was terrifying to all three of them. Birds were squabbling and bickering in a constant, collective scream, as they fought for prominence within the colony. Kirrick felt extremely daunted, and was afraid that, being so small, he would - inadvertantly be crushed in the melee of to-ing and fro-ing, without even getting to see Kraken himself.

However, finally, the pair of robins reached the nest site of the great gull. He was resting, surveying all around him, with an amused and benevolent air. His gaze fixed upon Kirrick and Portia as they approached. As he turned his head to face them, they saw that he only had one eye. The other eye socket was empty, courtesy of some long-dead rival, and a patch of feathers had grown over the empty hole, giving Kraken the look of a pirate.

'What brings you to such a dangerous place, my little friends?'

In his dungeon, deep in Slyekin's lair, Traska fumed in impotent rage. How dare he be treated in such a peremptory fashion! That fool, Slyekin, was not fit to be ruler. Traska could have told him so much that would have been vital. The magpies could have prepared themselves. But all Slyekin was interested in was his Great Feast, and the personal, vain-glory of the entertainment he intended to provide. The ego of that damned bird!

Traska caught himself. In his anger he had begun to mutter out loud, venting his feelings. That would be suicidal, and he forced himself to bite back his anger, and to stem his bitter outpourings, before any of Slyekin's watchers heard him and reported back to their leader. Traska had no doubt as to Slyekin's response to such treason. He must lock away his feelings and be patient. Surely, Slyekin would come to see reason and would seek his advice. In this, as in many things, Traska was deluding himself. Little did he realise the perilousness of his position.

Tomar was in a similar situation. But the difference was that it was of his own making. He had been brought before Slyekin and had been subjected to maniacal abuse. But he had deliberately appeared cowed and subdued and, in this manner, had dissipated some of the magpie's anger. Slyekin was disappointed in him. He had expected more spirit from the old owl. However, he gained an increasing sense of satisfaction and pleasure in the knowledge that he had so diminished the might of the Council of the Owls. Tomar's meakness just meant that it would be even easier to humiliate him at the Great Feast.

Slyekin decided that Tomar would be the last to die. His hatred of this particular owl was the strongest. Tomar stood for everything good in Birddom, and Slyekin despised him. After the owls had crowned him king of all Birddom, Slyekin would particularly enjoy seeing Tomar's face as he had to watch his fellow owls being slaughtered before his eyes, in the certain knowledge that he could not avoid the same fate. Slyekin would make him watch the Great Owl himself die. That would indeed be sweet, extinguishing the last hope for birdkind, and leaving Tomar to face his own end, utterly defeated.

Tomar had been dismissed from Slyekin's presence and had been taken to his own place of solitary confinement. He was actually quite glad of this. Being alone would allow him time to think. Now, more than ever, he needed that.

Kirrick's natural optimism was vanishing fast as he told his story to the great gull. He could tell that Kraken had little interest in the goings on of other species of birds, and he had a suspicion that the gull felt a certain admiration for Slyekin's schemes and power-seeking. The robin tried to emphasise the peril to all bird life unless the magpies' expansion was checked, but he could see that he was wasting his time. Kirrick felt desperate. It had been so easy with the falcons and the eagles. Darreal and Storne had understood the importance of his mission and had supported him with some zeal. But this bird seemed only interested in his own little kingdom. Portia could see that Kirrick was having little success, so she too joined in, exhorting Kraken to muster his troops and come to their aid. But the great gull was getting bored. He cared little for the robins' tales of evil doings elsewhere. He had enough to worry about in his own back yard! What did he care about magpies? Or robins, for that matter. The whole of Birddom could go hang, as far as he was concerned. Now, if any bird was foolish enough to attack him personally, it would be a different matter. But Kraken knew that the most likely source of such an attack would be from within his own hierarchy. For, as leader, he always felt the threat of rebellion and sedition, from within the massed ranks of his followers, and his one eye had to be permanently open to that danger, above all else.

So Kraken barely listened as the pair of robins pleaded urgently for his help and Kirrick began to see their chances of success evaporating before his eyes, like mist after sunrise. Suddenly, a raucous cry went up from an incoming seagull, and it was taken up by the birds on the clifftop until it became a deafening chant.

'The fishing boats are coming!'

A great wave of excitement swept over the colony, and all the gulls turned to watch their leader. Excusing himself curtly, Kraken stood up and turned his back on Kirrick and Portia. Then, after a momentary pause, he took off. A split second later, the whole cliff top erupted as hundreds of birds took to the air, the beating of their wings and their savage cries creating a wall of noise which buffeted the tiny birds. Within seconds, though, they were totally alone and watching, in silence, the departing flock of gulls as they headed out seawards towards the incoming flotilla of fishing boats. Kirrick turned to his mate.

'I'm sorry, my darling, but we have failed.'

'If only they had their brains in their heads, instead of in their stomachs!' fumed Portia.

Kirrick laughed. 'I think we've wasted enough time here,' he said. 'We'll have to make do without the help of this rabble. We must get back. The day is almost upon us. We shall need all speed to be in time.'

So, without further ado, the pair of robins took wing and headed back whence they came, but with heavy hearts. Everything now hung in the balance. Success and failure were weighted equally. Only time would tell the outcome of the battle ahead.

CHAPTER 12

It had taken more than a week for the insects to transport the phial of poison to the vicinity of Slyekin's lair. Thousands of the tiny creatures had marched ceaselessly and uncomplaining, with their enormous burden on their backs. When they had arrived at their chosen site, it had taken a further two days for them to eat through the cork stopper, with hundreds of pairs of mandibles chewing voraciously. Finally, however, the seal was breached and the virulent liquid seeped out on to the grass. Some of the insects rolled in the pool of poison. Others ventured into the bottle itself, coating their bodies with the viscous fluid. Every insect was meticulous in charging himself with a dose of the poison and it was several hours before the phial was drained of its lethal load. Then the bottle was dragged and pushed into a dense patch of undergrowth, and the legions of insects formed ranks once more.

Any onlooker would have been utterly amazed to see a glistening river of myriad varieties of insects, marching side by side, as, loaded with their deadly cargo, they set off into the surrounding countryside, to impregnate the carrion for miles around.

Tomar's instinct for the corvidaes' laziness had been unerring. Slyekin had sent out foraging parties to collect a veritable banquet of decaying carcasses for the Great Feast. But no corvidae ventured further than a few wing-flaps' distance from Slyekin's lair. Food was abundant in the locality and no magpie chose to travel further than necessary, or to waste energy in strenuous transportation of finer carcasses, to be gleaned from greater distances. The remains of hedgehogs, rabbits, squirrels, mice and even an unfortunate fox, butchered at the hands of sadistic humans on horseback, were piled high in the arena. This putrefying mound was already several feet in height, and more was being collected by the hour. No one would go hungry at this feast!

Tomar had been dragged from his dungeon and brought before Slyekin at first light on the eve of the Feast.

'Well, old one,' squawked the magpie. 'Tomorrow will be my crowning glory. The greatest feast ever known in the history of Birddom. It's only a pity that you probably won't enjoy it.'

'A day is a long time in a tyrant's life,' Tomar said to himself. 'Many things can happen between dawn and dusk.'

'This has been my destiny since birth,' continued Slyekin. 'It is my right. You can do nothing to prevent it, Tomar. You are completely in my power. Nothing can happen to interfere with my plans. I am invincible!'

'What part do you have for me in your plans?' asked the owl.

'You will be the instrument of my coronation. The Council of the Owls will meet again, and will choose me as its leader, and king of all Birddom. You will personally herald the news to all assembled.'

'An honour indeed!' muttered Tomar wryly.

'Once the announcement of my total authority has been made, the Great Owl will officially disband the Council. There will be no further meetings.' Slyekin strode back and forth as he spoke, gesturing wildly with his wings.

'What if the Great Owl refuses to do as you say?' queried Tomar.

'You must see to it that he does not refuse,' answered Slyekin, sternly. 'You must speak to him. He must be made to see that the power of life and death is in my wingtips.'

'I see that I have no choice but to do as you ask,' said Tomar, sounding weary. 'What will happen to us, once your rightful coronation has taken place?'

'I will have no further use for you,' Slyekin replied. 'You will be free to leave.'

'We are all old and I can see now that our time is past. All that we seek is to return to our homes and live out our lives in peace and quiet.'

Tomar spoke submissively, biting back the anger that seethed inside him. Slyekin laughed, and spat in his face.

'To think I used to be afraid of you. You are nothing. Go now, and prepare a pretty speech for my coronation.'

When Cerival was brought to him, Tomar was shocked to see how frail and defeated he looked. His eyes were bruised through lack of sleep, and his feathers, once so fine, were dishevelled and dirty. The claws on his left foot were hideously bent and twisted, courtesy of some playful torture by his captors. His head was bowed as he faced Tomar, and he could not meet his friend's eye. The weight of his failure, and personal guilt in forwarding Slyekin's ambitions by his patronage, was crushing him visibly.

Tomar greeted the Great Owl formally and in an ancient tongue, little used in the latter days of the Council, but well-known to them since childhood as the language of the Council of the Owls in olden times. Cerival's head came up when he heard this and there was a certain straightening of his posture. But he made no reply. Tomar then spoke to the Great Owl, giving such a message of hope that years seemed to fall from him and the light, that had been missing for so long, returned to his eyes. Tomar told Cerival all about Kirrick and of the plan that they had formulated together. He explained to the Great Owl about Kirrick's missions, to seek the aid of the falcons, eagles and gulls. Tomar was fulsome in his praise for the little robin's courage and expressed his absolute conviction that Kirrick would succeed in his quests.

Cerival questioned Tomar at length, seeking to reassure himself that every eventuality had been covered. But he could find no fault in his friend's plan. He began to thank Tomar, expressing his gratitude that one owl at least had retained the strength and moral courage to continue the fight for Birddom. But Tomar stilled him, telling him that every owl now had a role to play, and that Birddom needed his wisdom and leadership now, like never before. Cerival demurred, saying that the right of leadership had passed from him to another, but passion showed briefly in his face, as he vowed to support his dearest friend in whatever way he could. So Tomar then outlined his ideas to Cerival and the Great Owl nodded thoughtfully, in approval of the other's plan.

And all the while, the corvidae guards sat uncomprehending, amused by this ancient prattle between the two old fools. When, at last, a silence fell upon the pair of owls, one of the guards spoke to Tomar.

'Have you told him what the Boss wants? Does he know what to do?'

'Oh, yes!' replied the Great Owl in sonorous tones. 'I know what to do.'

The fledgling magpie looked up at his mother as she spoke. He was already surprisingly large for his age – Katya had worked tirelessly since his hatching to provide food for her offspring. He had not yet ventured out of the nest and his whole world was one of satiation and indoctrination. For, as she fed him, Katya spoke to her son, filling his mind with hatred for the magpie who had so savagely sired him. From the day of his birth, he had known only this: that he had been born to exact retribution upon that evil bird. As he opened his beak to receive more food, his mother spoke again.

'Venga, my son. Your life at this moment is simple. Your one aim for now is to grow big and strong. Take all the food that I provide. But, take also into your heart the words that I speak. For your life has been given to you by me and your purpose in life is clear. You will be my sword, Venga. You will seek out the magpie who took away my joy, and you will take away his life. For no one bird is less deserving of life than he. This evil magpie who knows no pity must be shown none in return. You must kill him. Kill him for me. So, remember this, little one. Your mother loves you. But she will love you even more when you have killed him and brought me back his head to decorate our nest!'

Two guards had been posted to watch over the huge mound of carrion, gathered in readiness for the feast. As evening drew on, the pair of magpies eyed the food with ever-increasing hunger. They knew that it was a huge risk. They themselves had been instructed to kill, without impunction, anyone who dared to raid the store of meat, before the day itself. But who was to know if they had a few choice morsels themselves? There had been far too much to count. No one would miss a small rabbit or two, from amidst this bountiful larder.

One of the guards kept watch whilst the second chose a carcass, whose gamey smell announced its advancing state of putrefaction. Pulling it from the pile, he set about it with avaricious relish. The second guard grumbled on seeing the other magpie already beginning his meal, but he, too, was soon devouring a rank carcass of his own choosing. Hunger, and fear of being found out, made the magpies feed fast, and, having stripped the bones clean of flesh, they carefully carried the pitiful skeletons some distance away, hiding them in the undergrowth. Then both guards returned to their posts.

The poison took about thirty minutes to take effect and the magpies took a further half an hour to die. A thousand pairs of eyes had watched this unfolding drama and, when the magpies finally lay still, and cold on the ground, a legion of insects marched into the clearing and carried the bodies, in solemn procession, into the undergrowth and away.

Most of the magpies would begin arriving shortly after dawn on the morrow, but hundreds had travelled from far and wide and were roosting in every available branch. There were so many corvidae about. Often the trees were blackened by their sheer numbers – a spectacular negation of Nature's spectrum of colour. Everywhere, there was black and white. The noise of their greetings to each new arrival, and their chatter about the upcoming feast, as they settled down on their perches, was deafening and unceasing. For excitement was in the air. This celebration was the culmination of their year's work, and every bird strove to outdo the others in their tales of the murder and mayhem, which they had carried out for the furtherance of their leader's ambitions.

For about half the assembled throng, this was their first Great Feast, but they gossiped eagerly about past events as if they had themselves parti-cipated in the debauches that they had only heard about. Many there had never met Slyekin, and those that had looked upon the others with disdainful reproach when they bragged about what they would do and say when they came into his presence. They would learn!

Discussion then moved on to how many species had been eradicated in Slyekin's drive for supremacy in Birddom. Estimates varied, but the general consensus finally set the figure at around eighty. And, truth to tell, this was not far from being accurate. It would have been considerably simpler to list the small birds still surviving, by name of individual, than to catalogue the species butchered to extinction by the corvidae hordes.

But two small birds, at least, had survived to survey this scene. Kirrick and Portia had finally arrived, and had taken refuge in a small knot hole, in a decaying old tree. It had no branches and was little more than a rotting stump, but it gave them cover and shelter, and it was a safe haven from which to watch the gathering of the massed ranks of their enemies.

'What do you plan to do, my love?' asked Portia.

'That's just it. I *have* no plan,' replied Kirrick. 'We've come all this way, and now I have no idea how to proceed.'

'Remember, darling. Trust in Tomar. You have done your part, as well as you, or anyone else, possibly could. I think that our best course of action is to wait for the eagles. We can fly into battle with them, if you wish.'

Portia's words made sense to Kirrick. Yes, they would wait for Storne and his company. But, as they settled down to rest, Kirrick realised that there would be very little sleep for him tonight. Tomorrow couldn't come soon enough. It would be the most important day of all their lives.

Slyekin woke early and was soon strutting around, posing and preening, practising his speech. This was his day, his destiny. To finally destroy the powerful Council of the Owls filled Slyekin with a delicious anticipation. He would eat their brains out of their skulls! The savage magpie clapped his wings as he thought of that. Maybe that way he would inherit their oh-so-renowned wisdom.

'Ha!' he laughed, spitefully, planning each moment of the pageant to come. 'To be king of all Birddom! To be recognised as such!' A frisson of pure pleasure tingled through his body.

Later, they gathered before him in their multitudes. A sea of faces, bright eyes, shiny beaks. Hundreds of magpies, crows, rook and other corvidae filled the arena and waited, in total silence, for their leader to speak. Slyekin's henchmen came up to him, and asked when everyone was going to eat.

'The feasting will start after my coronation. Everyone can eat as they watch the owls die. You'd better take some food now, for Traska. He's going to need his strength for later. But don't bother feeding the other prisoners. It would be rather a waste, don't you think?'

Slyekin and the huge crows cackled cruelly at this. Then, as his henchmen departed on their errand, Slyekin stepped forward, to address his audience.

'My followers. My subjects,' he began, grandly. 'This year's annual feast will, I hope, be a rather special one for us all. I know you will all, one day, tell your children about it. We have waited so long, and worked so hard to get where we are today. My genius has brought us this far, and will carry us on to ever greater glory. We have eradicated all but a paltry few of the lesser species of bird, and enjoyed doing it too, I dare say! We have defeated the old order. The Council of the Owls no longer dictates the law of Birddom, and today you will witness their utter destruction. Nothing can stand in our way, as we march forward together. No enemy will be strong enough to gainsay us. We are an invincible army, and whoever we chose to take on in the future, will fall before us.'

Slyekin paused for the waves of inevitable adulation that poured forth from the throats of the assembled congregation, noticing, however, the sections where the cheering was less enthusiastic than the others. His beady gaze focused on them, as he continued,

'I demand nothing less than total loyalty. But I promise you nothing less than total victory! Today, for your entertainment, you will witness the very last Council of the Owls. They have, in their wisdom, decided to retire. For centuries, they have been the Law Makers, the Law Givers. Now they are redundant. They have recognised that a superior intelligence to their own now makes the rules. Today, they will crown me as rightful king of you all, indeed of all Birddom. Then they will disband and abdicate. I assure you, their retirement will be short-lived. After that, we will feast from our not inconsiderable store, and, thereafter, you will have to make your own entertainment!'

A further raucous wave of cheering went up

from the arena. Each owl took his appointed place in the Council, but Slyekin usurped the Great Owl's position in the centre of the Council, and he was forced to fill the lesser position, vacated by the Council member who had died en route to the festivities.

While this preparation was going on, Slyekin summoned one of his henchmen to his side.

'You'd better eat something now, while the pageant is going on. You'll have work to do when everyone else is eating. Choose a dozen of their guards to take with you. I'm sure they'll enjoy the exercise after a good meal!'

With that, he dismissed the giant crow and stood once again before his audience.

'And now,' Slyekin proclaimed, 'let the Council begin.'

Traska waited in his cell. He knew that it was the day of the Great Feast, and he was fearful now of the part that he had been chosen to play. Obviously, Slyekin had little use for him, or the knowledge that he had so dearly wished to impart. Well, it was too late now. Traska's sole thoughts at this moment were for his own survival. For he was sure that, whatever the purpose of Kirrick's missions, today would see their outcome. And he had no intention of being caught in the conflict, which he knew would ensue.

So it was that, at this stage, Fate lent a hand, in the shape of his guard. One of the magpies had brought some food and Traska was grateful, as he was starving. But his guard took the proffered carcass, and kept it for his own.

'I've earned this, guarding a miserable bird like you,' cackled the massive sentinel.

Traska was weak from hunger, having been given only the barest rations since his arrival. So he had had no chance to recover his energies after his exhausting flight south, and was in no fit state to tackle this adversary. He could only look on, in abject misery, as the guard wolfed down *his* meal, laughing as he did so. Traska settled down in the corner, and closed his eyes, brooding malevolently. It was some time later when he heard the guard gasp, and he looked up to see the large bird contorted in agony on the floor. He was immediately puzzled. What could be wrong? Was this something to do with . . .? A smile of satisfaction played across Traska's beak as he relaxed, watching with interest the death throes of his captor. So! He wasn't missing out on all the entertainment, after all!

The coronation ceremony had managed to exceed even Slyekin's expectations. Every owl had played their part, following the lead given by the Great Owl and Tomar. Many of them seethed in resentment at the apparent complicity and surrender of their most respected leaders. But something inside them stayed their anger. It was all too unbelievable. Slyekin, in his vanity, noticed none of this. He had just been declared king and ruler of all Birddom. He had realised his greatest ambition and was revelling in the moment. But, even in his moment of glory, he recognised that the crowd wanted something more. The pageant and his coronation had been well received, but baser desires now needed satisfying.

Slyekin called for silence and announced that the feasting should begin. The assembled masses did not need to be told twice and fell upon the food store in their hundreds, tearing and ripping at the multitude of carcasses, in their frenzy of feeding. Hundreds more hovered impatiently nearby, unable to reach the feast for the throng surrounding it. Turning away from this spectacular orgy, Slyekin called for his guards. The time had come for the second part of his entertainment.

He explained to Tomar that it would be safer if the owls were escorted until they were a safe distance from his home, because of the vast crowds and their present temperament. Slyekin looked up in annoyance when he noticed that his summons had not been answered. He shouted once again for his henchman and their cohorts. To a bird, they were in no position to hear him, or ever would be again. Unscripted, but with perfect timing, Isidris chose this moment to vent his feelings over the charade, in which he had been so unwilling to play a part. He railed in anger at Tomar and the Great Owl, and was astonished to see them arrange the remainder of the Council in a protective ring around their newly-crowned king. Slyekin felt suddenly grateful for the barrier that they presented, for Isidris was a powerful bird, and Slyekin felt horribly vulnerable without his own guards. Isidris was incredulous, speechless with rage at the duplicity of his fellows, but, as he looked into Tomar's face, comprehension dawned on him, and he laughed.

Isidris looked out over the massed assembly – gorging themselves, and oblivious to all but their own gratification. Then he looked back at Slyekin, encircled by the members of the Owls' Council. Finally, he looked back into Tomar's eyes and, following his old friend's gaze, looked skywards. Two darkening clouds appeared to the north and to the west, moving too swiftly for the elements themselves. Tomar offered up a silent prayer of thanks.

'Look well, Slyekin,' commanded the old owl. 'Look and see the coming of your doom!' The magpie stared in terror and disbelief at the fast approaching squadrons of eagles and falcons, as they closed to the battle site.

An alarm went up among the corvidae on the ground, but was unheeded by many, who were too busy fighting each other for scraps of food to realise the imminent danger that faced them. However, hundreds of magpies, rooks and crows took wing and climbed to meet the incoming attackers. Battle was joined in a countless number of aerial duels. The screeching and screaming in the air above their heads alerted more of the corvidae to their peril, and many abandoned their squabbles for food to join their comrades in the skies in repelling the ranks of birds of prey.

Tomar had to shout to make himself heard above the noise of battle.

'You had planned a spectacle of death for the amusement of your followers. We must not disappoint them, though I suspect none will witness it. Let it now be done!'

And, at his command, the owls fell upon Slyekin and tore him to pieces. His reign as king of all Birddom came to an end almost before it had begun. Soon Tomar was left looking down at Slyekin's head on the ground, the eyes staring, unseeing, at the mayhem in the skies overhead.

'Aye, look well,' repeated the old owl. 'Look for all eternity upon your doom.'

Traska had waited until he was certain that his guard was dead. Then he had stealthily made his way out of his place of confinement, and into the open air. He was free! At that very moment, Traska had looked up and witnessed the arrival of the attacking forces. He had the wit to quickly duck back under cover as the mighty birds swept overhead. He had no intention of enjoining battle with this enemy. Let other fools fight, and expend their energy, and their lives. Traska looked on from the safety of his cover and snarled in his anger as he saw Kirrick flying in the midst of the incoming legions. Curse that infernal robin! He'd brought all this about. The robin – and that meddlesome old owl! Traska abandoned his temporary place of cover and retreated back into Slyekin's lair to find a better place to hide. And wait.

CHAPTER 13

Kirrick and Portia sat anxiously, watching the conflict from their vantage point in a nearby tree. Upon reaching the battle site, they had left the eagles and had alighted, knowing that their task was done and that others, more powerful, now held the hope and doom of Birddom. Things were not going well. In spite of the initial advantage of surprise and the fact that each of the attacking force was individually superior to their opponent, sheer weight of numbers was against them. Portia had to physically restrain Kirrick from joining the affray, knowing that he would stand little chance against the much larger foes. The owls, seeing the way that the battle was going, took to the air as a phalanx, and soon scored significant victories with their size and strength. Tomar and Isidris fought side by side, each protecting the other's flank from attack. Elsewhere, Storne was in mighty form and reaped a savage harvest amongst the corvidae. Darreal and his falcons held their own, but it soon became apparent that each eagle and falcon was taking on two or three black and white defenders. Why wasn't the poison working? Had Tomar's plan failed?

Some of the falcons had fallen, dragged earthwards by mobs of magpies and crows. Whilst many corvidae lay dead or wounded, it was clear that the attackers' numbers were slowly dwindling. For the corvidae had realised, at last, the desperateness of their plight. They had abandoned their orgy of self-gratification and had united in this fight for their very lives. Many among them were, by nature, cowardly and would have fled, had the opportunity arisen. But there was no escape and, now that they had no alternative but to fight to the death, most surprised even themselves by their fortitude, in the face of such fearsome opponents. They began to look around them, at the battles raging across the skies and see, here and there, signs of hope that they might yet be victorious. This bolstered their courage and they continued their fighting with renewed vigour. A huge cheer went up as the first of the eagles lost his fight, and plummeted to the ground. He was immediately set upon by a veritable swarm of magpies, who pecked the last vestiges of life out of his huge frame. Then, rejoicing, they took to the air once more, eager for another victory. Fearing that all would be lost, Kirrick turned on Portia.

'I can't just sit by and do nothing!' he pleaded.

As he turned to look again, he gasped in horror. The magpies had managed to separate the two valiant owls and now Tomar was surrounded. The old owl fought on alone and not without effect, but the odds against him were beginning to be overwhelming. It had seemed that for a while Tomar held back his foes with some unseen power, which belied his physical frailty. The magpies seemed reluctant to strike a blow, as if he had some magic which would undo them. But their bravado increased as they saw the anxiety in Tomar's eyes, and more and more they pressed forward, sporadically risking a direct strike and emboldened by their success. Kirrick could not let his mentor be brought down.

But, just as he took to the skies to race to the aid of his friend, two things happened simultaneously. The poison in the carrion began to take massive and deadly effect, with dozens of corvidae literally falling out of the sky, screaming in agony as they did so. And, in the same instant, a vast flock of screeching, cawing seabirds arrived from the east and joined the battle. The remaining magpies did not know which way to turn. The timely arrival of the gulls encouraged the falcons and eagles immeasurably and they rejoined battle with the corvidae, with hope refreshed and strength renewed. The magpies looked about them as bird after bird succumbed to the lethal fluid inside them, often dying before their bodies hit the ground. The tide of battle had turned irrevocably in favour of the attacking forces. The corvidae still fought savagely, but their superiority in numbers had already been wiped out by the poison. And the influx of fresh and fierce opponents left them overwhelmed. The combined effect of these two causes put the magpies to rout. Those that chose to stay and fight were no match for the sharp beaks of the gulls. The combination of their savagery, with the strength and power of the eagles and falcons, swung the battle in the attackers' favour. Many of those who fled were either caught by their pursuer or tumbled earthwards, as the poison's effect took hold from within.

Kirrick had not needed to strike a blow and yet, incredibly, it was suddenly all over. Only a very few of the magpies escaped, and fewer still without some wound, to always remind them of the battle. Storne and Darreal circled in triumph. The sky was theirs. Kirrick flew over to where Tomar had landed. The ground was strewn with dead or dying corvidae and the owl was hopping hither and thither, dispensing his own particular brand of mercy by despatching each agony-stricken magpie that he found still alive. Tomar smiled as he saw the little robin approaching.

Before they had a chance to speak, Kraken alighted and called out to Kirrick. 'Better late than never, eh?' He was slightly breathless, and his beak was bright with blood.

'How can I ever thank you?' asked Kirrick. 'I thought that I had failed in trying to persuade you to our cause.'

'You had, my young friend,' replied Kraken. 'The cause was purely personal. When you lose a child, you tend to want to take revenge upon the perpetrators.'

The gull went on to explain how ill news had been brought to him by his distraught son, telling how Traska had senselessly murdered his younger sister, Kraken's beloved daughter. That act of casual brutality had been paid in kind, ten times over. One evil bird's need to assuage his own ire had had a profound effect on all of them.

As owl, seagull and robin talked, they were joined by Darreal, Storne and Isidris. This mighty gathering of heroes conversed at length, exchanging news and expounding deeds of valour by one or other of the victors. Kirrick was suitably impressed when told the reason for the magpies' agony. Only Tomar could have had the vision to think of such a plan! Kirrick was honoured to be introduced to the Great Owl, Cerival, who had despatched the last of his opponents and had flown down to join them. The robin blushed more than once when Tomar sang his praises before such exalted company, but the owl's words were roundly endorsed by all there, and indeed each of these great birds saw Kirrick as their equal in terms of valour and marvelled at what he had achieved. Everyone was eager to recount his own story, and so, at length, the whole was known to all.

Amidst the satisfaction and self-congratulations Tomar voiced a note of caution. He had listened to Kirrick's tale, embellished by Darreal and

Storne, and he felt decidedly uneasy. In spite of not wanting to spoil the mood of celebration, he could not help but voice his concern.

'What happened to Traska?'

Five mighty beaks turned in the old owl's direction, as the heroes considered the implications of Tomar's enquiry. In one smaller head, however, a different question was triggered. Where was Portia? Kirrick realised, guiltily, that he had forgotten all about his mate. Where could she have gone? He remembered with regret that his last words to his love had been spoken harshly. The robin excused himself, unheeded, from the company and went off in search of her.

Storne was the first to answer Tomar, but his tone was defensive and unsure.

'Traska was last seen in my land. He was trapped in the rabbit warrens. I had a watch set, and my eagles would have reported to me if he had escaped.'

'Escape he did, however,' Tomar replied gravely. 'Kraken wouldn't be here at all if it hadn't been for Traska's brutal slaying of his beloved daughter.'

'Yes,' the great gull said, a deep anger in his voice. 'Would that your eagles' watch had been more thorough.'

Tomar interceded quickly. 'Let us not quarrel among ourselves. This is no time for recriminations. We have won a great victory. But my question remains unanswered. We must be sure that Traska is dead.'

'How could he have survived? We killed nearly every magpie here today,' squawked Storne, still bridling at Kraken's accusation.

'Nearly is not enough with an evil bird like Traska,' Isidris intoned. 'Of all birds here I have been the only one to come face to face with the magpie, and, in spite of our glorious triumph, I for one shall not rest easy until I am sure that Traska is no more.'

When Portia had been unable to pluck up the courage to fly into battle and fight beside her mate, she had turned away in despair. She simply could not bear to watch her brave love die. But the sounds of battle had carried to where she cowered and the portents had been unmistakable. Tomar's plan was working. They were winning. But would Kirrick survive? The thought of losing him had overwhelmed her and she had fled. Seeking darkness to cover her misery, she had hidden in the mouth of a dark tunnel and had let the tears fall unchecked.

Kirrick was becoming frantic with worry. On leaving the company, he had returned at once to the place where he had left Portia, and had then searched the open ground for some sign of her, but she was nowhere to be found. Calling her name, he had flown out over the battle ground, terrified that he might find her tiny body dead and cold among the fallen. She couldn't be dead, could she? After all that they had been through together?

Unsuccessful, he had returned to the treetop where, together, they had watched the eagles fly into battle. Where could Portia be? He couldn't lose her now! He wouldn't want to live without her! In great distress, Kirrick abandoned his search, and flew back to his companions.

Emerging from her hiding place, Portia saw the circle of great birds with Kirrick at its centre. A conflicting mix of emotions coursed through her veins. Pride in her mate. Shame in herself. She hesitated to join them, so she hopped out of the tunnel and into the undergrowth to compose herself and to find food for her conquering hero.

'Calm yourself, my young friend,' Tomar said kindly. 'What distresses you so?'

'I can't find her. I've looked everywhere for Portia, but I can't find her!'

A sense of foreboding prevented Tomar from offering the usual assurances. If only they had some word about the magpie. The old owl regretted his earlier compassion towards the injured corvidae. He could have interrogated one of them for news of Traska. But it was too late for that now. His thoughts returned to the distress of his friend.

'Where have you looked?' he asked.

'Everywhere!' cheeped Kirrick miserably.

'Then let us all help you. Seven pairs of eyes are better than one.'

The great birds each flapped off in search for

Kirrick's mate and the robin was left alone, at a loss what to do next. Then, out of the corner of his eye, he spotted the entrance to a dark tunnel. Kirrick had no idea that this was the lair of the despot, Slyekin, and what would it have mattered? Slyekin was dead and his stain had been expunged from the world. Yet Kirrick felt a dread. There was evil in that place, he was sure of it. But he had to find his love!

On returning, she saw, ahead of her, Kirrick going in to the tunnel in search of her. She tried to call out, but her beak was full and he disappeared without hearing her. A chill fear clutched at her heart. Portia knew, with an illogical certainty, that her love was in terrible danger. Dropping her carefully selected provisions, she raced to the spot where she had seen him disappear.

Kirrick was deep inside Slyekin's lair when he heard Portia calling. He turned around and began to retrace his steps. The distress in her voice spurred him to haste and he quickened his pace as he rounded a corner, heading towards the entrance.

Traska's black and white body towered over him. Kirrick had no chance to react, and the confined space gave him no room to manoeuvre. Traska had chosen his ambush well. His head lunged forward and his beak penetrated Kirrick's chest. A plume of bright scarlet fountained out of the wound and soaked his feathers an even deeper red. Kirrick fell back, mortally stricken. Traska wiped his bloody beak with one wing.

'That is for all the trouble you have caused me and mine, Kirrick. Never have I felt such pleasure in finishing off an adversary.'

And, with these words, Traska turned and disappeared into the dark.

When Portia found him, Kirrick was still breathing. But one look at the damage wrought to his body told her the worst. She went to him and, cradling his head gently in her wings, spoke softly to him. She told him of the depth of her love and she talked about their hopes and dreams for the future. She did not let him go, even when she felt his life slip away. His body lay still and cold, his heart beating no more and his eyes closed. Portia kissed him, over and over again, and then she wept, the pain of her tears racking her entire body with sobbing. Finally a shadow fell over her and, looking up, she saw Tomar's kindly face. His look of loss reflected her own, as he gently took her by the wing and led her away.

'Kirrick was the bravest bird that I have ever known. You must be proud to have been loved by him.'

The owl spoke gravely, and Portia replied in kind.

'Proud, yes, and honoured. Our love will never die, even though he is dead. Kirrick will always be with me, though his body becomes food for the worms which he once fed upon. He will live on in my heart, to the end of my days. Promise me one thing, Tomar. Let such a tale be made of this that Kirrick will be remembered forever. He deserves no less.'

'I promise you this,' answered Tomar, 'that while any bird still lives, Kirrick will be remembered!'

EPILOGUE

Katya watched with pride, as her young and powerful offspring practised his flight. He swooped and soared, spiralling in his joy at his own ability. Then he dived, pulling out late, and skimming the surface of the gully, before rising again and rejoining his mother on her perch.

'Well done, Venga. You are improving every day, my son. You are already strong and will grow stronger. Work hard, Venga, and hone yourself. Your enemy is very powerful. Yes, and evil. But you have the power of good on your side. And good will prevail. Nature knows that evil must not triumph for long. And I have been given a fine son to conquer that evil. A fine son indeed!'

The young magpie's chest swelled with the compliment and he launched himself once more into the air. How he loved to please his mother!

As dawn's light touched the treetops of Tanglewood, Portia sat contentedly on her nest. In the weeks that had followed Kirrick's death, she had mourned for her mate. But Nature's healing processes had eased her sadness and the two reddish-brown eggs

188

beneath her gave her a joy to match her sorrow. Theirs would be the future. Her children would be able to live in a world of freedom, thanks to the efforts of her Kirrick, their father. Portia spoke his name aloud, calling on him to be with her at this time.

'Kirrick, my love. I promise you that I will bring up our children to honour your memory. We had such plans, you and I. My wish was selfish, compared to yours, and I have what I wanted. But, in losing you, I have realised that you were right. Birddom is much more than a single pair of robins. So I vow to you, my hero-husband, that I will strive to follow your example and to work, in whatever way I can, for the good of Birddom. Wiser heads than mine will make the decisions which will affect our future, but I will do whatever is asked of me – and do so in your name, and in your memory. For, thanks to you, the evil has been swept away and right once more prevails. Thanks to you, my darling Kirrick, we are free!'

And so, as the sun rose majestically over the horizon, Portia tilted back her head, opened her throat and began to sing.

BOOK TWO

TWO FOR JOY

CHAPTER 1

Merion and Olivia looked on in hushed awe as they sat behind their mother at the very edge of the clearing. Portia had been invited as the guest of honour to the inaugural reconvening of the Council of the Owls. It was spring, a full six months since the Great Battle, when Slyekin and his magpie empire had been defeated. Throughout the late autumn and the long hard winter, survival had been uppermost in the thoughts of all of the leaders of Birddom. Sadly, some had not made it through to the weak but welcoming sunshine that lit up this particular day. The Great Owl, Cerival, had passed on contented into the next world, knowing that the last dreadful years of doubt and anguish had been expunged by Slyekin's downfall.

Tomar now led a Council whose number measured eight members. Three owls had fallen in the battle against the magpies, and a third of the strength and wisdom of the Council had been irrevocably lost. But, for this meeting at least, their numbers had been made up by some very notable birds indeed. Darreal and Storne had both made the long journey from their respective highland homes to be present on this momentous occasion. So, too, had Kraken, flying inland once more from the coastal fortress of his seabird colony. The final place was left empty, in memory of Kirrick, without whom no Council would ever have been held and no future would have been possible.

It would be wrong to think that no progress had been made since the battle against the corvidae. The eagles and falcons had traversed the country, disbanding those magpie covens that remained intact and searching, always searching, for Traska. But, of that evil bird there was no sign. He had completely disappeared. With the onset of winter, they had abandoned their hunt and had returned to their homes. The severity of the weather through December and January had meant that there had been a necessary hiatus in the new order. Birds, large and small, had concentrated on making it through to warmer times. Now spring had come and the thoughts of all birds could turn to the future.

The immediate task for the Council was twofold: to assess the threat still posed by the corvidae; and to make plans for the future of Birddom. Tomar had already decided that the first task for his own kind, led by their respective Council members, would be to carry out a census of the bird life remaining in the land. This was an onerous task indeed. But vital, in order to analyse the current eco-structure and assess the imbalance in the natural order that needed to be addressed. Yet how could such a restoration be achieved? So many species had, almost certainly, been wiped out by Slyekin's murderous armies. Would Nature ever be able to recover from such a loss?

Tomar's opening speech was simple, but eloquent. He paid a touching tribute to the robin, whose courage and commitment should, he said, be an inspiration to them all.

'Kirrick's achievements cannot be measured against his physical size, for he had a bigger heart than all the rest of us put together!' exclaimed the old owl.

Portia's chest swelled with pride when she heard her mate so described. But to the two young robins, Kirrick's offspring, it was not the words that impressed them. Never before had they seen such an array of huge and magnificent birds. Each of the owls was impressive, although Caitlin, the little owl, looked slightly comical by comparison to her fellow Council members. But Kraken, with his enormous black wings, savage yellow beak and piratical glare, scared them both greatly. And Darreal, with his keen, piercing stare and wickedly hooked bill, lost nothing by comparison. As for Storne, the magnificent eagle sat on his perch as if he owned the whole world.

Yet each of these three great birds were listening with due deference to Tomar, and they nodded in approval at the owl's eulogy to their late, heroic friend. Kirrick's loss had been a tragedy, even amongst so many other deaths. But the robin had left a legacy to them all. And they had a duty to see that Birddom went forward to a future that would be a fitting memorial to him.

'We must see to it that neither Kirrick nor any other bird who gave his life in the struggle against evil died in vain.'

Again, all around the Council, heads nodded in agreement at the wisdom of his words. Storne caught Tomar's eye, and indicated that he wished to speak. The owl nodded his assent.

'We have a great task ahead of us,' boomed the great golden eagle. 'Some very serious decisions need to be made. The murderous actions of the magpies have had a significant effect on all of us. Not only on the small bird population, which has been so cruelly diminished, but on the larger birds, whose natural prey included some measure of those same species. It may seem heartless to some of you here, but it is, or was, the natural order of things. We took them when we needed, killing only for food, and in that way maintained the balance in Birddom. But there is no longer any balance. The life of every single small bird must henceforth be sacrosanct, at least until a way can be found to restore their numbers.

This restraint must, of necessity, bring us into greater conflict with Man. For we will still need to eat and the deficit in our food supply will have to be taken from his stock. And therein lies great danger, as you are all aware. I talk not just of the needs of raptors like myself. The remaining birds will need to take a greater proportion of their food from Man's crops. For we must honour our agreement with the insects. Let no bird break with the oath that Tomar made. Any that do so will pay with their own lives.'

The eagle paused, and swept his gaze around the clearing. His pronouncement was clear and unequivocal. And Storne knew that its message would be carried back, across the length and breadth of the land, to every bird's home. The pact would hold, if the Council remained strong enough to enforce it. But Birddom needed to be given a reason to believe in the Council of the Owls. They needed to see a clear direction. A plan for the future. Storne looked once more to Tomar.

'May I ask what plans the Great Owl has in mind? The very future of Birddom is in his charge now and I, for one, am confident that it is in safe wing-tips. How do you see the way forward, Tomar?'

The old owl had indeed given many long hours of thought as to that future and he began, without further ado, to explain his ideas. As he spoke, Portia began to see that he had in mind a role for her. Birddom would need repopulating and Tomar believed that the only way to achieve this would be to encourage an influx of small bird species from Wingland, that vast continent beyond the shores of Birddom. Slyekin's empire had been very insular and it was unlikely the evil that had warped the corvidae in this land was also present in the wider world. Someone was needed who would be prepared to fly over the sea, and do everything in their power, once in Wingland, to persuade many species of bird to migrate to a new home in Birddom.

Portia's standing as Kirrick's mate made her, in the eyes of the Council and of Tomar in particular, the ideal candidate for such a role as emissary. However, the old owl was worried for her safety. In his mind, he had already been responsible for the death of one brave robin and, because of this, he balked at asking Kirrick's mate to put herself into danger.

Portia, for her part, felt torn between her desire to be a player in another great adventure – to be useful and important in the way that her Kirrick had been – and her maternal instincts. Merion and Olivia were beyond the fledging stage and becoming increasingly independent. But the bond between them was extremely strong and Portia would be sorely grieved to be parted from them. Even so, she knew that her destiny had chosen her to be more than just a mate and a mother and, when the subject was raised, Portia volunteered for the task without hesitation.

Tomar, with his usual perception and intellect, then offered Portia his own aid in looking after the young robins. Both Merion and Olivia were excited to be in Tomar's tutelage. He had such a great fund of stories, and knew so much about the history of Birddom, that their initial fears about being parted from their mother were swept away on a wave of noisy enthusiasm. Portia was relieved, if slightly piqued, to see that her children would be so easily reconciled to her departure, when it came.

Traska realised that he was taking a risk, coming to this wild and desolate place. The hooded crows, which dominated this part of the Isle of Storms, were huge and menacing. But rumour had it that they were also very slow-witted. Traska liked that in a potential ally. It would give him the control that he needed. He had learnt, during his brief period of captivity by Slyekin, the need for brute strength in order to provide a protective shield behind which he could weave his evil plans.

The irony of the fact that, in the final analysis, that same strength had been of no help at all to Slyekin was lost on Traska. He knew that the alliance formed against the corvidae empire were out for his blood. He had been hunted as mercilessly as once he had hunted for his adversary, the robin Kirrick. The magpie grinned malevolently as he recalled his act of murder. Killing that cursed robin had been so sweet. And it had been one in the eye for Tomar and his high and mighty Council of the Owls. Traska's insides knotted with anger as he thought of the old owl and of how his genius had robbed Slyekin of his victory and ruined the magpies' plans for domination. Thanks to Tomar and Kirrick, he had been forced to flee his homeland, to become a fugitive in exile. But Traska had no intention of spending the rest of his life in hiding. He wanted revenge. Revenge on Tomar. He wanted it so badly. And Traska always got what he wanted.

The hide-away of the hooded crows was in an extremely inaccessible, mountainous area, with scree-strewn slopes and precipitous-sided valleys. But, in spite of these precautions, their numbers were relatively small. Their attacks on lambs and other small livestock had made them hated by the island's farming community and a bounty had been placed on each of their heads. Whenever one was sighted by Man, it would invariably be blown out of the skies. Traska realised that he should be frightened by these giant corvidae, but he was supremely confident in his own, vastly superior intellect.

Without warning, two of the hooded crows alighted, one on either side of him. Their dirty cream and black colouring compared unfavourably to the jet black, pure white and startling blue of Traska's own plumage.

'What are you doing here, stranger?' one of the crows asked him.

'I've not come here to talk to the likes of you. I want to meet your leader!' barked Traska viciously.

'Oh, you'll meet him, all right. But only when

you've answered a few questions,' replied the other escort.

'I hope that this isn't going to take too long,' Traska snapped at them. 'I've important business to attend to. Your leader isn't going to be pleased with you when he finds out how I've been treated!'

'We'll take our chances,' the first crow answered back. 'Now. Who are you? Where are you from? And what is your business here?' Traska replied with withering contempt.

'My, my! Three questions all at once. That must have been tiring for you! My name is Traska. I've flown all the way from Birddom. And my business is certainly none of yours! Now don't waste any more of my time. Take me to your leader without further delay.'

So imperious and commanding was his tone that the two giant crows turned and, with only a curt call of 'Follow us!', took to the air and flapped away. Their flight was long and meandering, designed to mislead anyone who wished to try and mark their route for future reference. But eventually they led Traska to a site that he assumed correctly to be their destination. It was a massive cavern, the entrance well hidden from casual view by dense vegetation. Two giant trees stood like sentinels at the entrance to the cave, guarding its depths. In each of these trees, several roosts were sited – huge, haphazard structures, which served as both billet and lookout for the giant crows.

The cavern itself was dank and full of sound.

Its ceiling was high, and constantly reflected back, in echoes, the screeching of the birds, who used the cavern as the base for their operations. Several rank partial carcasses of lambs and calves lay rotting in the gloom. Not for nothing did the farmers revile these predators. Every now and then a solid-looking crow would hop over to the decomposing bodies and rip savagely at the flesh, gulping down large mouthfuls.

As Traska was led into the interior, he caught sight of a massive bird. Compared to this giant, the rest of the flock of hooded crows seemed almost diminutive in stature. Donal was the leader's name and Traska quailed in his presence. Then the magpie pulled himself together and began to appraise his opponent with a more critical eye. The head was huge, with a powerful black beak. It was set upon a thick-set neck and shoulders, the solidity of which made the thought of this bird in graceful airborne flight seem almost absurd. It was as if he were made out of the same rock as the cavern in which he resided. The eyes were, however, a dull black, with no gleam of intelligence. Traska decided to go on to the offensive.

'More time-wasting! When am I going to get through to you stupid birds? I want to meet your leader!'

'I am in charge here, and you'd better watch your tongue, or I'll rip it out, personally!'

'Give me your name then, and show a bit of respect for your superior!'

'What the hell makes you my superior?' Donal queried, laughing.

'Well, I've got a brain, for a start,' muttered Traska, under his breath. But to Donal he said, 'You may be the leader of this shabby band of flea-bags, though I can see little cause for pride in that. But I am king of all the corvidae in Birddom!'

'Well, forgive me, your Majesty!' the giant crow replied, bowing his head low. Then he turned to his hench-crows, and barked an order. Half a dozen crows swooped down upon Traska, quite prepared to rip him to shreds, at their leader's bidding.

'Break one of his wings.'

The pain was excruciating, as two of the crows pinned him down and a third forced his wing back at an unnatural angle until the bone snapped like a twig. Maimed, Traska rose once more to his feet and glared at Donal with contempt. He refused to let himself show how much the injury hurt.

'You are so brainless. Didn't you ever give a thought as to why I came here? You know your trouble? You're a moron, that's what you are!'

'I'm not the one with the broken wing,' Donal responded defensively.

'It'll mend,' Traska said. 'But now I'll have to remain here until it does. You've just got yourself a house-guest.'

'Why should I bother to look after you? If we turn you out, you'll soon fall foul of some hunter. And then I won't have to worry about you.'

'You still don't get it, do you? My coming here is the best thing that ever happened to you. I can offer you an opportunity better than any you have ever dreamed of.'

'Tell me about it!' commanded the massive crow.

Traska began to strut about arrogantly, in spite of the injured wing, which hung limply at his side.

'You are outlaws in this land. Living in hiding, in fear of Man. You are hunted and persecuted, constantly afraid for your lives. In Birddom, Man presents no real threat to us. We are lords of the skies. We can come and go as we please. There is so much space and food is plentiful. Come and join my corvidae. Our numbers are fewer than they were erstwhile and you will find little competition among us.'

'You are most generous, oh king of the corvidae. But I am left wondering why.'

The huge crow looked quizzically at Traska, who replied,

'Because I need some muscle. We corvidae have enemies in Birddom. Other birds, jealous of our power. They have waged war against us in recent times. We won, of course. But our numbers were diminished. We lost some fine birds in that battle and I want revenge. Your band of crows would give me the strength that I need to conquer my foes, once and for all. You, in return, will get a home where you will be free of fear and will be able to live in a manner far beyond your present meagre aspirations.'

'I have to say that I am impressed by your offer.' Donal's tone was conciliatory and there was less aggression in his posture. 'We have begun badly. But I believe that we have both seen the other's worth. Let me try and make amends for your ill-treatment, and for my rudeness. I am called Donal and I am, as you say, leader of this motley crew. My two lieutenants, Finbar and Shauney, you have already met.'

Donal indicated the two hooded crows who had been Traska's escorts upon his arrival. 'They tell me that your name is Traska.'

The magpie stifled a contemptuous retort concerning their powers of memory, and replied with a simple 'Yes.'

'Well, Traska. I hope that you will forgive us and will accept our hospitality, now that we are all friends.'

'I've never had a friend and certainly wouldn't choose the likes of *you*, if I wanted one!' Traska mused, masking his thoughts with a smile.

'I have travelled a long way and I am very tired. Perhaps there is some place where you would allow me to rest.'

Donal snapped an order to his two lieutenants and Traska was led to the foot of a smaller tree at the cavern entrance. There were many branches and several hung low to the ground. Finbar grabbed the end of one in his beak and pulled it powerfully downwards, allowing Traska to hop onto it, in ungainly fashion. Hindered by his wing, he was forced to climb up through the branches, using feet and beak to pull himself higher, until he reached a comfortable roost. There, exhausted and in pain, Traska collapsed and lay still. After a while, fatigue overcame the agony of his broken wing, and he slept.

CHAPTER 2

Portia spent many long hours in Tomar's company, as Kirrick had before her. And, in their way, the discussions between the two were every bit as crucial to the future of Birddom. They were planning a regeneration, an input of living resources back into the land that they cherished.

The first difficulty to be overcome was precisely how Portia was to make the journey, so vital for their future. Of course, she had travelled great distances on her journeys with Kirrick and Tomar did not doubt her endurance. But robins are a resident rather than a migratory species, and the old owl was worried that Portia's directional skills, so honed to inland flight, might go awry when crossing so vast a stretch of water, with no landmarks to guide her.

However, little choice remained. Most of the migratory birds had been slaughtered in the first wave of Slyekin's master-plan and the few individuals who had survived the onslaught had fled. Tomar had no doubt that they carried with them news of the terrible destruction and murder, prevalent throughout Birddom. These birds would hardly have been welcome heralds, then, for Portia's mission. She would have a daunting task ahead of her, persuading the Wingland bird populace that Birddom was now a safe and desirable place to live.

So, initially, their talks focused on her flight across the sea. Tomar had taken the opportunity, at the end of the Council meeting, to have brief discussions with Kraken. He had elicited information as to the easiest flight paths, dependant upon the prevailing winds at the time of the journey. The owl had stored this vital data in his computer of a brain, as the two of them went on to discuss the various alternative journeys that Portia might have to make. The robin herself was confident that she could achieve her objective, in all the possible scenarios set before her. The journey did not worry her.

But, having completed that task, monumental in itself, Portia's real problems would begin. In Wingland, she would be travelling in strange places, without companion or guide, and where there was little certainty of common language. Migratory birds were, of necessity, multi-lingual and could generally make themselves understood in all countries that they traversed. But resident populations tended to colloquialise their speech, and both owl and robin feared that this might make communication impossible.

After much thought, Tomar came up with the only reasonable solution to their problem. Upon arrival, Portia would need to seek the aid of one of the migratory birds, who had erstwhile visited Birddom in its annual wanderings. Once found, that bird could readily serve as a translator and mediator between Portia and the continental birds, whom she hoped to entice into returning with her.

During their discussions, Tomar searched the heart of the pretty young robin before him and was satisfied with what he saw. No difficulty presented to her was seen as insurmountable. No task was thought to be beyond her limits. She was a fine bird. Brave and stout-hearted, like her mate, with the same spark of resilience and humour. Kirrick had chosen well. Some members of the Council had raised doubts that Portia, a mere female of a small bird species, would be a fitting emissary for Birddom. Tomar had silenced these doubters with the severity of his rebuke. He declared that no other bird could have been appointed for this task and that no other was more equal to it. And now, talking to Portia, Tomar felt increasingly justified in his confidence in her. She would succeed, if any could.

Far away to the north, Katya, with a mixture of admiration and awe, watched her son in full flight. Venga was powerful in the air, but also unusually graceful, the long tail not seeming, in his case, to hinder his flowing movement across the sky. A young adult now, Venga still kept close to his mother. He would have liked to take a mate and settle down. But he knew that Katya saw another destiny for him. His life would know no peace until he had carried out his mission of vengeance. Katya had sought news from the local corvidae covens and had discovered that the evil magpie, who had perpetrated the terrible attack upon her the previous year, was not of local stock.

Her description of him swiftly drew a positive identification from several of her neighbours. From them she learnt that his name was Traska and that he had flown to these parts from far off to the south, in pursuit of a robin. She also learnt that Traska had been involved in a fearsome battle with the mountain eagles. A number of magpies quailed when they were asked about the fight and refused to talk. One or two bragged, though Katya got the distinct impression that they had not taken part in the conflict. But one bird gave her the news that she was looking for.

'Oh yes, I remember, all right. That Traska. He was a sly one. Bullied and berated us, he did. Acted big and lorded it whenever he could. But when it came down to a fight, he vanished without a trace. Some thought he'd died at the talons of one of those eagles and had been carried off. But I saw him, running for cover at the first sign of trouble. The coward ducked into a rabbit hole, and left us to face the music.'

'Did you see him again? Did he survive?' Katya asked, eager for more information.

'Oh, he'll have survived, all right. His type always

do. But he's not been seen around here again. He'll have gone back where he came from. Still chasing that bloody robin, I expect. He won't want to have returned empty-beaked. Not if you believed his story. Said he was a personal friend of Slyekin, if you please. Well, he's no personal friend of mine, and if I ever laid wings on him, I'd break his damned neck!'

Katya thanked the magpie for his help and flew back to her own nest, brooding over what she had been told. It wasn't much to go on, but she could not let the matter rest. Traska must be made to pay for his outrage. She would have to trust to her son's tenacity and commitment, if she were to have any chance of finding the evil creature who had so blighted her life. It was time for Venga to begin his mission.

After only a week in the company of these dolts, Traska was almost screaming. He had never encountered birds who were so slow-witted. Even Donal, their leader, showed little intellectual capacity and had difficulty in grasping the simplest of ideas that Traska put forward. The hooded crow's natural tendency towards greed and his instinctive cruelty and viciousness, should have been enough to make Traska's task much easier. But Donal simply couldn't make the connection between the benefits to be gained in Birddom and the actual action required in physically going there to reap those benefits.

Traska had worried initially that his ally might work out for himself that everything on offer could actually be reached out for and taken without the slightest need to provide aid to the magpie who proposed the deal. But now, Traska's only worry was that Donal and his crows were just too plain stupid to make the journey in the first place. He wondered that they had ever learned how to fly!

His wing still gave him a good deal of pain, although the alignment of the bones was good and they had begun to knit properly. Traska knew the vital importance of ensuring that his wing healed completely. For the journeys that he needed to make he would have to be fully fit, in every respect. So, he remained patient and let Nature do its work. For this reason alone he also kept his temper with the crows. He stifled all desires to rant and rave at their numbing stupidity. He knew that he could dominate them. But he knew also that they could finish him easily with one moment of casual violence.

Traska spent a good deal of time during his stay with the crows plotting and scheming against Birddom. Every single time that he thought about Tomar and Kirrick, bile rose into his throat and his chest constricted with anger. His conceit could not bear the thought that they had defeated him. No! Slyekin had lost. His plans had been sabotaged by that meddlesome pair. Traska himself had achieved the only victory amidst the debacle. He had triumphed over Birddom in all its sanctimonious righteousness. He had killed the robin. That act – the slaughter of a single, small bird – stood disproportionate in Traska's mind. An act of meanness and cowardice had assumed heroic status in the evil magpie's warped brain. And now, all of Traska's mental energy was directed towards finding a way to overthrow the Council of the Owls and thereby gain a victory over Tomar. The old owl had now replaced Kirrick as the focus for all of Traska's hatred.

So, as his wing slowly mended, Traska applied himself to the task of preparing a plan to reinstate the corvidae as the rulers of Birddom. With himself as their leader, of course.

Merion and Olivia spent as much time as possible with their mother. She recounted stories of her time with Kirrick and of his heroic deeds. Olivia pointed out to her mother that she had been every bit as brave as their father.

'Oh, no, my dear. Your father was very special.'

'So are you, mother. You are special too.'

In this way, her children helped to bolster Portia's confidence in the face of her epic task. And their closeness, in the time before her departure, strengthened the bond between them all. Portia knew that her children's love would go with her on her journey and this was a great comfort to her.

'Will you tell us the story about the rabbits?' Olivia asked, and Merion laughed, and clapped his wings, excitedly. It was one of his favourites. So Portia began to tell them of the time in the highlands when they had been pursued by the magpie hunters, and had cheated certain death only by the daring trick of using rabbit warrens as a means of escape.

'And the magpies thought that you had vanished into thin air!' chuckled Merion, unable to keep from joining in the story.

For, in truth, he knew it almost as well as Portia. The children had been fed the tales about their father with their first beakful of worms. They knew all about his exploits and could recite their mother's stories of Kirrick almost word for word. But this didn't lessen their enjoyment in hearing them told again, or Portia's in telling them. However, the two young robins were eager and excited about spending time with Tomar. For he, they both knew, was sure to have a great fund of stories to tell them, not just about their father, but also legends and myths from the beginning of time in Birddom. Like all children, they had both a great thirst for knowledge and a deep love of a good tale.

So the time passed for the three robins in cheerful companionship and, on the eve of Portia's departure, Tomar visited their home with some glad tidings.

'My dear Portia. How are you? Are you ready for your journey?'

'I think so, Tomar. It's a little bit daunting. More than a little, actually. But I so want to prove myself equal to the task.'

Portia's eyes betrayed a fear, locked deep inside

her, that she might not have the resilience of her beloved partner, Kirrick. Her deepest worry was not of the dangers that she would have to face, but of failure to complete the task allotted to her. Tomar saw this and sought to comfort her.

'I believe that Kirrick showed his greatest wisdom in choosing you for his mate. I have no doubts that I have shown equal wisdom in choosing you as my emissary. You face a hard road, Portia, and will encounter many difficulties and dangers. But you will be equal to them all, my brave young robin. I truly believe that loneliness will be your greatest foe on this journey, although I do not doubt your strength of mind. I only know that Kirrick's task was made immeasurably easier, once he had you to share it with him.'

'Kirrick will be with me on my journey,' Portia answered bravely.

'I hope, then, that he will not mind another companion!'

Tomar's eyes glinted with good humour as he delivered his news, with the deftness of a magician producing a rabbit from a hat.

'It was purely a coincidence, I can assure you,' he began, keeping the robin in suspense. 'You see, yesterday morning I had a visitor. Someone with whom you are acquainted. He came to see me, to offer his service to the cause of Birddom. I think that meeting you and Kirrick must have had a profound effect upon him.'

'Who is it? Who is it?' chattered Portia, as excited now as one of her own children.

'He is someone to whom merely scratching around for food and surviving the odd scrap with the local felines is now insufficient challenge. I believe that he once saved your life. It is a debt that I think will be increased 'ere this tale is told to future generations.'

'Mickey! It must be Mickey.'

Portia could not hide her pleasure at the prospect of seeing the young bullfinch again. Mickey had indeed helped Kirrick to save her life when she had foolishly tried to slake her thirst with sea water. His streetwise know-how and quick thinking had meant the difference between life and death for Portia. He had also been their guide on their journey to see Kraken, leader of the gulls and, although it had seemed fruitless at the time, it had been crucial to the final outcome of the Great Battle between good and evil. So Mickey had already had a considerable say in the preservation of everything that was right in Birddom. And, now that he had had a taste for action, it seemed that he wanted more.

'Mickey it is,' said Tomar. 'And he was delighted when I suggested to him that he should accompany you on your journey. He said that it would be a great honour for him.'

Tomar paused, and looked sharply at the young robin, whose features had betrayed a momentary flash of concern. He quickly divined its meaning, and sought to reassure her.

'My dear Portia. The arrival of Mickey was but a happy chance, and one that may well prove fortunate to all concerned, himself not least. But he was not the one that was chosen by the Council. Nor was his aid deemed necessary by any there. However, let us not turn our beaks away when a juicy worm wriggles before our eyes. Mickey is willing to be your companion and I believe that his cheerful disposition will help to lighten your mood in the dark times ahead of you.'

'I will be glad of his company,' Portia replied, simply. 'But you speak rather ominously of "dark times", Tomar. What is it that you fear? It makes me think that you have not told me everything.'

'I have told you everything that I know, my dear friend. But it is the unknown that worries me. We have no news. We are cut off from the wider world of birds. Since the decimation of the small bird species began, not one migratory bird has dared to venture to our shores, knowing that, in doing so, their lives would be forfeit. So we cannot be sure that you are not flying into a danger every bit as perilous as that which we have faced in Birddom.'

Portia looked truly alarmed. 'Surely you cannot believe that the corvidae in Wingland have been infected by Slyekin's evil?'

'No, I do not believe it to be so,' Tomar stated, adding, 'But I would be much happier sending you on your journey if I could be sure!'

CHAPTER 3

It took three further weeks before Traska's wing had healed sufficiently for him to attempt flight. But he applied himself to the task with grim determination, ignoring the pain. He initially favoured his stronger wing and had to continually correct his flight-path. Only supreme willpower made him use his damaged wing to its fullest extent. For the first few days he returned to his roost, exhausted by his exertions. But, gradually, his strength returned and he was able to attempt longer and longer flights. He ranged out far across the countryside, returning at dusk to a meal and sleep. Food was always plentiful in the company of the huge crows. For their part, they seemed to be in a sort of limbo, waiting for Traska to be well enough to make the journey of which he had spoken. On the few occasions when the magpie talked to his hosts, he took every opportunity to emphasise the attractions of his plans for them. He painted pictures of a land of abundance and a life of ease and plenty, with none of the dangers they now faced.

Traska's cause was helped greatly when two of the hooded crows became careless and were blasted from the skies by a farmer's double-barrelled shotgun. This was a most persuasive incident and Traska thanked the farmer, silently, for his unconscious assistance.

So preparations began for the long journey to Birddom. Donal decided that an initial band of twenty hooded crows should accompany Traska, with the rest remaining in their present hideaway. Donal himself would not go with the first wave of the exodus, sending in his stead his lieutenant, Finbar, to lead the crows. If, after a couple of months, everything in Birddom turned out to be as Traska promised, then three of the band would return with the news and Donal would lead the rest of his followers to this new land and home.

Traska was very pleased with this arrangement. He did not doubt his own ability to sow the seeds of treachery in the heart of Finbar. Even this slow-witted lieutenant would, with the magpie's insidious help, be made to see the advantages of becoming the leader of his small band. And in being seen to make this come about; in being the instigator of Finbar's pathetic little rise to power, Traska knew that he would win the loyalty of the huge crow. Twenty of these massive birds, cruel and powerful, but easily manipulated, would be more than sufficient for his purposes. He did not plan on outright war in Birddom. Not this time. There were other ways to be victorious against hated foes. And Traska hated Tomar the owl so very much.

★ ★ ★

Katya and Venga were deep in discussion. They had sat together for hours, while the sun had ridden across the sky and they had talked of little else but Venga's mission. Katya had begun by reaffirming her love for her now fully-grown son. Then, for the first time, she recounted to him the full horror of Traska's attack upon her.

She spared nothing in describing the details of the rape, the pain, the shame, the gloating indifference of Traska. She needed to crystallise Venga's anger, to focus his vengeance and hatred. She sobbed in the aftermath of remembrance and Venga held his mother gently while she cried. But, once her tears had stilled, they began to discuss in detail what Venga would have to do to find the evil perpetrator of such a terrible deed. They both knew the dangers that the young magpie would have to face in his attempts to track Traska and not only from the evil bird himself. Word had spread swiftly about the eagles' hunts for corvidae. Crows, ravens, and magpies were fleeing their homes in terror, or hiding in the desperate hope that they would not be discovered. Katya understood such vengeance. It was the very fuel that had kept her alive. The fuel she now ignited in the breast of her son. Venga would need to exercise extreme caution in his attempts to follow a cold trail, to find the magpie who was the object of their hatred. He would have to fly south for many days, to the site of the Great Battle. Tales of the clash between the alliance of the eagles, falcons and owls, and the full might of the corvidae, had spread like wildfire. It had already assumed legendary proportions, becoming the most famous event in all of Birddom's history. Every bird in the land knew some of the details and many embellished them, after their fashion, until the conflict grew into a fantastic struggle. Katya knew that Traska would have wanted to be at the centre of such a horror.

She also had no doubt that he would have survived it. Not for him the heroic deeds and glorious death in battle. She knew that he would have observed, feeding on the energy of violence and death, but aloof from the fight itself. In her mind, Katya saw Traska creeping about on the edges of the struggle, scoring small victories against wounded and maimed opponents, tormenting the dying and bathing in the blood of the vanquished. Venga would have to begin his search for Traska in that place. It would be a monumental mission. The aftermath of any war left behind it confusion and chaos. She did not underestimate the task that she had set her son.

Portia and her children were just stirring when Mickey's cheerful face popped into view. The bullfinch cheeped a greeting, then hopped onto an adjacent branch. Portia joined him after a few moments preening to make herself look respectable.

'Good morning, Portia. You look very beautiful today.'

'Well, thank you,' she replied, flustered but pleased by the compliment.

'I hope that you didn't mind me calling on you so early, but I've been eager to talk with you. I'm so excited about our adventure.'

Portia looked sombre, and her voice was subdued.

'It won't be easy, Mickey. We could be going into great danger.'

'I know, Tomar told me all about it,' replied the bullfinch. 'But at least we'll be together. Two heads are better than one, and all that.'

'Yes, that is a great comfort to me. Thank you for offering to accompany me. I'm not sure that, when it came to leaving, I would have had the courage.'

'Of course you would, Portia. You've more courage in your smallest claw than I have in my whole body. I'm relying on your bravery. Wherever we go, I'll be right behind you!'

Portia knew from experience that Mickey was no coward, but his joke made her smile. She had no doubts that he would make a good companion.

'But when do we leave, Portia?' Mickey asked, eagerly.

'We set off on our journey at daybreak tomorrow. I believe that Tomar has planned quite a send-off. I hope that, in the end, we can justify his faith in us.'

'I know that you will do yourself great credit. I am worried that I might let you down. I certainly will be of no great help when it comes to the language. Blimey, I can barely speak the Owl's own tongue, let alone communicate in foreign speech.'

'There are more ways of communicating than with words, my friend,' Portia replied. 'I truly believe that you were well chosen, if chosen is the right word. Your good humour and cheerful disposition may well turn out to be the most effective language that we will have in Wingland.'

'Thank you. But I believe that you exaggerate my importance.

I know that I am merely a companion to the emissary. You are the important one, Portia. The one that was chosen. I'm just tagging along for the ride. Besides, if humour and cheerfulness are good communicators, I know a more powerful one.'

'And what is that?' Portia asked, playfully.

'Beauty,' answered the bullfinch, and laughed at Portia's blushes.

Tomar had called for all the members of the Council of the Owls to be present when Portia and Mickey began their journey, and now the two small birds stood, at first light, in the midst of the circle of eight. Tomar called for silence, then began to speak.

'Today is an historic day for Birddom. For, once again, we must rely on a robin to perform great deeds for the good of our kingdom. Your mission, Portia, is a more positive one than that which faced your mate, and I am more hopeful of the outcome. You are the equal of Kirrick in our eyes. You have undertaken freely, as he did, to fly into the unknown, with the risk of great peril. If you had chosen to set aside this burden, none here would have blamed you. So, take with you our thanks and admiration for your courage and resolve. And as for you, Master Mickey, guard her well and keep her safe. But, above all, bring her back to us, along with one or two others if you can manage it!'

Laughter and good cheer rang around the clearing and the formality of the gathering dissolved as each owl bade the brave pair farewell. Portia hugged her two children, trying not to cry. They, in return, beamed proudly at their mother. How lucky they were to be the offspring of two such heroes. Then, suddenly, all the goodbyes were said and the time for departure had come. Portia and Mickey took one look into each other's eyes and then they were airborne, circling around the clearing before disappearing over the treetops.

There was little ceremony for Traska's departure with the small band of hooded crows. Once the magpie's wing had healed completely and had regained its strength, Traska went to visit Donal to make arrangements for their flight. Traska got the distinct impression that the leader of the crows had begun to regret his decision and now wanted the adventure to be very much underplayed. So Donal agreed at once that there was no point in delaying – they should leave that very evening. Traska would have preferred to wait until morning. He knew that they would not be able to fly very far before having to find a roost for the night, with all the inherent dangers that that posed. But Donal seemed most eager that they should be gone straightaway. Traska was becoming far too popular for his liking. And popular meant powerful in Donal's eyes. Traska knew better, however, than to argue with his host, or to try to usurp Donal's position on his own territory. So, with only a cursory farewell, the band of huge and menacing corvidae took to the lowering skies and flew off east.

Traska flew alongside Finbar and, engaging him in seemingly idle conversation, wasted no time in denigrating Donal for his incivility.

'Do you think that he was jealous of you?' asked the magpie. 'It seemed to me that he was very keen to get rid of you, altogether. I expect that he saw you as a threat to his own position. A powerful bird like yourself.'

Traska's flattery worked like a charm and he could see that he would have very little difficulty in bending this rather stupid bird to his will. Traska smiled thinly as they flew on. When it became too dark to see easily, Traska asked Finbar's opinion on where it would be best to alight for the night. He had already spotted a likely roost some time previously and had been subtly steering them towards it. But he wanted to give Finbar the impression that he was the one who was making the decisions.

Finbar's own, less than profound thoughts on the subject, with the ideal option staring him right in the beak, concurred with Traska's, and the band of corvidae descended into the chosen treetop to rest for the night. As the birds settled, Traska raised his voice so that all there could hear the words that he spoke to Finbar.

'A wise choice of roost, if I might say so. I begin to feel so much more confident, now, about our journey. With you to lead us, I know that we will not go far astray.'

Finbar's chest puffed up with conceited pride and Traska picked up, from here and there around him, affirmations from the other crows.

'Yes. That Finbar's a good chap. We won't go far wrong with him around. Traska obviously thinks highly of him, at any rate. And that magpie is nobody's fool.'

When Venga finally took leave of his mother and flew south to begin his search for Traska, he felt a curious mixture of emotions. Since his birth he had known no other companion, so fear was uppermost in his mind, big and strong as he was. However, this feeling was soon replaced by one of excitement. At last he was set on his course, actively pursuing his destiny. He had a great adventure ahead of him. He would see places, experience sights, face dangers of which he had so far only dreamed. The more he thought about it, the more the feeling of excitement welled up inside him, making him want to shout to the skies. But, as he opened his beak to let out the sound, the feeling changed subtly and he realised with a shock that his overriding feeling was one of relief.

He had never known anything except the claustrophobic love and anger of his mother. But now he was free. Oh, he was still bound by his duty, by the constraints of his mission. But he had escaped from her physical presence and the feeling of relief was overwhelming. He opened his throat and cawed his joy to the clouds, the sun and the trees. He sang to the mountains and valleys. He flew without restraint. Without a care in the world. Vigour coursed through his veins, and his wings beat the air relentlessly.

His first flight covered many miles and only the lack of light prevented his continuing. He felt that day as if he could have flown on forever. But, as dusk descended, he began to look for a suitable spot to alight for the night. He had taken little notice of his surroundings and knew only the direction of his flight from the general position of the sun, now low in the sky to his right. The light became gloomy and Venga gave all of his attention to the task of spotting a roost.

The hawk hit him hard. She had swooped down on him from above, at great speed, and her talons buried themselves deep into his flesh. Venga screamed as the pain registered and then began to struggle wildly, in a desperate effort to free himself from the hawk's clutches. The fury of the young magpie's struggles hampered the raptor's flight. Venga was heavy and powerful. Gradually the talons were loosened from his body, but the claws did terrible damage. In an effort to hold him, the hawk tried to move one of her feet, to improve the grip on the magpie's body. Venga thrashed in terror and fury, twisting his wings free and spinning the two of them around in the air.

The hawk had had enough. She would look elsewhere for an easier prey. But, as a parting shot, she flicked her head sideways, near to Venga's face. Her curved beak hooked into the magpie's left eye, ripping it from its socket. The agony of this terrible wound, on top of the damage wrought to the rest of his body, caused Venga to mercifully lose consciousness.

If he had done so a moment sooner, the hawk would have felt it and held on to the limp body. But she had already dropped the magpie. Venga fell like a stone, oblivious to the impact of his body on the hard ground below, cushioned only by a scant layer of vegetation. Exposed and utterly still, Venga lay on the hillside, awaiting his fate. Death had only to choose from its many options. Venga had no say in the matter.

CHAPTER 4

On the first evening after Portia and Mickey had left on their mission, the children were very subdued. Immediately after the robin and bullfinch had flown away, Tomar had made a point of introducing Merion and Olivia to each member of the Council of the Owls. Every single owl had something wonderful to say about their mother and father, and the two young robins were effusive and excited, too full of awe to be immediately affected by their mother's absence. There had been no further ceremony, although several of the Council members had urgent business that they wanted to discuss. But Tomar felt that it was imperative that he should devote his fullest attention to his charges for the time being.

Tomar and the young robins had been the first to leave, as the old owl wished to avoid a lot of goodbyes, which might remind Olivia and Merion of their mother's departure. He had flown slowly, flapping his huge wings with great deliberation and keeping his pace to theirs. And, while they flew, he had talked. Tomar had told them about the founding of Birddom, and of the first Great

Owl. Time passed quickly as he spoke, and the two children were too enthralled by his words to feel tired from their journey. They peppered his tales with questions, limited only by their occasional lack of breath from flying so far and asking so much!

They stopped only once on their journey, for food and water. Even with their beaks full, Merion and Olivia chattered away, asking about the heroes of the past, and wanting to know more, always more. Tomar felt exhausted. Their thirst for knowledge, for information and entertainment, left him drained. Fatigue in his aching old bones from the flight was nothing by comparison to the mental strain of trying to keep up with two quick, young minds, ever eager for more stories.

But, once they reached Tanglewood, which Kirrick had found so daunting on his first visit, the pair of young robins fell quiet. Perhaps the long flight had tired them more than they showed, but neither Merion nor Olivia displayed any inclination to explore their new surroundings. They thanked Tomar when he brought them some food, remembering their manners, but ate listlessly. And afterwards, the pair of them huddled together, heads down. They looked thoroughly miserable.

Tomar had avoided talking about either Kirrick or Portia to the young robins during their journey, not wanting to remind them of the absence of both their parents. But now he saw that they were missing their mother greatly and so the old owl decided to tell them a tale about their father. Tomar asked the young pair if Portia had ever told them about Kirrick's escape from Traska, when he had hidden on the back of a swan to avoid detection by the watching net of corvidae, who had been gathered by the malicious magpie in order to trap him. On finding that the children had, indeed, been told that story, the owl asked them if they knew the tale about Darreal and the mouse. Once again both Olivia and Merion enthusiastically chorused their affirmation.

Tomar, in his wisdom, knew all along that Portia would have raised her two young children with such tales about the heroic exploits of their father. But he was skilfully drawing the young robins out of their unease and depression. However, the old owl realised that he would have to find a story that they hadn't heard to keep their minds occupied. So, he decided to embellish a simple tale, told by Kirrick in the immediate aftermath of the Great Battle, when he had sat with Tomar, Cerival, Storne, Darreal, Isidris and Kraken, swapping stories of all that had preceded their momentous triumph.

Kirrick had, in fact, only provided the bare bones of the tale. In the midst of such heroism, it did not seem anything out of the ordinary. Kirrick had told it in a self-deprecating way, to indicate the extent to which luck had played its part in his adventure. But all the birds there realised the peril that Kirrick had faced and doubted that they would have dismissed it so lightly. For Kirrick had seen a fox and at rather too close a distance for comfort. Now Tomar knew that foxes do not usually pose too great a threat to wild birds. He was aware that they would, of course, eat eggs out of any nest that they could reach and, likewise, take young fledglings. He knew too that, as skilful hunters, foxes could sometimes kill an unwary adult. But Tomar had learnt as a young owl that their known preference was for larger, domesticated poultry which, being pinioned, provided easier targets as well as much more substantial meals.

Kirrick's experience was confined to a close encounter with one of these large predators, after he had made an ill choice of resting site, following an exhausting flight on his journey north. He had been numbed with fatigue as he had only recently recovered from illness and delirium and, in the gathering gloom of evening, he had picked a low roost in a willow tree. Kirrick had been too tired to search his surroundings for signs of danger and had barely folded his wings before he had fallen asleep. The tree in which he had chosen to alight was adjacent to a large bank of earth. Careful examination would have revealed to the robin an entrance, in the side of this bank, to a fox's den. Had the prevailing wind been in the right direction, the smell alone from the hole would have alerted Kirrick to the danger.

The robin had told how he had awoken the next morning to the sound of snuffling, to find a large, bushy red tail brushing past, inches from his beak. The fox was returning to its lair, carrying its prey. Its jaws were stretched wide in an effort to hold the plump body of the chicken. It had seen Kirrick on his roost and had paused momentarily, thinking to lay aside its burden for a quick snack, but, fortunately for the robin, it had already eaten well during its night's excursions and hungry young mouths waited in the den below. So Kirrick had escaped, flying off immediately upon waking and realising his danger.

Tomar looked at the two young robins waiting eagerly for a story, and asked, 'Did your mother ever tell you about Kirrick and the fox?'

'No, never,' Merion and Olivia cheeped in unison, thrilled that they were going to hear a new tale about their father.

'Would you like to hear it?' the owl teased, knowing the answer full well. The robins beamed, their earlier depression forgotten. So Tomar began his story.

'Kirrick awoke with a start. Something had disturbed him from his deep sleep. A noise, close at hand. The first thing that he saw when he opened his eyes was a large black nose. It quivered in front of his beak and Kirrick looked down from it to a long, pink tongue, lolling from between the fox's jaws. The robin realised that, at any second, those jaws would open and snap shut again around his small body. He pecked sharply at the beast's nose, and the fox yelped in pain and backed off slightly, surprise written all over its face.

'What do you mean by waking me up like that? I was having such a nice dream.'

'Aren't you afraid of me?' asked the fox.

'Why should I be afraid of you? You're only a fox, aren't you?' Kirrick replied.

'But I'm so much bigger than you are. I could swallow you whole, and not even feel your body as it slipped down my throat!' the fox barked, bridling at Kirrick's apparent insolence.

The robin realised that he was playing a dangerous game, but continued, 'Oh, I don't think so. You obviously don't realise who I am.'

Uncertainty clouded the fox's face for the first time, and Kirrick paused significantly, before carrying on, 'Do you think that I would have been foolish enough to roost here, right on your doorstep in such a perilous position, if I were a mere robin that you could just gobble up like a biscuit?'

The robin puffed up his feathers to their fullest extent, and assumed a look of self-importance on his beak.

'Who are you, then?' asked the fox, with a touch of respect in his voice.

'All in good time,' Kirrick replied. 'First of all, tell me your name.'

'I am called Reykard.'

'Well, Master Reykard. I am Kirrick the Wise, a great wizard and magician, though I say so myself.

I am the possessor of great powers and could transform you into a toad as soon as look at you, so mind your manners. I merely took this guise for ease of travelling through this countryside without frightening poor, dumb creatures like yourself.'

Kirrick's tone was utterly dismissive and helped him to establish his dominance over the fox, who began to look decidedly uneasy. But, even so, Kirrick realised that the animal remained close enough to eat him, in a flash, before he could make good any escape. He'd had no time since waking to preen the kinks out of his feathers, or to stretch his wings. He was still so vulnerable, and only his wits were keeping him alive.

'Perhaps, young cub, there is something that you might do for me.'

The fox was a full-grown adult and being referred to, in such imperious tones, as an adolescent, further undermined its confidence in the confrontation.

'What could I possibly do for a wizard?' asked the curious animal.

'Well, I am looking for wild garlic plants. As everyone knows, they possess healing properties and are of great use in a lot of my potions. Do you know where any might be found?'

'I have quite a wide-ranging territory and I think that I remember seeing some garlic on my travels. But those plants were several miles to the north of here.'

'Were they plentiful? I wouldn't want to waste

my time on a few miserable specimens. I need to gather a good quantity for my spells.'

'Oh, yes,' replied the fox, enthusiastically. He seemed pathetically eager to please.

'Very well then,' the robin continued. 'I am still rather weary and, as you were rude enough to wake me from my repose, you can carry me there on your back. Or would you rather spend the rest of your life as an earthworm? It wouldn't be too long a life, I can assure you!'

'I will carry you, oh great wizard. Hop onto my back. I can run very fast. We should be there in an hour or two.'

'Well, stop yapping. I've no time to waste. Perhaps I can catch up on my sleep while I ride on your mane.'

And, so saying, Kirrick jumped down from the branch, and onto the fox's smooth back. He dug his small talons deep into the animal's luxuriant fur and held on, as the fox set off at a gallop.

It was a dizzying ride, and Kirrick took quite a battering, being constantly bumped about as the beast that he rode leapt over obstacles, or squeezed through narrow gaps in the vegetation. Reykard continually looked over his shoulder at the robin, as if fearful that the wizard might grow angry at the roughness of the ride and perform some hideous spell on him.

'Are you all right?' panted the fox. 'We're almost halfway there.'

'Well, I cannot say that it's a comfortable ride,

236

albeit that it might be a swift one. But you carry on, young pup. I can tolerate a few bumps and bruises. As long as you are sure that our journey will be worth the discomfort.'

So the fox bounded on and Kirrick sat on its back, gaining several miles in his journey with very little effort on his part. Finally, they arrived in a damp wooded grove, where the pungent odour of the garlic plants was sufficient to make Kirrick close his nostrils.

'Here we are,' barked the fox. 'I hope that you are pleased with me.'

'It will do, I suppose,' Kirrick responded, diffidently.

'How are you going to carry all the plants that you need?' asked the fox.

'Do you think that I am a wizard for nothing?' replied the robin. 'A little magic will provide me with a basket big enough to carry a whole field of garlic. And perhaps I will transform you into a horse, so that I can ride you all the way home again!'

The fox looked frightened, and thought about bolting. But it was afraid that the wizard might carry out his threat before it could get away. Besides, Reykard was intensely curious and wanted to see the wizard as he really was, and to watch him perform his magic.

'But that would be unfair' Kirrick continued. 'You have been kind enough to carry me this far. I will not ask more of you. Indeed, I feel that you should be rewarded. I am too tired to begin my tasks here straightaway. Too little sleep, you know. But, before I catch up on my rest, I think that I can manage just a little magic. As a thank you for your service to me, I will grant you a wish. How would you like a den full of plump and tender young ducklings, already plucked so that you won't have the bother of a mouthful of feathers? I could give you enough to last you and your family for a whole month, if you so wish.'

The fox's eyes glittered greedily at the thought of such a ready supply of food. He could do with a week or two of ease.

'I would like that very much. Thank you, oh kind wizard,' replied Reykard.

Kirrick closed his eyes, and pretended to concentrate. Balancing on his perch, he spread his wings wide and began to chant in a strange tongue, as if speaking an incantation. The robin was actually using the ancient language of the owls, for he had learnt a smattering of words from Tomar before he had set out on his journey. After a few moments he opened his eyes again and looked directly at the fox.

'That's all there is to it, Reykard, my young lad. Simple enough when you're a wizard. Now, off you go back to your den and let me get some sleep.'

'Just how many ducklings will there be?' asked the fox.

'You'll be really surprised,' replied Kirrick. 'You won't be able to count them!'

Reykard positively drooled as the robin spoke

and, quickly voicing his thanks, raced off in the direction that they had come. And Kirrick hopped up into a higher branch of the tree, and began to preen, preparing himself for his next journey.'

Tomar was quietly pleased with himself. His little story, whilst apocryphal, was suitably in keeping with Kirrick's heroics. And it also served its purpose well. Merion and Olivia were enraptured and now showed no signs of the sadness that had come upon them on their arrival at Tomar's home. The old owl bade them goodnight, promising more tales in response to their eager pleading.

Once the children had settled, Tomar flapped his great wings and set off for a brief flight around his territory. His huge eyes scoured the terrain for food, but he was also watchful for any other activity. Although it was at his suggestion, Tomar felt that a significant burden had been placed upon his ageing shoulders. The two youngsters had been given into his care in complete trust. Portia had shown absolute faith in Tomar and had willingly undertaken a journey fraught with potential danger, safe in the knowledge that her young would be well looked after. It was a heavy responsibility and weighed upon the old owl in equal measure with his duties as Great Owl and leader of all Birddom. For these young robins were very special. Their father was a hero, the greatest of his line. And who could say that their mother, Portia, might not yet outdo the heroic exploits of her mate?

But above all to Tomar's eyes, Merion and Olivia were symbols of the rebirth of Birddom. They were the very first children born into a world of renewed peace and hope. The very first fledglings who did not know the fear of tyranny. They were born to take ownership of this new world. Tomar was but its temporary guardian, in the twilight of his life. But he vowed that night, to himself and to the two sleeping young robins, that he would strive to deliver into their wings, when the time came, a world fit for their generation. Birddom would grow strong, prospering in his safe-keeping, and their future would be a bright one.

CHAPTER 5

Portia and Mickey had flown east when they had taken leave of the Council and of the robin's two children. Sadness weighed heavily upon her and the pair flew in silence for a long time. They were heading back towards Mickey's home territory, where Portia and Kirrick had first encountered the ebullient finch and, from there, towards the coast itself, following the route that the three of them had taken on their urgent mission to seek the aid of the seagull flock. It would be a good place to stop and rest, before their daunting flight to Wingland. Besides, Kraken could give her the latest information as to weather conditions and prevailing winds. Few knew the seaward skies better than the great gull.

Portia only hoped that her welcome would be warmer than on that previous occasion, when Kraken had, quite literally, turned his back on the pair of robins who had so needed his help. Of course in the final analysis he had come in the nick of time, and had been instrumental in achieving their great victory over the corvidae. But Portia still felt a little uncertain about bothering him again. It was her sense of doubt that finally broke the silence between them, much to the relief of the usually garrulous Mickey.

'Do you think that Kraken will help us? It is such a perilous journey and neither of us has had any experience of sea-flight before.'

'You underestimate yourself, Portia. Why, it's not so long ago that you were flying halfway across the country. And as for Kraken, well, he's a cranky old sod, there's no denying it. But he's our friend now. Don't forget that he was one of the Council that originally decided to send you on this mission. It is his duty to help us, in whatever way he can. And if he refuses, I'll peck out his other eye!'

Portia cheeped in merriment at this and Mickey strove to keep the mood light by an absurd impersonation of the great black-backed gull. An onlooker would have been astonished to hear the rasping caws that emanated from the usually melodious throat of the bullfinch in flight. For her part, Portia giggled helplessly and struggled to maintain an even course in the air. Finally, Mickey finished his imitation.

'Ouch!' he gasped. 'That made my throat sore. No wonder that Kraken is such a grouch, if that's what talking in gull does for you! I need a drink.'

The two companions flew on, their eyes searching the terrain for a suitable place to stop and refresh themselves. Soon they spotted a small, secluded pond and, after checking for possible danger, alighted and settled down to drink.

The thought struck them both simultaneously, but it was Mickey who voiced it. 'Blimey. I've just realised. We're gonna have a rare old thirst by the time that we get across the sea. All that bloody water, and nothing to drink!'

As they neared the coast, it seemed to the pair that the fates were conspiring against them. A strong breeze sprang up, chill and buffeting, and holding the threat of inevitable rain. The weather deteriorated quickly, until Portia could barely see in front of her beak, even though it was the middle of the day. It seemed that, at any moment, the heavens would open and they would have to find shelter. But their luck held and it was not until they landed on the cliff ledge that was Kraken's home that the torrent began. Good fortune held there, too. Or good sense, on the part of the giant gull. The topography of the site meant that the ledge was protected to a large extent by an overhang of limestone. And this kept the worst of the rain from the backs of the smaller birds. Portia peered out into the stormy gloom, then poked Mickey playfully with her wing. 'What was that you were saying about no water to drink?'

Kraken, however, concurred fully with the amiable bullfinch, when he sat huddled with the two travellers, discussing their options.

'It's different for us gulls. We are used to the taste of salt water. Most of our food comes from the sea. Our bodies are adapted to it.

But even we need fresh water to drink. That is why our forays are usually confined to coastal waters. We need a land base to survive. But you small birds would have a real problem, even if the weather were not so foul. You live here. You are not natural travellers, like some other birds, and Wingland is far, far away.

Your size, and, more importantly, the size of your wings, means that the distance that you will have to fly across the sea will seem much greater than it would to a gull. A flock, flying together, gathers strength from its sheer numbers. But two birds only are not enough to generate that collective energy. In addition, being smaller, it will be crucial for you to take on sufficient water to last you through your journey. Otherwise you will undoubtedly dehydrate and die. Absurd to think of in all this rain, but true, nonetheless. Be in no doubt of that, my friends.'

Kraken stared solemnly at them with his one good eye, as if appraising their worth, before continuing,

'There is one more, crucial difference. When a seabird is tired, all it has to do is alight on the ocean and ride the waves. Our feathers are water-proofed and we are as comfortable on water as on land. You, however, will have no such luxury. To obtain any rest at all, you would need to find something man-made to land upon and, in the wide vastness of the sea, that in itself would be an incredible stroke of good fortune. But even then it would be of no avail if the waters were too rough. You would just be washed away and drowned.

No. With all this rain, I fear that your task is now nigh on impossible. This weather is set to last. It is no passing shower. And it will be far worse out to sea. I see no possible way of your surviving an attempt to cross the waters to Wingland on your own. If only you weren't such small birds!'

Just at that moment a raucous clamour arose from the cliffs around them, as eager ears picked up the sounds of the incoming fishing boats. And, from further out to sea, there came the low mournful hoot of a klaxon, as a channel ferry cruised away, unseen, into the distance.

Kraken almost laughed. 'Well, praise be that your size is as it is!' he remarked, cryptically.

Both robin and bullfinch stared at him, looking puzzled. Portia especially so. She had fully expected the imminet source of food to totally occupy Kraken's mind. It was at this point on her last visit that she and Kirrick had been ignored, as Kraken had led the flock towards the incoming boats.

The huge gull read her mind. 'Oh, that hungry bunch of scavengers can wait for a few minutes. I think I've solved your problem.'

Kraken quickly outlined his ideas to the companions, and was satisfied to see their evident relief at the logic of his solution.

'Well. Now I'm wet and I'm hungry. So, if you'll excuse me, I'll be off. We can talk in more detail when I've had my meal. At least you'll have plenty to think about while I am gone.'

And, with that, Kraken took wing and the entire cliff top erupted with noise and motion, as a hundred pairs of sodden wings flapped away in eager pursuit of their food.

Destiny is sometimes hard to deny, even if its course is altered by events. So it was with Venga. The first thing that he registered on regaining consciousness was overwhelming pain. He had lost a good deal of blood from his wounds and the rents in his flesh screamed excruciatingly when he moved. The movement was a panic reaction, a reflex response from his body to the sudden terror that flooded his mind. Venga could not see. He remembered the awful moment when the hawk had torn out his left eye, just before he fell. But he could not recall any similar damage to his right. Had he been further injured when his unconscious body had crumpled onto the hard ground?

With no eyes Venga was as good as dead. His mind reeled at the appalling prospect of being taken by a predator that he could not see. There would be no warning. No chance for escape, or even for a show of defence. He shrank against the earth, pressing himself into the ground as if, by some force, he could lessen his solidity. He wished that he could merge with the very fabric of his surroundings, to hide from the inevitable. Venga was bewildered that he had not already been killed. There must have been a veritable army of voracious predators in these parts and he presented such an easy target, exposed and vulnerable as he was.

But, unknown to the injured magpie, humans were about on the hillside. Although several large carnivores had smelt the blood of the hapless bird and had seen the wounded body, none had been courageous enough to risk exposure on that same hillside. For the humans carried guns and every creature in the animal world knew that guns meant death. So, salivating in frustration, many who would have enjoyed a meal of magpie watched on with hungry eyes and bellies.

The man and his son walked side by side, the latter a half-sized version of the former, in attire and demeanour. Each carried a shotgun in the crook of their right arm and the boy held on tight to the legs of a brace of pheasant, whose limp bodies hung down heavily by his knees. He struggled manfully against their weight, forcing himself to keep up with his father's large stride. Then they both stopped, unsure of what lay ahead in the gloom and the man illuminated the ground in front of them with his torch. The beam reflected off Venga's brilliant white feathers, and picked out the sheen of gore that coated much of the magpie's head and body.

'Wow. Cool!' shouted the boy, in his excitement. 'Look at all that blood, Dad. Is he dead?'

'I don't know, son. Go and take a look.'

The boy needed no further encouragement. He

followed the beam of light, slowing a few steps from the stricken bird.

'Awesome!' he breathed.

The sound of the boy's voice alerted Venga to his peril. He fluttered feebly, attempting to move away from this new source of danger, trying to ignore the agony that such movement inevitably caused.

'He's alive, Dad. I saw him move.'

'Well, we'd better put him out of his misery, then.'

'No, Dad. Wait! We can't eat him, like the pheasant. Can't we keep him? Look at his wings and tail. He's beautiful!'

'I'll tell you what he is,' replied his father. 'He's a bag of fleas. And a vicious blighter, too. You've seen what magpies are like on the roadside. Worse than vultures, they are. Besides, he'll never recover from those wounds. Look at him. One of his eyes is missing, for Christ's sake!'

'I want to keep him, Dad. I'm not leaving him here to be eaten and I won't let you shoot him. I can look after him. I'll clean him up and keep him in that old cage. We didn't get rid of it when Sammy died. It's in the shed with all the other junk. I'll feed him, and everything. Can I keep him, Dad? Please.'

'It'd be kinder to finish him off quick, now . . .' began the man, but one look into his son's face told him that this perfectly sensible course of action was not an option. 'All right then, lad. But

248

you'll have to carry him. Give me over those pheasants. I still think that you're mad, though. Whoever heard of keeping a magpie as a pet?'

Crossing the sea from the Isle of Storms proved a far more tiring and difficult journey for Traska than it had been when he had fled Birddom in the wake of the Great Battle. His injured wing hampered him and the weather was foul. Strong winds and rain buffeted his small band of corvidae and, even though the distance between the tip of the island and the north western coast of Birddom was a mere fourteen miles, the crossing took more than two hours. Finally, however, exhausted by their exertions, the band of crows and the solitary evil magpie alighted on the rocks surrounding a lighthouse, taking what shelter they could from the dreadful weather. Free from the need to concentrate solely upon their own survival, several of the hooded crows recovered sufficiently to begin bemoaning their decision to follow Traska to this benighted land. Discontent rumbled through their ranks, and a few of the more belligerent among them threatened to fly straight back home 'as soon as this bloody weather improves!'

The inclement weather turned out, however, to be in the magpie's favour. For, on the high promentory overhanging the raging waters, a lamb was blundering about, driven to distraction by the high winds and driving rain, and separated from its mother. Its pathetic bleating carried down to where the twenty huge crows huddled near the water's edge. Traska was the quickest to react.

'I must apologise for the welcome that my land has afforded you all. It is most unusual. Perhaps Birddom has been weeping for the absence of its king. But, is it not, as I promised, a land of plenty? For, even in its sorrow, we are provided for. Hear how our next meal calls out to us to come and eat it!'

The magpie's cruel laughter carried to them all, cutting through the wind like a scimitar. Once again, their faith was bolstered by a display of arrogance and confidence. Traska wasted no more time on words, but flapped off in search of the stranded lamb. The others followed and soon a grisly black curtain descended around the unfortunate animal. Traska hopped back and forth around the periphery of the group as they fed. He had not had the stomach for the actual slaying of so large a creature himself.

'Let these great oafs do all the heavy work,' he thought. 'That's what I brought them here for, after all.'

However, he had exercised his dominance over the band of crows, by selecting a few of the choicest morsels – the tongue and the eyes – for his own consumption. After all, this was his land, and hadn't he provided the bounty that they all now enjoyed? Traska knew, however, not to push his luck too far, so he let them feast without further ado.

And, while they sated themselves, beaks flashing

and craws swallowing, the voice of the magpie was insidious behind them.

'I told you that my land was a wonderful place. There are no farmers here to blast you with their deadly pellets. Man doesn't rule in this land. I do!'

The relief that flooded through Venga's body when he found that he had some measure of vision after all was indescribable. From the moment that he had been hit in mid-air, by the hawk's cruel talons, his world had turned into nightmare. Everything had been pain and terror. But now, even though the magpie quailed at the child's gentle touch, a glimmer of hope flickered weakly in Venga's heart. He was alive – and he could see!

The boy was washing the caked and crusted blood away from the magpie's one good eye. It had run across his beak from the terribly wounded socket when he had lain on the hillside and had congealed and hardened over the eye, like a carapace, blocking out all light. But, under the child's careful ministrations, Venga's sight, though monocular, was restored. When the boy replaced the magpie on the floor of the cage, he was delighted to see his patient respond for the first time.

Venga shook out his feathers. Then he hopped, slowly and painfully, across the sanded surface. The bird cage had erstwhile housed a grey parrot, which, due to carelessness, had escaped into an environment totally alien to such an exotic species.

It had not lasted the week. Fortunately, the boy never knew. In his imagination, his pet had flown the incredible distance to his homeland and was, even now, squawking and talking to his fellow parrots about his kind young master. Venga opened his beak, accepting gratefully the steady stream of wriggling worms and beetles that were fed to him. Then, ignoring the pain that returned with a vengeance due to this increased activity, he slept, dreaming of his mother.

CHAPTER 6

The huge coil of rope reeked of pitch and its strong odour made the two tiny birds hiding within gag at the stench. Portia already felt very sick. The motion of the ferry, as it was rolled from side to side by the waves, turned her stomach as much as the smell. Other things distressed her also. The incessant rain. The noise of the ship and the proximity of so many humans. Portia began to think that Kraken's idea had not been such a good one, after all.

Mickey cheeped quietly into her ear, trying to comfort her.

'At least we're safe and sound, and letting someone else do all the hard work.'

'But what if we're discovered? What if the men catch us?'

'They can't fly, can they?' was Mickey's ebullient response. 'Stop worrying, Portia. Enjoy the ride!'

Enjoyment was not a word that the beautiful robin would have chosen at that precise moment. But she let it pass. It was no good snapping back at her companion. This was just a necessary, albeit uncomfortable, part of their journey. The crossing to Wingland had to be made, and she was prepared to endure anything that would help to achieve their aim.

The rain finally abated, but no sun penetrated through the cloud cover to ease the chill in their bones, and their slow passage across the sea was a joyless one. The two birds took turns to keep watch, allowing the other to snatch some sleep. It was hard to stay awake – the rolling motion of the ship induced a state of somnolence. More than once it was only the dousing from a sudden cloud of sea spray, as the ship pitched and tossed on the waves, that roused the designated watcher from approaching slumber.

Meanwhile, back in Tanglewood, Merion and Olivia were exploring their new surroundings with renewed vigour and enthusiasm. Tomar's stories, and their natural resilience, had enabled the pair of young robins to cast off their feelings of doubt and unhappiness and now they played gleefully among the trees, chasing each other in and out of the branches in an exhilarating game of tag.

Tomar watched this strenuous activity from the comfort of his perch. A satisfied smile spread across his beak. He allowed his great mind to turn to matters other than the immediate needs of his charges. Tomar wondered how Portia and Mickey were getting along. He estimated that their journey would now have taken them halfway across the vast stretch of water that separated Birddom from

Wingland. Looking about him at the far from perfect weather conditions, he hoped, with all his heart, that things were more favourable for his two friends. Their flight would be one to test them to their limits, in even the mildest weather. And Tomar knew well the vagaries of the coastal climate, from his discussions with Kraken. The old owl offered up a prayer for the continued safety of the robin and the bullfinch, then turned his attention back to the simple pleasure of watching the young at play.

Neither robin was hungry, as Tomar had not long since provided them with a breakfast more than sufficient to fill their bellies. But both Olivia and her brother were entranced by the wriggling caterpillar that made its slow progress along the branch in front of them. It was vividly coloured in green and black, and covered all over with fine hairs.

Both robins salivated without knowing the reason. Neither had ever eaten a caterpillar before. In fact, they had never had any meal that moved! Born into a world where insects were no longer a part of the food chain, the robins did not know the taste of living flesh. But the very movement of the wriggling creature before their eyes triggered a subconscious response. Everything about it said 'Eat me!'. The pair of robins looked greedily at their prize, and it was Olivia who spoke first. 'That's not an insect, is it?'

'No,' replied Merion with false assurance. 'Insects have wings and six legs. This creature has got dozens!'

'Do you think that we can eat it, then?'

'What do you mean "we"? I saw it first, and I'm going to eat it.'

Merion's tone was belligerent. It was the only way with his sister, for Olivia was the larger of the pair and naturally the stronger. But she was gentle of temperament and Merion knew that he could bully her into giving in.

'Can't we share it? There seems more than enough for both of us.'

'No!' repeated the young cock bird, in a tone that would brook no denial. 'It's mine. I am going to eat it all!'

Merion glared at his sister, defying her to challenge him. It was a risky game to play and he decided to change tack.

'Besides,' he whispered, 'It might be dangerous. The creature might be poisonous. Far better that only one of us should be made ill. And I love you too much to let you risk such a fate. Anyway, if I find that it is safe to eat, I promise that I will find another one, especially for you.'

Olivia was somewhat mollified by what her brother said. She had indeed considered the dangers inherent in eating something entirely alien to their diet. And she still wasn't sure, in spite of Merion's denial, that they should be thinking of eating this creature at all, whatever it was.

Satisfied that there would be no further argument from his sister, Merion hopped imperiously onto the branch, where the undulating body of the caterpillar beckoned him. The young robin hesitated, unsure of what to do next. He had never killed anything before. How did you do it? Which part should he attack? What if this creature had some way of fighting back? Merion suddenly felt considerably less tempted by his prospective meal, but he did not want to lose face in front of his sister.

Tomar's timely intervention decided the matter. The old owl cuffed Merion unceremoniously about the head with his wing. It was a restrained blow, but still powerful enough to knock the robin from his perch. Merion landed in an undignified heap on the forest floor, and looked up with fear in his eyes at the owl who was staring angrily down at him.

'What do you think you were doing? Do you not know the law? I personally made a solemn promise that no insect would be taken as food by any bird. Do you want to break that vow? Does the word of the Great Owl mean so little to you?'

'I am sorry, Tomar. We didn't know what the creature was. It certainly doesn't look like any insect that I've ever seen.' Tears filled Merion's eyes, from the blow to the head, and from the severity of the old owl's admonishment.

Tomar shook his head, ashamed now of his own anger. What had he been thinking of? This was the pair's first spring. It was entirely logical, therefore, that neither robin would have seen a caterpillar. Of course, their mother would have taught them from birth about the ban on eating any insect, and would have shown them many examples of creatures that they were to avoid. But, the seasons being what they were, Portia would not have had the opportunity to teach her children about the larval stages of insect development. And now Tomar had sent their mother away from them, before she had had the chance to complete their education.

The old owl was thoroughly ashamed of himself. 'Forgive me, Merion!' he said, in a voice full of contrition.

'I am the one who should be sorry, Tomar.'

'Well then, we are both sorry, and there's an end to it. Come back up here, and I'll tell you both a story. And then, if your head has survived its battering, I'll teach you more about the other creatures that make up this wonderful, bewildering world of ours.'

There were times during the crossing when Portia believed that she would never again see dry land. On several occasions she had begged Mickey to let her simply take to the skies and trust to luck, and to her own instincts and innate skill as a navigator. But the bullfinch had been firm with her.

'I am sorry for you, Portia, and I know that you are unwell. But we have chosen this course and we must stick to it. Unpleasant though the journey may be, it is taking us in the right direction.'

'Well, I've had a bellyful of it!' replied Portia petulantly.

'If my memory serves me correctly, you had a bellyful of the sea once before!' was Mickey's pointed answer.

Portia bridled at the bullfinch's reminder of her foolishness when they had first met. How dare he try and tell her what to do? He was her companion on this voyage to Wingland, but she was Birddom's chosen emissary. The robin turned her back on her friend, and would not speak another word. Mickey, realising that he had upset and offended Portia, decided that silence would also be the best policy. So the two birds slumped miserably on the deck, each lost in their own thoughts. Gradually, Portia's temper cooled and she began to think more rationally. Tomar had once again shown his wisdom in choosing the brash bullfinch to accompany her. She might not like what he had said to her, but she realised the wisdom of his words.

Impatience was their greatest foe when the ferry finally eased into the harbour and began the slow, tortuous process of docking. It took nearly an hour for all of the humans to disembark, and the combination of the fumes from their cars and from the ship itself laid a choking cloud over the immediate area. Again and again Mickey had to counsel caution and Portia chafed against the delay. She was anxious, now that they had made dry land, to be on her way and this forced inactivity was galling.

But, finally, the bullfinch cheeped, 'Let's be off then.' And the disparate pair took to the skies, to begin their first journey over the foreign soil of Wingland.

They had two priorities. The first was to find a safe roost that they could use as a base for their operations in the immediate vicinity. It was entirely possible that they would have to journey much farther afield before their quest was over. But they had to start somewhere. Their second need, as urgent as the first, was to find and befriend a transient – a migratory bird – who would be able to interpret for them in their discourse with the local resident birds. Of the two, this was the far harder proposition. Roosts at least were static. But the very nature of migration meant that the type of bird that they sought spent most of its life on the wing, journeying vast distances from their summer to their winter homes. Tomar had chosen the time of their departure to best match these seasonal odysseys. The old owl had reasoned, without firm proof, that these travellers, who had historically spent their summers in Birddom itself, would now have chosen this part of Wingland as their best alternative. But so much depended upon climate and the availability of food resources.

Now that they were back on dry land, albeit a foreign and frightening one, Portia took the lead in searching for a temporary home. Keeping together they flew far and wide, identifying likely sites only to discard them as too dangerous, or too exposed, or disadvantageous in some other way. It was fortunate that both birds were able to thrive in similar habitats and were gregarious enough, by nature, to benefit from the proximity of humans. They finally chose a thick hedge of thorns bordering a winding but little-used man-made road. There were plenty of human dwellings close by, but none near enough to present any real danger. Adjacent farmland and an apple orchard in early bloom would provide sufficient food.

'This will do very well,' Portia announced, as they alighted, swiftly hiding themselves from view amongst the dense vegetation, and Mickey did not demur.

Life for Venga became an interminable cycle of boredom. At first, he concentrated solely on his own physical recovery. The boy was kind and provided the magpie with a regular supply of food and water. Venga's wounds healed quickly and, as they did so, his strength returned. It was no longer agony to hop around the base of the cage, but flight was virtually impossible within its cramped confines. A single flap of the wings was all that was required for the magpie to attain the perching pole, which was placed halfway up the side of the cage. Sitting there, Venga's long and beautiful tail could at least be straightened out, even though the tips of its feathers still touched the floor.

Whenever he flexed his wings, stretching them wide to maintain the circulation of the blood and to exercise his muscles, the wing-tips brushed against the bars, providing Venga with a constant reminder of his captivity. Time passed, the days blurred into one another. The magpie longed for the freedom of the skies. For unrestrained flight. But his home now seemed a million miles away. Venga fretted and worried about his mother. For all of his life, her one obsession had been revenge for the heinous cruelty of the outrage that Traska had perpetrated upon her. Venga had become the symbol and the implement of that retribution. The central core of his life was now being denied to him and Venga feared that Katya might die of old age, bitter, frustrated and let down by her own son. Such heavy sorrow was hard for a magpie to bear. For his circumstances seemed hopeless. There seemed no way out. It occured to Venga that, in the face of such a futile and depressing existence, Death might as well visit him, before it took his mother to its black breast.

Traska's black and evil heart beat inside his breast to its own twisted and perverted rhythm. He had led his band of incomers across heather-clad uplands, through dank forests, and over serene lochs. This menacing and brutal legion had wreaked havoc as they journeyed, slaying at will any small bird or animal that they encoun-tered. After the hiatus of peace that Birddom had experienced following the Great Battle, it was a shocking reminder of the corvidae's rise to power. News of their passage spread like wild-fire and ahead of them great tracts of land emptied, as the scant remaining populace fled for their lives.

But this was no band of hunters bent on the systematic destruction of all small bird life. It was merely a whirlwind of violence, which caused great damage then passed by. Something to be avoided, rather than feared. But still word of their coming went ahead of them. These huge crows were alien to Birddom's shores and news necessarily became exaggerated. They doubled in size. They had beaks that could crack stone. They ate their victims alive.

This was just as Traska had hoped, for it helped to create an aura of invincibility about his troops, which, for now at least, was not borne out by the reality. They lacked numbers. In a battle with the eagles of this region, for example, his own side would be hopelessly outnumbered. But Traska did not plan any such outright confrontation with his enemies. Although it rankled deeply that his personal reversal had come at the wings of those accursed raptors, the evil magpie was not looking for reprisals. Or, at least, not by such direct means as battle. He would engineer their downfall, and, more importantly, that of the leaders of Birddom as well, the Council of the Owls.

Traska was sure that news of his return with his menacing army would make its way south, and finally would reach the ear of the one bird in the land that he hated above all others. Tomar. He wanted the old owl to know that he was back. That Traska wasn't afraid of the high and mighty

Council, or of its lordly supporters. But the magpie also wanted to mislead Tomar as to his intentions. To draw the owl's mind and eye away from his real plan. Subterfuge would be his weapon, sleight of wing would fool his opponent. And then he would strike. He would hit them where it would hurt the most. And then his revenge would be complete.

CHAPTER 7

It had all seemed so plausible, so easy, when the great and wise had devised the plan. A simple task for Birddom's emissary. To fly across to the vast expanse of Wingland and persuade a few dozen birds, to begin with, that life would be better for them if they would accompany the robin back to her homeland.

But, in reality, it was an idea fraught with difficulties, not the least of which was deciding where to begin. Two weeks had passed since Portia and Mickey had scoured the locality and had chosen a suitable base for their operations. The local bird populace had been neither hostile nor friendly. To a large extent, they had ignored these strangers to their land and had carried on with the normality of their lives. Such attempts as there were at making contact were all instigated by the robin and the bullfinch. But every attempt fell down because of the language barrier. Portia and Mickey simply couldn't make themselves understood.

To make matters worse, at no time since their arrival had they even had a glimpse of any migratory bird to enlist. They searched the skies daily for a sighting of a swallow or martin, serin or swift. But to no avail. It seemed that those birds who had previously traversed the seas to Birddom were now far more cautious about journeying even close to its shores. They had deserted not only Birddom itself but also, it seemed, the part of Wingland in closest proximity to it.

'We have underestimated our task, Mickey,' Portia said solemnly, as the pair reviewed another fruitless day. 'There are birds aplenty here. Enough, indeed, to repopulate every part of our land. But none will come with us while we are unable to communicate with them. And yet, conversely, there are birds who can understand us, and who we could talk to, if only we could find them. I am glad now that we made our sea voyage in such a leisurely fashion, for I fear that we will have a great deal of flying to do in these lands before we complete our mission.'

The robin looked earnestly at her companion. The pair had kept up each other's spirits since their arrival from Birddom and had talked together at length. Mickey had gradually lost his facade of chirpy coarseness. Such serious discussions called for more than a brash manner, and the beautiful robin was glad to learn that Mickey evidently possessed a keen mind. Portia had begun to suspect that her companion's way of speaking was a contrivance to hide his intellect.

But it was obvious he had taken their failure badly. The normally ebullient bullfinch was very crestfallen and withdrawn. He felt very inadequate, as if, in some way, he had let his companion down. Portia smiled in encouragement at her friend.

'I am relieved you are here with me, Mickey. I could not face a single mile without you. You can always make me laugh. I know that we will need your good cheer in the days and weeks to come.'

'Thank you, Portia. I am gratified that you see me as an integral part of our mission, even if only in the role of the fool!'

'I value you as a friend, Mickey,' the robin replied. 'Now let us plan our next journey. Which way do you think that we should travel?'

The bullfinch considered their options for a while before replying, 'It is still early in the season for large numbers of travellers to have reached these northern climes. I think that our best option would be to travel south, in the hope of a chance encounter on their flight-paths.'

'Sounds good to me, mate,' chirped Portia, in an awful impersonation of the bullfinch's accent.

Tomar thought long and hard about the information that he had received earlier that morning. He sat quietly in the bole of the crooked fir tree, which had been his home for more years than he cared to remember. Merion and Olivia were playing a game, flitting in and out of the nearby shrubbery, and the old owl watched them with deep affection. But his attention was elsewhere.

News had been brought to him of Traska's re-appearance and of the mayhem being caused by his band of thugs. Not that Tomar was seriously worried about them. They were insufficient in number to prove any real threat to the sanctity of Birddom, and their violent actions were of minor significance, compared to the return of their companion.

Tomar recognised his own failure, as Great Owl and leader of all Birddom, in allowing Traska to escape from his talons after the Great Battle. The malevolence of this magpie knew no bounds and the owl had come to fear Traska more than he had Slyekin, his megalomaniac leader. That magpie had been corrupt and insane. But Tomar knew, with a chilling certainty, that Traska was truly evil. And it was not just the callousness of the magpie's actions in murdering Kirrick that made the old owl's blood run cold. He knew that this dreadful bird meant to inflict more malice against the just and natural order of the land. But what was his specific purpose in returning to Birddom? The numerical weakness of his cohorts persuaded Tomar that Traska had not come back for a fight. The re-emergence of the Council of the Owls, and their strong alliances, forged during the confrontation with the corvidae, gave the owl confidence that Traska would not dare wage outright war. The question remained: What devious plan was now fermenting in Traska's mind?

★ ★ ★

Traska needed news. He desired information about Birddom, and had his own peculiar way of obtaining it. While the small bird populace had been decimated by the corvidae, those remaining had taken great heart from the victory over that same enemy. The whole of Birddom knew about the Great Battle, and particularly of Kirrick's role in the overthrow of Slyekin's evil empire. The brave robin was a hero throughout the land and the birth of his two offspring had been the cause for great celebration.

Equally important for birds everywhere had been the reformation of the Council of the Owls. Many a bird slept easier in his nest knowing that Tomar was the leader of Birddom. News of the first meeting of the new Council, and of its agenda, spread far and wide. Tomar's plans lifted everyone's spirits and a sense of joy and optimism reigned throughout the land. Portia's mission was the talk in every treetop in Birddom and, in truth, Traska could easily have obtained all the information that he wanted by patient eavesdropping. But patience was not a virtue that the magpie possessed, if indeed he possessed any virtues at all. Besides, it was much more fun doing it his way.

The unfortunate recipient of Traska's attentions was a young starling, who had lingered too long over a tasty morsel when her flock had become airborne, alerted to danger by their lookouts. They had seen the dark shapes of the huge crows, as they penetrated the valley where the fifty or so starlings were feeding. Engrossed in sating her appetite, the unfortunate starling had realised her peril too late. The hooded crows had mobbed her as she tried to flee and now she cowered, helpless, in front of Traska. She was not a very brave bird, and the violence inflicted upon her was far in excess of any requirements. She would have told Traska everything that he wished to know with much less 'encouragement'. But the magpie's bloodlust filled his mind. Every question was accompanied by a vicious peck, drawing blood from the terrified starling.

But Traska was careful not to kill his captive before he had extracted every scrap of information from her. Three times she pleaded with him to finish her, to release her from the agonies that he was putting her through. But Traska knew that this was an opportunity to impress the giant crows who watched the proceedings with eagerness. The magpie knew that mercy was not on the agenda. Not that any such charitable act would ever have entered Traska's mind. He was enjoying himself far too much. However, there came a time when the little starling simply had nothing left to tell him, and Traska vented his disappointment at the ending of his entertainment by casually stoving in the starling's skull with a stabbing thrust of his powerful beak.

The evil magpie sat quietly and pondered the information that he had gleaned. His original plan would have to be altered. He had intended to go after Portia, but now she was out of his reach. But the young robins . . . now there was a thought. So that blasted robin's bloodline lived on, did it? Well, he would see about that!

Finbar and the other hooded crows were also enjoying themselves hugely in this new land. Although reliant on, and, in reality, led by Traska, Finbar still revelled in his portion of power as their nominal leader. These massive corvidae talked incessantly amongst themselves about the opportunities that had been placed in their paths.

'There's so much food here, and we can fly where we like without being blown out of the skies by Man,' said one.

'Traska was right,' continued another. 'This is the land for us. We'll not want for anything here.'

There was, indeed, a general consensus of opinion among the hooded crows that their individual and collective lot had been much improved by following the magpie's advice. Traska had chosen his route inland from the coast with considerable care. He wished at all costs to avoid contact and conflict with Man, not only because of the inherent dangers, but also to help create the impression in the dull-witted minds of his companions that this was a much better habitat than they had left behind. So, an air of contentment reigned among the corvidae and, for the time being at least, they were happy to leave Traska to his plans while they explored their new home.

* * *

A germ of an idea had been forming in Traska's mind ever since his interrogation of the starling, and it crystallised his vague intentions of harm towards the pair of young robins into something far more specific and satisfying. He knew now exactly how he could bring about the downfall of the high and mighty Council of the Owls, and exact a fitting revenge upon his enemy, Tomar.

But, in the meantime, he explored the territory minutely, looking far afield for a fortress of his own, which would allow his small force to repel any retributive attack once he had carried out his evil design. It was on one such excursion that Traska found himself in familiar surroundings. He was flying over a tract of land at the foothills of the high mountains where he had suffered ignominious defeat at the wings of Storne and his eagles. Immediately below him was the very spot where Kirrick and Portia had gone to ground in the rabbit warrens, and where the hunting magpies had so nearly caught up with them.

'Curse that robin!' He had been the bane of Traska's existence, and continued to dominate the magpie's thoughts and feed his hatred long after his actual death. Traska flapped his wings strongly for a few beats and veered off his present course, wanting to flee the haunting memory of Kirrick's goodness and valour.

Katya recognised him the instant she became aware of his presence and her heart froze with fear.

But Traska did not know her. She had been an object when he had raped her, a mere receptacle for his lust. Now those base feelings were latent and Traska's loneliness made him seek contact with another magpie. He had spent too long in the company of strangers and desired greatly to be with one of his own. Besides, Traska had swiftly realised that the female that he approached was very beautiful indeed.

'Good morning, my dear lady,' ventured the evil bird, honey dripping from his tongue. 'This is a fortunate meeting.'

'How so, sir?' Katya replied. She had seen no gleam of recognition in his eyes, and this hope made her bold. 'Who is the recipient of this good fortune?'

'Both of us,' responded Traska, slightly taken aback by the tone of her reply. 'I have been searching the land without knowing why. Now I have my reason. My quest is self-evident. I was meant to find you.'

'Pretty words, sir. But why should meeting me affect you so? You know nothing of me.'

'Oh, I know you well enough!' answered Traska, and Katya quailed at the thought that, after all, this devil had known all along that she had been his victim and was now cruelly toying with her. But his next comments reassured her of her anonymity.

'I know that you are the one bird that I have been looking for all of my life. What is your name, my lovely?'

'I am called Katya, and I am definitely not your lovely!'

'Forgive my forwardness. I did not mean any offence, Katya. Your beauty merely made me speak from the heart.'

Traska looked at her shyly as he spoke. With utter astonishment, Katya realised that this foul creature who had so blighted he life was in love with her. It had to be that. She knew only too well that he was still more than capable of forcing himself upon her, there and then, as he had done so horribly before. But there was respect and admiration in his gaze and Katya saw a way to succeed in her plans. But the thought of the necessary action repulsed her. She would have to accept the advances of this malicious, vile bird. Even encourage them. She would, she knew, have to become Traska's mate, until Venga returned to save her. She looked up into Traska's eyes, with a demure expression.

'You mistake me, sir,' she replied. 'I took no great offence. But now you have the advantage over me. You know my name, but, as yet, I do not know yours.'

'You must forgive me once again, Katya, for such rudeness. My name is Traska.'

'Traska,' she repeated, and her smile belied the bitter taste of that name upon her tongue.

'We might as well give up and go home. We have failed in our task, and let down everyone in

274

Birddom!' Portia sobbed, in despair. 'Whatever made me think that I could be like Kirrick? He was a hero.'

'Yes, he was,' said Mickey. 'And one thing that he would never have done is give up. So let's not have any more of that kind of talk. Of course you're depressed. Of course you are disappointed. But we've come a very long way, and I, for one, am not going back to Birddom without a whole host of birds following on behind me.'

The bullfinch puffed up his chest feathers, his bold eyes daring Portia to argue with him.

'I hate it when you are always right,' she laughed, breaking the tension that had started to build.

'I am sorry, Portia. I know that the onus of this burden falls upon your back, not mine.'

'Our backs,' the robin contradicted, no longer surprised by her companion's eloquence and wishing to mend any damage to their relationship that her former harshness and self-pity might have caused. This was a lonely and frightening land. Portia knew that their friendship was all that stood between her and failure. 'Enough of this brooding then, Mickey. Let's keep looking. Where haven't we tried?'

This was a good question, for the robin and the finch had covered a great deal of territory in their search for a migrant to mediate between them and the natives of Wingland. They had flown many miles, casting their net wide while systematically journeying south. But the skies and the trees had

275

remained deserted. Mickey smiled at her, a twinkle in his eye. 'Just keep your beak pointed into the wind,' he said. 'And I'll be right behind you!'

With Katya's help, Traska eventually found what he was looking for. The terrain in the narrow and steep-sided valley was similar to the hideaway where Donal and his band had remained so well hidden and safe, in spite of their persecution by Man. It was here that Katya had made her nest after Traska's horrifying attack upon her. Her need then had been to shut herself away from the world, to hide her shame and sorrow. Traska clapped his wings in delight when he saw it.

'My dear Katya. It is absolutely perfect,' he crowed. 'No bird, large or small, could over-fly this base unnoticed. And, more importantly, none could gain entrance to our home with my friends around to discourage them!'

Traska used the word 'home' in a tone that was far too familiar for Katya's liking, but she swallowed her disgust. 'I'm glad that you approve. Traska. I've always been very happy here.'

'I must say that I'm surprised to find so beautiful a bird living all alone,' Traska oozed. 'Have you never had a mate, my love?'

Katya held back the retort that would betray her true feelings, and turned away from him. She did not trust herself to look at the evil creature who spoke so possessively to her. But her words, when they came, were very much to Traska's liking.

'I think that I was waiting. Waiting for you.'

He closed upon her then, and she shuddered at his touch. Their coupling was brief, but not brutal as it had been before. Indeed, if the awful memory of the rape had not precluded it absolutely, Katya might have felt some pleasure. Traska was not gentle or tender. He did not know how to be. Instead he was dominant and powerful, and exuded a confident masculinity that might, in different circumstances, have thrilled and excited her. Katya had to remind herself that the only pleasure left to her would not be released until this foul bird in her wings was dead and cold, food for worms, if his fellow carrion eaters left anything for them to eat.

Traska mistook her sigh for one of contentment. 'At last!' he thought. 'Everything is going my way!'

CHAPTER 8

Venga lay motionless at the bottom of the cage. He had superficially soiled his beautiful feathers so that they now appeared matted and dull, and agonised breaths rasped from his throat. He looked near to death. But his one good eye was bright, as he watched and waited. He knew that the little girl would come. She always followed the same ritual each day before leaving for school. She would pass by his cage and pause to talk to him. Although Venga understood nothing of what she said, he responded by emitting a loud caw in answer. This always made the little girl giggle.

Venga could see that she was tempted on occasion to pet him, but was afraid of his sharp beak and claws. Initially, he had made a game out of frightening her by jumping up against the bars of the cage. This made her run off screaming, giving Venga a small measure of satisfaction. But the next day the little girl would return, undaunted, to stare at the magpie in the cage once more. Eventually it dawned on Venga that a different approach was necessary. More docile and friendly now, he encouraged her by his calls and so, cautiously, established the beginnings of a bond between them. And all to one end.

Venga's field of vision was much restricted following the injury suffered at the beak of the hawk, and so he had positioned himself carefully on the cage floor so that he could use his good eye to its best advantage. He saw the little girl's face as she looked into the cage. Concern for him spread across her features like a cloud and he could see that she was about to run off to get help from one of the other humans. The pitiful sound that emanated from Venga's throat stopped her in her tracks. It seemed to the little girl that the magpie was calling out to her. The tenuous bond between girl and bird, so assiduously cultivated by Venga, now bore fruit. She stopped and came back to the cage. Hesitating only for a moment, the little girl unfastened the latch on the cage door, and opened it wide. Putting her arm through the gap, she reached down and touched the stricken magpie. Venga held himself still as she stroked his feathers.

'Not yet,' he counselled himself. 'Wait!'

And then, as he had hoped, the girl reached fully into the cage with both arms and picked up his limp body. Her hands were trembling and she was clearly frightened by what her kindness was impelling her to do. Venga let out another soft cry of pain, to encourage her in her actions. The little girl gripped his body awkwardly, but held on as she drew him out through the cage door.

Now, unconfined by bars, Venga began to struggle in her grip. Freeing one wing, he fluttered and thrashed, and, at the same time, screamed a savage caw into her terrified face. The little girl jumped back in fright and dropped the now not so limp bundle. Immediately, Venga was upon her. His wings beat about her head. His claws caught in her hair, as he scrabbled for purchase. The long period of confinement had wasted some of the muscle in his wings, and he flapped them a few times, building up strength before he could take off and fly. The girl screamed in fear and her arms came up above her head, to brush him off her. In his surprise and anger, Venga lashed out at her hands with his sharp beak, drawing blood. He had had no intention of harming the child, but now the noise of her, and the threat of recapture, made him attack. He flew away from her head, circled, and then dived back towards her. Breaking easily through the barrier that her slender arms created, flung up as they were to ward him off, he struck her small face with a savage blow from his beak. In doing so, he inflicted upon the little girl a wound identical to his own. Blood spurted from the damaged eye socket and the girl dropped to the floor, covering her face with her hands. Aware that the screaming must soon bring other humans rushing to her aid, Venga looked around desperately for a means of escape. His ragged flight took him across the room and through an open door. Seeing a man approaching from one direction,

Venga turned away and flapped in panic along a narrow corridor. Fortunately, the kitchen door had also been left open.

There were humans in the room: the boy who had found him and his mother. She had risen to her feet, hearing her daughter's screams and the roar of anger from her husband. But she was so startled to see the dishevelled magpie flying towards her that she was slow to react. Using all of his speed, Venga fled across the room towards an invitingly open window – and out. He was free!

Not pausing for a second, Venga flew as fast as his wings would carry him. He needed to put some distance between himself and the humans. Fear drove him on and he expected, at any moment, to hear the bang of the shotgun, to feel the deadly pellets thud into his body. But, after he had flown for a mile or so, Venga knew that he was safe. Incredibly, he had escaped. He slowed his flight from the headlong rush into a more measured progress. Even the short distance that he had covered seemed to have required huge labour. His body, used to the confines and limits of his captivity, was exhausted. Venga knew that he would have to find somewhere to alight. He chose a high perch in a solitary pine to allow himself maximum visibility. Caution was paramount. He was still very vulnerable to attack. While he folded his wings to rest, Venga scanned the surrounding countryside for signs of danger. Seeing nothing to cause him immediate concern, he allowed himself to relax and think.

Venga knew that the man would soon begin his hunt. He would gather others too. They would want revenge and would kill him without compunction. He would have to put a great distance between himself and his pursuers. Venga's thoughts returned once more to his mother, Katya, and to his original mission. It had been his purpose to fly south, seeking for news of Traska, and now he realised that no other course of action was open to him. He must continue his quest without delay. So, in spite of his exhaustion, he launched himself once more into the sky.

Just when it seemed that their quest was hopeless, and that Portia and Mickey were staring certain defeat full in the face, they saw her. She was still a long way off but, even at that great distance, the speed of her flight and the unmistakable curvature of her wings, confirmed her as a swallow. Her flight path was bringing her towards them. Portia almost cried in her relief. Then she and Mickey took to the skies, creating a commotion to attract the swallow's attention. It was a risky but necessary strategy. For, while their noise might also have attracted the less welcome attentions of a predatory hawk or kestrel, they knew that they could never hope to keep up with the swallow in flight, if she flew by them. Fortunately, however, their efforts were not in vain. Luck had finally chosen to be on their side.

The swallow veered from its course, slowed, and alighted on a telegraph wire, folding her wings gracefully behind her back as she did so.

Portia landed on a high branch, at an unthreatening distance from the intrigued swallow, and hailed her.

'Good morning, my dear. I am so glad to see you. Do you understand what I am saying?'

'Your language is quite easy to comprehend,' the swallow replied. 'But your meaning less so. Why are you glad to see me? Do I know you?'

'Please forgive me. I will explain myself. My name is Portia, and my friend here is Mickey. We come from Birddom.'

At the mere mention of that word, the swallow began to show signs of agitation and started to flap her wings, preparing to flee.

'Please!' exclaimed Portia urgently. 'Do not go. We have journeyed so far and have searched for so long to find you.' The swallow appeared intrigued and settled herself on the wire.

'All right. Let me complete the introductions. My name is Swoop. You say that you come from Birddom. That name is very dark in my thoughts and in my heart. My sorrow still weighs heavily upon me. For it was in that fell place that I lost my mate, Bewla. He was ambushed, and murdered by a mob of crows.'

'I share your burden of sorrow,' Portia replied simply. 'I too lost my mate to the corvidae.'

'But they have been overthrown!' Mickey

chirped, unable to resist joining in. 'Birddom is a fair place once more. And free.'

'I find that hard to believe,' answered Swoop. 'We have heard no such news.'

'How could you?' asked Mickey. 'No migratory birds have dared to venture near our shores since the rise of the magpies and their cousins.'

'It is as my friend says,' continued Portia. 'That is why we have come to Wingland, on so perilous a mission. We are emissaries, sent by the Council of the Owls to seek out small birds who will be willing to return with us and make their home in Birddom. But we have failed so far because of our inability to communicate with the birds that are native to this land. Now I hope that you can see why we needed to find you.'

'I understand,' said Swoop. 'But I am still much afraid. It could be that you have been sent from Birddom as a trap and that, in aiding you, I would be sending thousands of birds to their doom.'

Mickey bridled, but Portia silenced him with a stern look.

'You are wise not to place your trust in us so readily. Your caution does you credit and you have reason enough, in your personal loss, to be afraid of Birddom. I do not know what I can say that will persuade you. In my naiveté, I had hoped that my face was one that could be trusted.'

'A fair face can often conceal a foul heart,' Swoop began, and once again Mickey bristled in anger. But Swoop smiled at him, as she continued. 'There is at least one bird here who has no doubts of you. And I am inclined to take his loyalty as proof enough that you are genuine, Portia. But you ask a great deal of my trust, on such little evidence.'

'I do indeed ask a great deal, and yet I will make no apology for it. We need your help as a translator and without you our mission will fail utterly. But I am convinced that we will only succeed in persuading others to come to Birddom if you can say, with conviction, that our land is a safe one. It is an insoluble dilemma.'

'Portia, forgive me,' Mickey interrupted. 'But I may have a solution. We ourselves are ill-equipped for travel. But Swoop here has spent her life on the wing.' He turned to the swallow. 'I know that it would be arduous, even for one like yourself. But your great speed will be an asset.' Mickey stumbled over his words, as he tried to explain his thinking.

But Portia caught hold of his idea, and expounded it enthusiastically. 'Yes. What a wonderful idea. Do you follow, Swoop? What Mickey is suggesting is that you fly to Birddom to see for yourself. I promise you, my friend, that you will be in no danger. Birddom is free and at peace. The law is upheld by the strength and wisdom of the Council of the Owls. Have no fear.'

'It is not an easy thing that you ask,' replied the swallow, after a long silence. 'But I see that it is the only way. I cannot stand face to face with any bird and lie. I need to see the truth for myself. But what will you do while I am gone?'

'We shall have little choice, but to do what we have spent most of our time doing since our arrival,' Portia said, wryly. 'We shall wait.'

Waiting was something that Traska was no longer prepared to do. For one thing, his hooded crows were becoming restless. And, more importantly, so was he. Traska was eager to carry out his plan. He wanted power. He craved it. And now he had a queen to rule by his side, in the new order that would follow when he had crushed the Council of the Owls. How he had crowed with pride when he had told Katya about his scheme.

She was appalled by the thought of such violence and slaughter. She had taken no part in the insurgence of the magpie battalions and in the genocide that they had perpetrated. And now, here was her evil tormentor, her most hated foe, boasting of his plans for further murders. But Katya knew that she had little option but to join him. She had to stay by his side, keeping him interested long enough for Venga to return and exact retribution. Entirely satisfied of her complicity, Traska called a council of war. He stood facing the rabble and singled out Finbar from among the expectant crowd.

'Finbar, my friend. Come and join me. For are we not joint leaders in this enterprise? I as king of this land, and you as head of your band of villains here.' Traska paused as a ragged cheer rang out from the throats of the hooded crows. 'I see that you like my choice of description. For villains you are, and blacker than any villain seen in Birddom before. Your exploits will ring out across the land and strike fear into the hearts of the Council of the Owls. You see, I have a mind to murder.'

Once again the birds facing him erupted in noisy endorsement.

'My band of blooded brothers, here is what I propose to do.'

It was a most unusual and unnatural sight. The band of hooded crows crept through the undergrowth with the utmost stealth, stalking their prey. Then, at Traska's signal, they stopped, stock-still, and listened. In the cluster of bushes ahead, a cacophony of bird song could be heard. Hundreds of chaffinches and goldfinches occupied the branches, feeding excitedly in their communal gluttony. The day was warm and languid, and the finches flitted from bush to bush, chattering gaily to their neighbours, entirely unaware of their mortal danger.

Traska's eyes glittered with bloodlust. At his second signal the crows crept closer, until they had formed a ring surrounding the bird-laden bushes. Traska held them back deliberately, increasing the delicious tension and sharpening their appetite for mayhem. Then, finally, he gave the third signal. A piercing caw that sent a chill into the heart of every small bird, as if each recognised the sound of its own doom. In seconds, the giant crows were among them, tearing and rending, then discarding the dead carcasses in favour of more living flesh. It was a massacre that left the trees red with blood. In a matter of minutes, it was over.

Traska flew up to a branch overlooking the site of the atrocity and grinned in satisfaction. The jubilant crows gathered before him and parted as Finbar came forward, carrying a solitary goldfinch in his beak. The tiny, jewelled bird fluttered in terrified agony and cowered as the hooded crow flew up and placed it before Traska, like an offering to a god. The magpie, however, had no intention of killing this sacrifice.

The goldfinch had been spared for a reason.

'Do not be frightened, my little friend,' Traska began. 'I will not harm you. Indeed, I need you to do me a great service.'

The little goldfinch shivered in fear at the tone of Traska's voice, but looked up at the magpie with a glimmer of hope in his eye.

'I will do whatever you ask, oh Great One.'

'I like that. Yes. I like that very much!' laughed Traska. 'A fitting title, don't you think?'

The hooded crows roared their assent.

'Well, my tiny messenger. It will be your honour to carry my words to the lords of Birddom. Go, and tell the high and mighty Council of the Owls that I, Traska, challenge them. I am back, and there is nothing that they can do to stop me. Inform them of the outcome of our little *game* here today, and tell them to expect more of the same. Now go!'

The goldfinch sat, stunned momentarily by terror, then shot into the air as if in fear that Traska might change his mind and kill him after all. He flew off, uncertain of where to go, but desperate to be away from that dreadful place of death.

Traska knew that his message would reach the ears of Tomar. The old owl would then have no choice. He was so honourable, so predictable. He would have no option but to come north, to face the threat that Traska posed. And then Traska would deliver his masterstroke and gain his long-sought victory and revenge.

CHAPTER 9

There was a terrible solemnity and sorrow among the members of the Council of the Owls as Tomar spoke.

'There are those among us who believed that we had put all of this behind us, with our victory over Slyekin. But I have long been troubled by our laxity in allowing Traska to escape from justice. And now he seeks my ruin and our destruction. Once before the Council was forced into despair and turned its back upon Birddom. That will not happen a second time. We are being tested. We must not fail!

But I am troubled by the nature of Traska's challenge. The slaughter is terrible, but he has insufficient forces to pose a real threat to Birddom. What, therefore, is his purpose in provoking us? I have never been more in need of your wisdom, my friends. For I am at a loss to divine his intentions. Speak up, members of the highest body in the land. What is the magpie up to?'

But little response was forthcoming. The rest of the owls were as bemused by Traska's actions and intentions as the Great Owl himself. No one offered a theory that held water, and the circle degenerated into frustrated mutterings. Finally, Tomar called the Council to order.

'It is clear that we are not as wise as the rest of Birddom gives us credit for. The meaning of Traska's provocation confounds us all. But he cannot be allowed to get away with it. We must respond before he takes it into his evil head to repeat his bloody message.' Tomar's face was a mask of anger as he continued to speak. 'So here is what I propose. I will lay aside my position as Great Owl, for I do not feel at present that I am worthy of the name. But I do not follow my friend Cerival into despair and blackness. I will reclaim my title, when I have earned the right. My business with Traska is unfinished. And it is personal. It is me that he challenges. For some devious purpose of his own, he taunts me with his callous murders and outrages. Well, I will face him.'

It was Isidris who spoke first in the silence that followed Tomar's decision. He smiled gently and fondly at his friend.

'Tomar. Of everyone here, I have known you the longest. You have always been the voice of reason among us. So now, listen to my counsel. You are wise, but you are no longer young. A rash one to one challenge is not a sensible course to follow. You would surely not prevail and it would increase Traska's triumph mightily to kill the Great Owl himself. Let me go in your stead. I have already had one brush with that awful magpie and I quite fancy another.'

'Thank you, Isidris. But this burden cannot be carried by another. Do not fear. I may be old, but I have not entirely lost my faculties. I can assure you that I have absolutely no intention of engaging in a personal confrontation, or trial of strength, with Traska. Unless it is a battle of wits and minds. I will seek the aid and support of Storne and the eagles. They will look after my frail old body. But it is my intention that the Council shall remain here, in the heart of the land, lest I fail and fall. Isidris, I charge you with the leadership of Birddom, in my stead.'

'But what of your charges, Tomar? Portia's children are in your care.'

'I am sensible of my duty towards Kirrick's offspring,' Tomar replied. 'I have decided that they will fly north with me and there I shall lodge them in the safekeeping of the eagles, while we oppose Traska's evil. I know that each of you would willingly care for them in my absence, but each of you has important work in your own region. Besides, Merion and Olivia were placed into my care. They will be company for me on my journey.'

It was the news that Traska had been waiting for, even if the timing of the interruption had been most unfortunate. For Traska had prepared his speech most carefully. The realisation that he was in love with Katya had been almost like a physical blow. His whole life, since his mother's death, had been solely concerned with the well-being and promotion of one bird only – Traska himself. He had never felt anything like this before and it sent his mind reeling. Love formed no part of his plans. It seemed at odds with the evil that Traska did. That he was.

But it also seemed to complement his cruel schemes. To be king and lord of all Birddom, and to have the love of this beautiful creature as well? That would make up for all the misfortunes and miseries that had befallen him in his life. Traska's conceit would not allow him to consider the possibility that Katya might not feel the same way about him. He was everything that a magpie should be. Proud, intelligent, dominant and, if he said so himself, a masterful lover! What more could Katya possibly want from a partner? She must love him too! He would wait no longer to declare his love and reveal the remainder of his plan to her.

To the evil magpie there was no sense of wrong in what he suggested to Katya. Traska had carried out his intentions and had passionately declared his love for his beautiful companion. Katya had expressed reciprocal feelings towards him and Traska had preened himself in satisfaction at her words. Then, as he proceeded to unfold her role in the evil scheme that would surely undermine Birddom in all its sanctimonious goodness, a messenger from among the hooded crows entered the glade, which Traska had chosen with such care as a backdrop for his declaration of love. Without so much as a by-your-leave, the crow had snapped out his message and now stood expectantly, as if waiting for instructions or thanks. The oaf had entirely spoiled the delicacy of the moment.

And yet Traska could not help but be thrilled. Tomar, the Great Owl himself, had been sighted crossing the border in the company of two young robins. It was everything that the evil magpie could have hoped for. Traska almost cheered. 'The old fool!' he exclaimed. 'He's flying straight into my trap!'

The gleam of absolute triumph in his eyes made Katya shiver, but she smiled back at him as he turned and dismissed the crow. Alone once more, the pair of magpies sat, momentarily silent. Then Traska continued to outline the charade that he wanted Katya to play for him. When he explained his idea to her, Katya froze in the fear that, after all, he had known all along who she was. But then she realised that he was still unaware, and she shuddered at the awful irony. For he wanted to use her as bait for his trap, a bait that Tomar's kind heart could not resist. Katya hated Traska all the more then. And she felt a deep sense of self-loathing too. What they were planning to do was so wrong. So evil. But what could she do? Katya knew that she would play any part in order to have her revenge upon Traska. And that could only be achieved, for the moment, by her co-operation in his dreadful schemes. She prayed hard for Venga to come back, somehow.

'You must return, Venga my love. The evil one

is here. We have him in our clutches. We can finish it at last. Come home, my son. Come home soon.'

Watching the skies had long since become a boring chore for the robin and the bullfinch. But they had little alternative. And nothing else to do. Frustration had turned to resignation. At times, both Portia and Mickey had doubted that Swoop would return. After all, why should she help them? They had offered her nothing in return, except for a long and tiring journey. What hope was there that the swallow would keep her promise? But both birds kept these thoughts to themselves, for to voice them was to finally admit defeat. Their mission would be over. Then a small dot in the sky caught their attention. Portia's pulse quickened. The dot quickly grew larger, transforming into a familiar and most welcome shape.

'Swoop!' they cheeped together, as the swallow raced to where they waited and circled briefly before landing.

'Welcome back. How was your journey?' Portia asked politely, her mind seething with other, more urgent questions.

'Oh, I wouldn't call that a journey! To a bird like myself, Birddom is but a flap of the wings away! But I am glad that I went there. For you spoke truly, within the limitations of your own knowledge.'

Portia's face registered instant concern, and the swallow continued quickly, in order to reassure her, 'Do not worry. Birddom is still at peace.

The Council of the Owls rules, as you said. I spoke to a wise old owl, who confirmed everything that you had told me.'

'Tomar!' Portia exclaimed, gleefully.

'No,' replied Swoop, a shadow passing behind her eyes. 'Tomar was not there. I was told that he had gone away on a journey to the north.'

'Why would he do such a thing?' Mickey asked, puzzled by the owl's unusual behaviour.

Portia's concern was more personal. 'What about Merion and Olivia? Who is looking after my children?'

'They have gone with the Great Owl. It seems that there has been some trouble. A magpie called Traska has been causing a little mischief, and Tomar felt obliged to deal with it personally.'

Swoop saw the look of horror on Portia's face.

'I see that you know the name that I spoke.'

'Traska was the evil bird who murdered my mate, Kirrick,' Portia cried. 'To hear that he is still alive, and has returned to plague Birddom once more, is dreadful news indeed.'

Mickey did his best to comfort her. 'Yes, Traska is indeed evil. But he is only one bird. The power of the corvidae is no more. What real harm can he do? However unpleasant his mischief-making, he cannot prevail against the might and right of Birddom.'

'You are right,' Portia said, trying to calm her fears. 'Tomar is wise. His mind is more than a match for one magpie. But my children! Why does he take them into danger?' Her distress seemed once more to overwhelm her. 'Mickey. We must go home! I cannot stay here a moment longer. Olivia and Merion are in peril!'

'Portia, your feelings as a mother do you credit,' said the bullfinch. 'But you are more than that. You chose to be so. Your role here is, in many ways, more important than that which Nature herself gave you. You cannot abandon the needs of Birddom. But do not fear. What you said a moment ago was right and true. Tomar is wise. He would not endanger the offspring of Birddom's greatest couple. Be glad that your children are with him. I would be far more afraid if they were not.'

Portia seemed slightly mollified by her companion's confident words. 'What would I do without you, Mickey? What you say is quite right, of course. My role is here, as emissary for Birddom. I must fulfil my obligation to all those who have placed their trust in me. And I must set aside my fears and put my own trust in Tomar. No harm will come to my children while Tomar is by their side.'

CHAPTER 10

The flight north had been long and arduous, especially for ones so young. But the enthusiasm of Merion and Olivia was infectious and the time had passed quickly. Tomar had told them many more of his stories about Kirrick, their father, as they had travelled, and the young robins had revelled in the tales of his heroics. To think that they were following in his footsteps, flying north to the land of their mother's birth. It was all so exciting.

And now, as they flew over mountain and glen, enchanted by the beauty of this wonderful land, Merion and Olivia had another reason for their enthusiasm. For they were going to see the eagles. The young robins remembered vividly their first impressions of Storne at the Council meeting. They had never seen a bird so lordly or imposing. And now they were going to meet him in his mountain home.

Olivia could hardly contain herself. 'Are you sure that we will be allowed to stay with Storne, Tomar?' she asked breathlessly.

'I know that he will be only too delighted to

have your company. And honoured too. Do not forget who your father was, or who your mother is, my young friends. You are a very special pair of birds. I am certain that Storne will welcome you with open wings.'

Tomar smiled at the young robins, who were blushing at his description of them.

'How much further is it to Storne's eyrie?' Merion asked.

'We could not possibly hope to complete the journey before nightfall,' answered Tomar. 'We will have to begin looking for a suitable roost for the night. Keep your eyes open, children, and don't be afraid to call out if you see something.'

Though it was not Tomar's intention when he spoke those words to his two young charges, Olivia did indeed call out to alert the owl to a potential danger. For the pretty young robin had spotted a magpie. Terrified that it might be the evil Traska, Olivia's voice quailed, as she cheeped in alarm. Tomar quickly looked in the direction of her frightened gaze. It was a magpie, all right. But it was not Traska.

This bird was a female and seemed to be in terrible distress. Her feathers were dishevelled and matted with sweat, and she lay abjectly on the ground, as if uncaring of the dangers that such an action could provoke. Tomar called to the two young robins to follow him and flew down to the lower branches of a tree, close to the magpie's prostrate body. She was alive, Tomar was sure of that. He had noticed feeble movements when he had first caught sight of her.

Now, nearer, the owl could hear her anguished sobs and his heart went out to the stricken bird. Enemy or not, this magpie was in need and he had to help her. Cautioning the robins to stay on their perches in the tree, Tomar swooped down to the ground, landing a few feet from the magpie. She turned her eyes to look at him and Tomar's heart constricted at the tortured gaze which met his own, unblinking stare. The old owl knew that something appalling had happened to her. He moved closer, speaking softly to the stricken magpie as he did so.

'There, there, my dear. Calm yourself. You are safe now. There is no more danger here. Nothing can harm you. I mean to help.'

Tomar's tone was friendly and soothing, but the magpie's eyes held his own, with a stare of pain and misery.

'How can I help you? What is it that ails you? My name is Tomar and I am a friend, if you will let me be so. Please tell me what has happened to you.'

And, between the sobs, the magpie began to tell her tale. It was a harrowing story and she held nothing back. Tomar soon realised that her story would cause distress to his two charges. Already Olivia was crying as she listened to the description of the savagery done to this beautiful bird. But it was the mention of Traska's name that made up the owl's mind for him.

'Wait, please. Do not tell any more for the moment. I must see to something. But I will come back.'

Tomar flew up to rejoin the pair of robins, and told them to stay where they were, and to await his return. 'I will not be far away,' he said.

Then, gliding down to the ground once more, Tomar helped the female magpie up.

'Come with me, my dear. Just a little way. I need to hear your story. But it is not for everyone's ears.'

So saying, Tomar led the magpie a short distance off into the undergrowth, out of sight and out of earshot of his charges. Then he settled her in a comfortable spot of soft leaves and grasses, and bade her continue.

It was as awful as he had feared. The young bird in front of him had been brutalised and raped by Traska, and her description of the attack was graphic and hideous. Traska could not have hoped for anything better. Dreamed up as a contrivance to separate Tomar from his charges, the tale was, however, no more than the truth and Katya's anguish upon reliving it was genuine. Her tears were real. Her terror was real. It would never leave her.

Tomar's eyes filled with tears. He wanted to fly away, so that he wouldn't have to listen to the rest of her terrible story. But he couldn't. Her need was so compelling. He had to listen. And he had to help her.

Olivia's screams sliced into his brain like a knife. Too late, Tomar realised the trap that he had walked into. Lured away from his charges by his pity for the cruelly abused magpie in front of him, he knew now that he had been fooled. Looking into her eyes, Tomar asked a single question. 'Why?' He did not wait for an answer. In his heart, he knew that he was already too late. But Tomar turned away from her and flapped off to go to the aid of the two young robins. Immediately he was set upon by several large and menacing crows, who descended upon him from all sides. Soon the old owl was fighting for his life. However, it appeared that, after the initial ferocity of their attack, the hooded crows seemed to remember their instructions. Now they contented themselves with containment.

Tomar was no match for his opponents, in any case, and was glad of the respite. But frustration seethed in his breast. What was happening to the children? He was powerless to help them. What evil was being done to Olivia and Merion by that poisonous villain, Traska? For Tomar knew, with absolute certainty, that the foul magpie was behind all this.

The robins' cries grew quieter, then fell silent altogether. Fearing the worst, the owl resumed his struggles to reach them with renewed intensity. And his efforts seemed to be the signal for the hooded crows. Secure in the knowledge that Traska's plan had been carried out to the letter, they now decided to enjoy themselves. Once again, Tomar found himself fighting for his very life. The crows drove him back with brutal efficiency and, when others joined in the battle, the old owl was encircled by a ring of muscle and flashing beaks. Soon he was bathed in his own blood.

'This is it,' he thought. Tomar had brooded somewhat, of late, on the manner of his death, when it came. But he had not envisaged this. To die in this manner – tricked and humiliated – was intolerable to him. 'But, if I am to die today, I will make it a memorable death. Forgive me, my young friends. I have failed you and placed you into the wings of danger. Forgive me, Portia. Forgive me, Kirrick. I come to join you, my friend!'

Traska pecked viciously at the legs of the two young robins. Typical of their breed, they were defiant in the face of peril. But inside they quailed with fear. This was Traska! The cruel and wicked bird who had murdered their father. And they were at his mercy, though both Olivia and Merion knew that they could expect precious little mercy at this bird's wings.

However, they were still alive. When Traska, and four of the most frightening birds that they had ever seen, had fallen upon them, they could not have hoped for more than a swift despatch from life. But it seemed that Traska had other plans for them. He did not mean for them to die. But his innate cruelty would not be denied in a lesser degree and the magpie allowed himself the pleasure of inflicting a generous helping of pain upon the two unfortunates.

Through her tears, Olivia bravely spoke up. 'Why are you doing this? We have done nothing to you. What do you want with us?'

'So many questions!' Traska exclaimed contemptuously, and pecked the young robin on the side of her head. 'Let's take them one at a time, shall we? Why am I doing this? Because I can, that's why. Because there is no bird in the kingdom that can stop me. You have done nothing to me. That is very true, but it is your misfortune to be the progeny of a bird who did his very best to thwart me. Unfortunately for him, his best wasn't good enough.

And what do I want with you? Another good question. I might want to eat you. But no. What kind of bird do you take me for? I might want to play with you, though I am not sure that you'd like the games that I really enjoy. Or I might just want to keep you, as pets, like humans do. Yes, that's it. You two shall be my pets. Unless, that is, your great uncle Tomar can offer me something else instead. Something that I'd much rather have!'

Traska's laughter was bitter and brittle, betraying increasing madness. He was so close now! By kidnapping the robins, he had the leverage to bring Tomar to him. And Traska knew that the old owl would do anything, sacrifice everything, in order to ensure the safe return of this young pair.

Tomar regained consciousness slowly and painfully. He was surprised to find that he was still alive, but realised that Traska had a great many more indignities to heap upon his ageing head before this nightmare was over. Weak through loss of blood, Tomar staggered about looking for any signs of the two robins. At one point he saw two small skeletons and a huge wave of despair swept over him. But the owl quickly realised that these birds had been dead for a long time. Besides, their body shape was not that of a robin. Anger replaced the grief as he thought of Traska, deliberately and cruelly, placing these pathetic corpses where he would discover them.

Tomar ceased rushing hither and thither and sat back to think. If the children were alive, and this wicked joke seemed to make that prospect more likely, then Traska must have captured them. But why? What did the foul magpie want? The power of the corvidae had been smashed in the Great Battle. Surely Traska wasn't deluded enough to want to continue with Slyekin's mad plans for total domination of Birddom?

And, if not that, then what more personal reason could Traska have? Did he hate robins so much after his encounters with Kirrick? If that were the case, then there was little hope for the children. But Tomar had to keep hoping. There was nothing else left for him. He had to believe that the robins were alive and would remain so until Traska's devious plans were satisfactorily concluded.

Tomar spread his wings wide and shook the aches out of his feathers. 'Think, you old fool. Think!

Traska has Merion and Olivia in his clutches. So what are you going to do about it?'

But, try as he might, the owl could not come up with an answer to that question. He had no ideas, no flash of genius, as was always expected of him. He had never felt older, or more tired. More importantly, he had never in his life felt more useless. A black cloud of despondency smothered him, choking out the flame of his hope. Tears fell from his huge, haunted eyes and splashed, unnoticed, onto his chest feathers.

A tiny voice, the sound of reason, prodded him, and pricked at him. 'Don't give up. You cannot give up. You are the only hope that Merion and Olivia have left. You must think of a way to save them.'

It was a small voice, weak and thin. An exhausted voice. Even so, it spoke the truth. Tomar suddenly nodded to himself, then launched his body abruptly into the air. His injured muscles screamed to his brain, but he ignored the pain and flapped his wings urgently, soon gaining sufficient height to emerge from the tree cover and into the clear evening sky. Tomar set his course towards the mountains. He needed help, and he needed a friend. Storne.

CHAPTER 11

'**M**y friends,' Portia cheeped, in a slightly tremulous voice. 'Thank you for coming here today.'

The beautiful robin looked around her at the multifarious array of small birds who had assembled in the vineyard to hear her speak. Swoop was at Portia's side, translating. The swallow had worked tirelessly over the previous few days, contacting representatives from each separate species and ensuring a full attendance at this crucial meeting. Portia took a deep breath to steady her nerves.

'In Birddom we have faced a time of great horror. I will not lie to you. The rise of the corvidae, and their murderous assault upon your kind in my country is, I am sure, well known to you all. Bad news travels quickest as they say. But good news can, and should, be heralded with equal vigour, and I stand before you today as the bringer of just such news. The magpies' reign of terror is over. They have been utterly defeated. Birddom is safe once more. If you do not believe me, you can ask my friend Swoop here. Is it not so? Have you not seen it with your own eyes?'

The swallow nodded several times in the affirmation of Portia's words, and the assembled throng murmured appreciatively at the heartening news.

'The corvidae in Birddom pose no further threat in my country, or here in Wingland. Your own magpies and crows were unaffected by the madness engendered by the villainous Slyekin. So it must be difficult for you all to appreciate the wanton destruction that he perpetrated. Thousands of birds died under his tyranny. Tens of thousands.' All around the robin, heads shook sorrowfully.

'The magpies' murderous acts have left Birddom bereft. Stripped of many of its jewels. But therein lies a golden opportunity for you and your loved ones. Birddom, at peace, is a beautiful country. But it is a country without song, without a voice. We need you to provide us with that voice. All that I ask is that you go back to your communities and tell them about Birddom. Persuade them that they can have a future there, if they so wish. It is a land waiting for them. Full of riches, but empty without them. Birddom needs small birds in its trees and its bushes, in its fields and its hedgerows. To make it whole again. To give it life.'

Portia's impassioned plea touched the heart of every bird there. Though they could not understand her words directly, all recognised the strength of her feelings and were moved. For that moment, in spite of the need for translation, the robin held them spellbound. But then the moment passed. The spell was broken. A mistle thrush voiced the simple question that dashed all Portia's hopes.

'Why?'

And, in reality, she had no answer, beyond her love of her own land. Why should these birds leave the safety and comfort of their own homes, to begin their lives again in a strange country? What reason could she give them that could compel them? There was no danger for them here. And Birddom had gained a fearsome reputation as a dangerous, even deadly, place for any small bird who flew in its skies. Yes, the robin might tell them that Birddom was safe once more. And it might indeed be so. But what did she offer them that they did not already have?

The simple question seemed unanswerable. The need was Birddom's, not theirs. Why should they uproot when their own lives were not being threatened? This attitude spread like wildfire through the crowd and Portia stared at them, open-beaked with dismay. Swoop did her best to translate the comments passing among the audience, but there was really no need. Portia could see clearly for herself that she had failed. Mickey's consoling wing was of little comfort to her. She could find no more strength. Her passion was spent and she turned away, as if unable to face her defeat.

Swoop exhorted the throng to give heed to the robin's words and to think of more than just their own immediate needs. But, slowly, the crowd began to drift away, as bird after bird flapped off to their homes and families, muttering, 'Birddom may need us. But we don't need Birddom!'

Robin, bullfinch and swallow sat in a miserable huddle, as they watched their hopes vanishing along with the departing birds. What could they do now? Portia had done her job. She had fulfilled her role as emissary for Birddom. No other bird could have done more, or guaranteed a different outcome. Now she was emissary no longer. All that remained was motherhood. She had suppressed the vague fears for the safety of her children, had sublimated them to Birddom's need. But, now that she had performed her appointed task, albeit failing in that role, she knew that she should go home. Her unease at the news that Swoop had brought from Birddom welled up inside her. Portia finally spoke her fears aloud.

'Well, Mickey. I have done all that I can for Birddom. Now, I must think of myself, and of Olivia and Merion. My place is with them. I want to go home.' There were tears in the robin's eyes, as she looked at her friend. 'Please!' she pleaded. 'Let's not waste any more time. My children need me. And I need them!'

The bullfinch's resolve crumbled as he looked at the desperation in Portia's eyes. He had thought to persuade the robin to give it one more try, although, in his heart of hearts, he knew that such an attempt would be futile.

'Very well, Portia. We will leave in the morning. Let's get some sleep now.'

The pair of travellers took their leave of Swoop, thanking the swallow for her unavailing efforts. Swoop promised to visit Birddom and they parted in friendship. Mickey placed his wing around Portia, as they watched the silhouette of the swallow's body recede into the darkening skies.

It was a council of war. The golden eagles, led by Storne, had gathered to hear Tomar's story. They sat, still as the stone of their mountain homes, as the old owl told of Traska's evil act. But rage built up swiftly among the assembly when they learned of the peril now facing Kirrick's offspring. Before them, Tomar looked utterly defeated and lost. His failure to protect his charges weighed very heavily upon his ageing frame and he seemed to sag, limp as an autumn leaf, under the eagles' gaze.

It was Storne who, seeing the distress of his old friend, sought to offer him comfort with his words.

'Tomar. You are the Great Owl. The leader of all Birddom. You have shown your wisdom and proved your worth, on occasions too numerous to mention. And, as Great Owl, it falls upon your shoulders to make decisions for the good of all of us. You feel now that you made an ill choice and fear the consequences. But do not doubt yourself, my friend. Your redemption is only an inspiration away and I know of no other bird more capable of providing it.'

'Thank you, Storne, my friend,' the old owl replied, and he straightened his shoulders, as if he remembered once more who and where he was. 'But words, however kindly meant, will not bring the young robins safely back to us. We must devise a plan for their rescue. And swiftly. Storne, you must send out scouts to find Traska's lair, although I am sure that it will be well chosen. And well defended. The sheer size and mindless brutality of the hooded crows will make them fearsome opponents. And, if the terrain is on their side, then our task will be all the harder. Unlike the Great Battle, we will not have an element of surprise on our side. Traska is ready for us. He has planned and prepared for this encounter. We must do likewise. Send out your scouts, my friend. And then we must sit together and think of a way to defeat this evil.'

The report, when it came, was exactly as Tomar had feared. The hideout that Traska had found, through Katya, was virtually impregnable to an aerial assault. Oh, a full scale attack by the eagle battalions could overwhelm and destroy the brigand band of hooded crows. But not without huge loss of life. And not without guaranteeing the deaths of the two young robins. Tomar and Storne discussed the options that were open to them. But every variant on the plan based upon attacking Traska in his hideout led them back to the same conclusion: The robins would be killed.

And that was not acceptable to the old owl, even if it meant also that Traska would die.

'Let us assume that the children are still alive. Traska would not have gone to so much trouble just to kill off Kirrick's offspring. He is much more devious than that. The young robins are pawns in this game. Bargaining chips that he will use to obtain what he really desires.'

Storne looked into the owl's huge, troubled eyes. 'Do you know what it is that he wants?' he asked.

'I am not sure. But I do not think that the death of Olivia and Merion is his ultimate goal. I believe that, after he had tormented me with his wicked schemes, he seeks my death also.'

'We will not allow that. Traska's triumph would then be complete indeed. He would succeed where Slyekin failed. He cannot be permitted to win in any way.' Storne's eyes flashed dangerously.

'That is not your choice to make,' Tomar reminded the eagle sternly. 'I must decide my own fate. I am old and more than ready to die, if, in so doing, I can guarantee that Birddom still has a future. I would willingly trade my old bones for the robins' freedom.'

'But that is madness!' Storne squawked. 'You know that you cannot trust that evil magpie. He will never let the young ones go. By delivering yourself into his clutches, you will merely add your own death to the inevitability of theirs!'

'My friend,' Tomar replied, in soothing tones, 'All death is inevitable. But every creature should die when Nature intends and not before. Trust in that immutable law. I do not intend to sacrifice myself in a futile gesture. But I do intend to secure the release of Portia's children, at whatever cost to myself. But, for now, we need to think of a way. We have a little time. For I believe that Traska plans to send us word. He will have seen your scouts. He certainly made no attempts to hide his whereabouts. The hooded crows that your eagles spotted seemed almost to have been placed there deliberately. I think, perhaps, that Traska hoped to force us into a rash act. But now he knows that we are waiting for him. His vanity will like that. He will feel in control. We must just hope that he overreaches himself in some way. In any case, we must wait to hear Traska's terms.'

Merion and Olivia clung to each other for comfort. They were both terrified of the sadistic magpie, who seemed to gain a cruel pleasure from their pain and humiliation. Traska had broken one of Merion's legs, with a vicious peck from his powerful beak. The pain was overwhelming, but the young robin fought back his tears.

'My, my! What a brave little bird you are!' Traska sneered. 'Every bit the hero. Just like your father – the late, great Kirrick!'

Olivia's eyes flashed, defiantly. 'Our father was a true hero. After all, he defeated you, didn't he?'

Her head snapped back, as Traska's wing hit her hard.

'No one defeated me!' the magpie roared. 'Least of all Kirrick. He's the one who's dead now, isn't he?'

'Yes. Murdered by *you*, you butcher!'

'True. Although I prefer the word "executed". Your father deserved to die. He thwarted me once too often. So did that damned owl, Tomar. But defeated me? Never! You're mistaking me for that fool, Slyekin. His plans were not mine. Too grandiose. Too unrealistic. Power is wasted on visionaries, isn't it? I am of a far more practical turn of mind. Baser metal, you might say. My needs are simple. I live for revenge. It is the sweetest food of all. I took my revenge upon your father. Now, I will have my revenge upon his mentor. I will teach Tomar who is the true ruler of Birddom!'

CHAPTER 12

It was a chilly and miserable dawn that greeted the robin and the bullfinch on their return to their homeland. Birddom was under a pall of grey, unrelenting cloud and the gloomy weather matched perfectly the mood of the two dispirited birds. Depressed by their failure in Wingland, but, in some indefinable way, feeling the need for urgency, they did not stop to exchange news with Kraken, but by-passed his cliff-top home, and journeyed on.

From what Swoop had told them, the pair had realised that it was to Isidris, the snowy owl, that she had spoken. Tomar must have asked him to stay on, rather than return to his own home in the western mountains, when the Great Owl had decided to journey north to meet the threat of that insidious magpie, Traska. Therefore, it was to Isidris that they must report their failure and from him seek wisdom and guidance. The Council of the Owls would be desperate for news, but would surely want happier tidings than those they had to offer. Having rested on the ferry boat during the return crossing, neither bird was tired. But both felt emotionally drained. It took a supreme effort of will for Portia and Mickey to cover the final few miles to the Council site. Isidris was waiting for them, as they flew in over the treetops and dropped down onto a roost.

The snowy owl had hunted unusually early that night, as if he had anticipated that the pair would return and have need of him. He greeted them traditionally, in sonorous tones, and they returned the courtesies, although with heads hung low. Isidris did his best to comfort them.

'Well met, my friends. But why such downcast faces? Is the end of the world to be visited upon us so soon? Remember that we have faced, and defeated, that shadow.'

Portia's eyes welled with tears as she answered, with an agonised question of her own. 'Isn't it true that the shadow still lives and now threatens to destroy my children, as it did my husband?'

'Peace, child. The threat that Traska poses is negligible, when compared to the all-encompassing evil of Slyekin's schemes. Birddom is whole once more.'

Portia's anger surprised Isidris. 'How can you sit there and say such a thing? That magpie is evil, and Birddom can never be whole while such evil remains. The sickness from one rotten fruit can spread to blight a whole tree. Don't you dare tell me that the danger to my children is insignificant!'

'Forgive me, Portia. I meant no such insult to you, or to your family. I counted it a great honour to have met Kirrick and would do or say nothing that could offend his memory.'

'Yes, I know that, Isidris. Tiredness and frustration have given me a harsh tongue.'

'Then rest for the moment. We will talk again later. I know that you are anxious to be reunited with Merion and Olivia. But you will need your strength for that journey.'

'Now tell me,' Isidris began, when Portia sat before him some hours later. 'Your adventure in Wingland did not go according to our plans, is that not so?'

'We failed utterly,' replied the dispirited robin.

'Do not be so sure, Portia. You have planted a seed that may yet grow. But I do not believe that any bird living could have achieved any greater success on such a mission. And if the Creator decrees that it was not to be, then we must think again and make plans anew for our future. It may be that our hopes will not be realised for many a generation and we ourselves may all be dead when they come to fruition. All of this I cannot foresee. I have not the gift like Tomar. Perhaps that is why he is Great Owl and I am merely one of the troops.'

'How can you speak that way?' Portia blurted out, upset at Isidris' self-mockery. 'Throughout the land all the members of the Council of the Owls are held in the highest esteem. Do not doubt your worth to Birddom. It is one hundred-fold greater than my own.'

'You shame me with your courtesy, Portia. But

there is no advantage or benefit to be gained in an argument as to whose life is of greater value to Birddom. Let us just agree that, in the vast scheme of things, both of us remain utterly indispensable to her future and that, when we pass from this world, Birddom will diminish greatly!'

In spite of her misery and anxiety, Portia found herself laughing along with the snowy owl. It felt good to shed her burden, at least for a moment, and the merriment swept through her like a gale, purifying her spirits. Her eyes were bright and shining when she regained control of herself and looked at Isidris, and the owl felt glad at heart that such resilience still held sway in the little robin. She would have great need of it in the days and weeks to come.

'All of that, however, is hopefully far ahead of us,' Isidris continued. 'There are more immediate and pressing concerns. Another long journey now faces you, but do not be afraid. You will not have to face it alone. I know that Mickey would follow you to the ends of the earth, if it were asked of him. But, if you would accept my company, I would be honoured to fly north with you. My beak itches for action, and I believe that I could be of some help to my friend, Tomar.'

It was the bullfinch who spoke up, in typically forthright manner. 'I was chosen by the Council to be Portia's companion on any and all perilous journeys, and I believe that I have proved myself equal to the task. And, as for being of help to the

Great Owl, surely he charged you with the responsibility of leading Birddom in his absence. Is it meeting such responsibilities to go gallivanting across the country, as you suggest?'

'Well. It is a humbling experience to be put in my place by one so small in stature, if not in courage. You speak wisely, my friend. It seems that wisdom is not the prerogative of owls. Though inactivity grates with me, I will stay here and carry out my duties, as you say. Portia needs no other companion to ensure her safety. She could have no truer friend than you, Mickey. But enough talk. I have been properly put in my place. Yours is far from here, at the side of your children. Go now.'

The further south that Venga journeyed, the more dangerous that journey became. Magpies were truly not welcome in any part of the land, but it seemed that Birddom's vigilance was greater in its heartland. Venga was forced to proceed almost entirely under the cover of darkness, which held great perils of its own. Night was not a natural time for travelling, unless you were an owl, or a predator on the lookout for a tasty meal of magpie! The corvidae that he met were few and far between, and he learned little from them. To a bird, they were scared and showed scant concern for anything beyond their own survival. It took a great number of dispiriting encounters before Venga gleaned any news of Traska. The evil magpie was, it seemed, reviled even by his own kind for his cowardice in the Great Battle, where his abundant sense of self-preservation in avoiding any direct confrontation with their enemies was not viewed favourably. His name was spat out with scorn by the survivors of that conflict to whom Venga talked. It seemed that, once the battle was lost, Traska had fled and vanished without trace.

So, where could Traska have gone? Exhaustive questioning revealed nothing further concerning the evil magpie's probable whereabouts. The trail was utterly cold. It was hopeless. Venga, in his naiveté, had never even considered the possibility that he would not be able to find his foe. It had been at the very core of his existence, awake and asleep, since his birth. The confrontation. The fight to the death. The victory. And now he had failed even to find his adversary. Traska had completely disappeared. Dejection swamped the young magpie. Venga thought about his mother. She had placed her trust in him. His whole life was dedicated to her revenge. He could not, and would not, fail her.

So, Venga remained where he was, risking capture in pursuit of his destiny. He cast his net wider and finally made the attempt of finding information from sources beyond his own kind. Birddom's loathing of the corvidae – with good reason, he knew – precluded open discourse between the magpie and any member of the small bird populace.

Venga was forced to adopt similar though far

less brutal tactics than Traska, in order to elicit the information that he needed. Only by threats could he gain the necessary knowledge for his pursuit to succeed. But each act of aggression raised the stakes for Venga. His activities would very soon bring retribution upon his own head. The young magpie desperately needed a break.

Finally, when he had all but given up hope, Fortune smiled upon him. Fleeing the immediate vicinity of his enquiries when the owls began hunting for him, he travelled several miles to the north, before falling, exhausted, into a clump of bushes at the edge of a fast-flowing stream.

Anisse's shock, at seeing the magpie so close to her nest, was palpable. The grebe had suffered grievously at the wings of the corvidae, when she had aided Kirrick. The physical scars of the assault upon her were faded and healed, but, emotionally, she was still red-raw and bleeding. Her first thoughts were to kill the magpie while he slept. It would merely be justice, after all that had been done to her by his kind. But the grebe's essential goodness balked at such an act of barbarism. No matter the cost to herself, Anisse could not take another bird's life.

Venga's first impressions, upon waking, were of a needle-sharp beak and a glint of hatred in the grebe's eye.

'Why do you look at me like that?' the magpie asked. 'What injury have I done to you?'

Anisse was somewhat taken aback by the

magpie's tone of voice. It had a strength and directness that reminded her of her previous encounters with the band of magpies who had harmed her, and of their vicious leader in particular. But the voice held no threat. There was no trace of aggression in the questions that he asked. Anisse forced herself to meet his gaze and, on doing so, could immediately see that he had suffered much himself. His one good eye returned her open stare.

'He is not afraid, and he does not wish me to be so,' the grebe thought. 'You really ought to take greater care, traveller. These are not friendly regions for a magpie. Indeed, few places are. Your race has done much ill in the land.'

'While I draw breath I will always carry the regret inside me for the actions of my own kind. Birddom has suffered terrible loss. Much more so than I could ever have imagined before making my journey.'

Anisse could see the look of genuine sadness in Venga's solitary eye and she decided that here was one magpie that she should help, if she were able. 'You speak of a journey. From the look of you, it would seem to have been a perilous one indeed. Why have you taken the risk, when all of Birddom is set against you?'

'I could not do otherwise,' the magpie replied. 'There is one of my own kind – corrupt, evil, and iniquitous – that I must find and kill if I can. His name is Traska. He raped my mother.'

At first Venga thought that Anisse's sharply

hissing intake of breath was as a result of shock at the vile action of the magpie that he hunted. But he quickly realised that the grebe had recognised the name. 'You know this villain?' he asked.

'Better than I would ever have wished to,' she replied, showing him the scars of her encounters with that terrible bird.

'My wish to kill him for what he did to my mother, Katya, is strengthened by seeing the harm that he has done to you. He deserves to die!'

'I can scarcely take this all in!' Anisse breathed incredulously. 'Surely, the Creator works in mysterious ways, when magpie seeks retribution upon magpie. But you will need an extremely long beak to wreak your revenge from here, my friend!'

The young magpie's head snapped up. 'You know where he is?' he demanded.

'I know only that news has recently reached the Council of the Owls of a resurgence of mayhem and violence to the far north. It is thought to be Traska's work. The bird that you seek is there, not here.'

Shock and disbelief registered on Venga's face. Traska was in his home? His mother's home! It was too terrible. Katya's mission for her son had sent away her only protection. But how could they have foreseen that the danger would be right under their beaks? He must go now. Immediately. And pray that he would not be too late!

CHAPTER 13

The two hooded crows were massive. It seemed to Tomar that flight ought not to have been possible for ones so solidly built. But whatever they lacked in grace, they more than made up for in confidence – even arrogance. The old owl watched with Storne while the pair of crows made their leisurely approach. They would not be hurried and were disdainful of the eagles who had joined them on either side, in escort.

Finally, they alighted and hopped forward to face the Great Owl and the leader of the eagles. It was Finbar, in his position of loaned authority, who spoke. 'I bring a message from the King of this land.'

Storne started forward, angry at the presumption, but Tomar stilled him with a touch of his wing. 'And who may that be?' he asked, smiling.

'What sort of bird is it who does not know his King? I speak of Traska, King and Lord. Master of all that you survey – and much more. He sends greetings to his lowly subject, Tomar.'

'For which I thank him,' responded the owl, through gritted beak.

'I will convey your thanks. Or perhaps, better

still, you would care to express them to him in person? Traska invites you to meet with him. For some reason, he believes that someone who has lived so long may have knowledge that is worth learning. Though what a peasant can teach a king is beyond me.'

Finbar smirked at this insult to the Great Owl, but Tomar swallowed it whole and his expression did not change.

'I am always ready to instruct those who are errant in their ways, if I believe that they are capable of improvement. But I feel that I would be wasting my breath with your master.'

The steely edge in the owl's voice flustered the huge, but dull-witted crow.

'You must come. Traska demands it.' A thought then struck him and his self-confidence returned. 'Besides,' he continued, 'There are two others with him whom you will surely want to see again.'

Now it was Storne's turn to restrain his companion. Tomar shook his head several times from side to side, as he fought to regain his composure.

'You are right. I very much want to see my young charges again. It is so good of Traska to have looked after them for me. Are they well?'

'As well as can be expected!' snorted the giant crow. 'They are still alive, at least, but for how much longer I cannot be sure. That is entirely down to our King's mercy.'

'The Creator help them, then,' muttered Tomar,

under his breath. But to the crows he replied, 'I shall come with you now.'

Storne looked aghast at his ancient friend. 'You cannot . . .' he started.

Tomar shook his head. 'I must,' he stated, simply. 'We have no other choice.'

Still unaware of the peril that her young children faced, Portia flew, nevertheless, with a desperate urgency and concentration of will. The miles bled by. Each rest was begrudged, a raw wound to her nerves.

'Can't we go any faster?' she complained to her weary companion.

'Oh, sure. It's not as if we've done anything like travelling halfway round the world and back, is it? I'm flesh and blood, you know. And both of them are knackered!'

Portia cast a frustrated glance at Mickey, which softened when she saw the extent of his distress. 'You are right,' she said. 'Another half an hour will make no difference either way. Rest on, my dear friend.'

Mickey needed no second invitation, but slumped back against the trunk of the tree into which they had alighted, as if unable to support his own weight. Almost immediately, he fell asleep. Portia watched the bullfinch for a while. What a special, treasured friend he had become to her. She had asked so much of him, and he had always given her more.

'Let him sleep,' she told herself. 'We've still got such a long way to go, and who knows what we may face at the end of this particular journey? Oh, Tomar. Look after my children. I am so afraid for them.'

'Is this what you have come to? Mistreating children?' Tomar had never been face to face with Traska before and he was genuinely surprised at how ordinary the evil magpie looked. His deeds had magnified his physical persona in the mind of the Great Owl, but in the flesh he was unprepossessing. There was, however, no doubting the malevolence that flowed from the magpie. Tomar looked from Traska to his female companion. 'May The Creator forgive you!' he whispered, holding her transfixed with his terrible stare.

Breaking free with an effort, she cast her eyes downward, away from his accusing gaze. Katya had never in her life felt such shame. Her glance fell upon the two young robins, cowering under the threat of Finbar's raised claws.

'Let them go,' she begged. 'You've got what you want. There's no need to harm them further.'

'There's every need, if I say so!' snapped Traska. 'They are Kirrick's brats, and I am of a mind to dispose of them as I did their father.'

'You cannot allow this!' Tomar's tone caught Katya's attention once more.

'I cannot prevent it,' she sobbed miserably.

'I know that you are not an evil bird,' the owl

continued. 'How can you stand by this monster, and allow his cruelty to continue, after all that he did to you?'

'You stupid, witless old fool!' laughed Traska. 'That was all a fabrication. A device to lure you away, so that I could kidnap those pathetic little robins. To force you to come crawling to me!'

'No. Katya was not lying when she told me of your atrocities against her. No one is that good an actress.'

'My darling mate is the greatest pretender in the world!'

'How dare you! How dare you call me your mate!' Katya spat out the words with venom, as she glared at Traska. 'You *did* rape me! You stole my life. My joy. You extinguished everything that was good and decent within me. You smeared my soul with your filth. Corrupter! Violator! I hate you! You disgust me. Don't you dare call me your mate!'

The shock on Traska's face was unbounded. At first caught, open-beaked, he shook his head in utter disbelief at what he had heard. 'No. It's not possible. What are you saying? Katya, my love. I would never hurt you.'

'There's nothing left to hurt,' she replied. 'You left nothing. You took it all.'

'But when?' he stuttered, still unable to take it all in.

'You don't even remember!' she screamed at him. 'But why should you? You've gone through your whole life raping the world, in one form or another. Why should you remember one single act of savagery in such a spree?'

'I didn't know. I didn't. I love you, Katya.'

'You are incapable of love. You need to have a heart to feel it!'

Traska felt as if he had been suddenly plunged into a void. Cast adrift in total darkness. His ears rang with the harshness of her accusations.

'Your soul is in hell, Traska,' intoned Tomar into the silence. 'You are damned beyond redemption.'

The owl's condemning words sparked one last demonstration of the magpie's malevolence. 'Well, at least I can take these two with me!' Traska screeched, moving rapidly and menacingly towards Merion and Olivia.

Before Tomar could react, the vile magpie slashed at the pair with his talons, missing Olivia's head by the merest whisker. But it was Katya who responded. Inside her head, something snapped. All restraint was gone now, replaced by a primal savagery. With no thought for her own safety, no consciousness beyond an incoherent and terrible violence, Katya fell upon Traska in a killing rage. Her loathing gave her a strength well beyond her measure and the evil magpie fell back under her assault.

Traska was astonished and appalled. He loved her! Why was she doing this? He only wanted to hurt his enemies. But he had wounded the one who meant the most to him. The only one who meant anything in his life. And now she too hated him. Enough to want to kill him! It was too much to bear! Traska could not find the anger to fight back. He refused to use his superior strength and experience against her. Katya's fury was uncoordinated, and he found that he could avoid the potentially lethal blows from her beak and claws. But his passivity led to him receiving grievous wounds. Traska's head and neck dripped with blood as Katya relentlessly continued her attack. Her bitter anger was not assuaged by the sight of his blood. She wanted him dead. Wanted to rid the world of this disgusting creature.

Then, just when it seemed that she must succeed in her murderous attack, she suddenly found herself fighting for her life. It had finally dawned on Traska's ponderous henchmen that their leader was in danger. Slow-witted they may have been, but they were also immensely strong. Katya was no match for the four hooded crows who pulled her away from Traska and set upon her. The beautiful magpie was slaughtered in seconds. Traska stood motionless as Katya's body was torn apart in front of his eyes. Eyes that bled tears as she died. And, as he watched, every trace of cunning and malice disappeared from his stare, washed away by the horror of his love's murder. It was over in an instant, but, to Traska, Katya's death would play forever in his mind. Over and over. Blocking out all other thoughts. The violence. The rended flesh. The heart ripped from her beautiful body. And the pathetic remains, when the hooded crows had finished with her. She was gone! He had lost her. He had lost everything!

The four murdering crows looked to their leader for approbation. For thanks, even. After all, they had saved Traska's life, hadn't they? But the magpie remained totally still, rigid with shock. He was alone in the world once more and he did not know how he could bear it. Turning his back upon the appalling carnage that he had been forced to witness, Traska hopped slowly away.

While the hooded crows were squabbling over what little was left of Katya's body, Tomar rushed over to the two young robins and ushered them quietly away from the scene of the bloodshed. He feared that, at any moment, Traska would rouse himself from his stupor and raise the alarm. 'Are you all right, my dears? Can you fly?' Anxiety spread across the owl's face, as he looked at Merion's injured leg.

'I cannot walk, but I think that I can fly.'

'So like your father!' Tomar gasped at the sudden memory of Kirrick, attempting to suppress the laughter that threatened to sweep through his old frame. But he recovered himself quickly, aware of the inappropriateness of such a response in the face of ever-present danger. His eyes darted this way and that. 'We must go now. The blood-lust will soon be off these crows. But what they will do without Traska to lead them, I am not sure.'

The owl and the two tiny robins took to the air, heading back to Storne's mountain stronghold.

Traska watched them go. It did not matter any more. It was over. His life was over. Ashes, where once a bright fire burned. A fire that had threatened to engulf the whole world.

'Are you Traska?'

It was more of a challenge than a question. The evil magpie looked up at the bird who had just alighted in the tree beside him. A magpie like himself, but one with fire still in his belly. Traska looked into an eye, full of blazing hatred. And he knew. He could not have said why. But he knew with absolute certainty. The tiniest flame in the depths of his soul guttered once more to life. There was something left. Some hope. Someone to live for.

'My son,' he said.

'Where is my mother?' Venga asked, in tones as cold as the grave itself.

'She is dead, my son,' Traska replied. 'We are alone now. All that we have is each other.'

Venga's stare chilled him to the very core.

'I am your appointed executioner. My mother's death will not have been in vain if I fulfil my destiny. Katya will not be alone in death this day.'

CHAPTER 14

As the young magpie flew down to face him, Traska assessed his opponent. He certainly approved of what he saw.

'What a fine strong son I have,' he thought. 'Well built and muscular, yet agile too. From here, his beak looks razor-sharp. All in all, I'd prefer not to take a closer inspection, but it would seem that I have no choice.'

In the tree, and in flying to the ground, Venga had presented only his profile to his enemy. Now, as he turned to face Traska fully, the older magpie felt a mixture of emotions on seeing Venga's damaged eye. Sadness, that such a fine specimen should, after all, be flawed. Triumph, for now he knew, beyond doubt, that he could defeat the younger bird. And anger. Anger against the world. This feeling, above all, surged through his veins. Anger. For taking away Katya, whom he had loved. For forcing him to fight. To kill his son.

For a brief moment, Traska considered refusing to fight, allowing, instead, his son to dispatch him without opposition. But it went against the very grain of his existence. Traska's instinct for survival had been paramount since birth. His eyes flitted quickly around, assessing the lay of the land in the fighting zone. There was a large-enough area of open ground, sparse of vegetation and fairly even underfoot. He would keep the fight grounded. In the air, Venga would have superior agility and speed. On the ground, Traska could manoeuvre his foe into positions of disadvantage, because of the younger bird's visual impairment.

'Are you ready?' asked Venga, in a stern tone.

Hopping slightly sideways to maximise his opponent's disability, Traska rushed forward, lunging at Venga's shoulder and striking a telling blow. Retreating just as swiftly, he called out, 'Never do that again. If you live to fight another time, strike first, then talk!'

Traska nearly tripped over his own tail as Venga came at him, with startling speed and ferocity. The beak was every bit as sharp and deadly as the older magpie had feared and only desperate evasion allowed Traska to avoid its thrust to his heart. Side-stepping once again, the evil magpie sliced open a gash in Venga's cheek, drawing blood for the second time, without reply. But, if he had expected his son to become enraged at his initial failure, Traska was to be disappointed. Actually, what he felt was considerable pride, as he watched Venga gather his wits, regroup and begin to probe for weaknesses in the older bird's defences.

The battle raged back and forth, as beaks flashed and talons ripped. Venga was suddenly aware of an audience. He quailed a little to see the massive hunched backs of the hooded crows, as they crowded around the arena to watch the fight.

'One against one,' he cawed out to Traska.

'Of course, my son. I wouldn't have it any other way.' The older magpie danced on his toes, never taking his eyes off his opponent, but calling out for all to hear, 'He's mine. No one is to kill him but me! I don't need any help with this young whelp!'

The crows laughed and jeered in a ragged and raucous chorus of malice. But Venga ignored them all, focusing on the job in hand. Seeing this, Traska felt a frisson of fear. Perhaps he had underestimated his foe. The boy certainly seemed determined enough. But that eye! 'That's it,' he counselled himself. 'Concentrate on that eye. That weakness will be his downfall. He cannot defeat you with one eye missing.'

Traska's reverie was savagely interrupted. Once again, he had misjudged the younger magpie's speed and, this time, a talon tore into his flank. An inch lower and his leg would have been maimed. As it was, the wound merely served to remind Traska of the size of the task that he faced. He began a strategy of constant movement, always in one direction, keeping the battle in circular motion and only changing direction when precipitating a sudden, brutal attack. In and out. Drawing blood. Weakening his enemy by degrees. Never getting close for too long. Blood now covered Venga from head to foot, and Traska marvelled at the strength of his son. 'Hell, but the boy has got courage!' he smiled.

But it was the sight of that smile, which Venga misconstrued as mockery, which finally caused that courage to fail. Tears flowed as despair took hold at last, and he rushed clumsily at the evil magpie. 'Die!' he screamed, as he put his remaining strength into that last, desperate charge.

It was Traska's change of direction that undid him. Venga had expected his opponent to dodge once more to the right, keeping him on the younger bird's vulnerable left flank. But, too late, he realised Traska's intention. Propelled un-stoppably by the force of his headlong charge, Venga was unable to turn away, as the older magpie sidestepped in the opposite direction and lunged with his own, cruelly-sharp beak.

Venga screamed in terrible agony, as total dark-ness closed in upon him. Blinded, he stumbled around the clearing, groping pathetically for his enemy. Traska stepped back and watched his son's torment, sickened to the very pit of his stomach. He knew that it would be a kindness to his son to end it there. One blow would be enough, now that Venga was defenceless. He should give him an honourable death. The boy had earned that, at the very least.

Traska turned his back upon the sight of Venga's stumbling, shambling agony. 'Finish it!' he called to his assembled cohorts. Then he took to the air and flapped exhaustedly away.

The reunion between mother and children was a heart-warming sight for the old owl. He had made so many misjudgements and thanked the Creator that no one else had been made to pay too dearly for his mistakes. Merion's leg would mend quickly enough and neither young robin seemed to be at all traumatised by their experiences. Indeed, like all young children, they competed with each other in the telling of their adventures, their eyes gleaming with excitement as the words flooded out. Portia hugged the pair of them to her breast. Tomar smiled with satisfaction, before withdrawing to allow the family some privacy.

Thus it was from Mickey, the bullfinch, that Tomar learned about his emissaries' adventures in Wingland, and of the obstinate refusal of the small bird population there to uproot and fly to a new home in Birddom.

'I am saddened by the outcome. But it should not have been wholly unexpected. The attempt had to be made and no two birds could have tried harder than yourselves to make a success of your mission. The sacrifices that you made will not be forgotten, and the whole of Birddom is grateful to you for your unstinting efforts. I will tell Portia so later. For now, she has her children to comfort her and I would not intrude upon their reunion.

But we will wish to honour you both. You are a

pair of fine, brave birds, and a credit to your home-land. You are living proof that it is not necessary to be big in size, as long as your heart is large enough. But it must be said that the future is very bleak for Birddom. We needed a massive influx of small birds to redress the natural balance that Slyekin tried, so terribly, to destroy. And it galls me to think that he may, after all, have succeeded in at least one part of his evil plan.' Worry furrowed the owl's brow, and he looked very old indeed.

Mickey was extremely concerned for his companion. 'Tomar, my friend. You must rest. You look absolutely done in! Have you eaten?'

'There's been too much of importance to be done for me to worry about my stomach!' the old owl laughed.

'Well. It'd be a fine thing for Birddom if it lost its leader, the finest mind in all the land, because he forgot to feed himself!'

'You are right once again, Mickey, and your wisdom shames me. I will eat, then rest. Tomorrow is soon enough to begin the future of Birddom.'

The venerable members of the Council of the Owls sat once more in the sacred oak trees ringing the clearing of the council chamber. The original eight, who had presided over the proceedings at the inaugural meeting after the troubles, were supplemented by four eager young owls. They had each been inducted with solemnity into the Council of the Owls and had taken their places alongside their elders. The strength of the Council was now complete once more and, judging by the brightness of eye and quickness of mind of this younger generation, its future seemed assured.

Tomar, the Great Owl, looked around the circle, with pride and pleasure. 'If only the future of Birddom looked so healthy,' he mused. Then, casting aside these doubts, he began to speak.

'My friends and fellow members of the Council of the Owls. We are met here today with two purposes. The first is to honour the very brave and resolute pair that stand before you.'

Twelve pairs of unblinking eyes focused on the robin and bullfinch in the centre of the ring.

'Portia and Mickey were unable to accomplish the task that we, the Council, set for them. But then we all knew just how difficult to achieve that task would be. Birddom could not have made a better choice for its emissaries, and I am proud of their efforts.'

A chorus of deep, sonorous voices joined the Great Owl's in voicing their thanks and support for the robin and the bullfinch. Tomar raised his wing for silence, then continued, 'But now we have to face the facts. The task remains unfinished. Birddom is in grave danger. Unless a way can be found to entice small birds to our shores in huge numbers, the future is very bleak. The natural order is crucial to continuance of life as we desire it. We have already committed ourselves to one breaking of this natural law, though I maintain

340

that it was crucial to our success against Slyekin, and I refuse to rescind my promise. We will stand by our decision not to take any insect for food, at least while I remain Great Owl, and, I hope, well beyond that, if the Council wishes to retain its honour.

Which brings us to our second purpose. Perhaps our newer members will be able to think of a way for our aims to be achieved. Fresh minds with fresh ideas are always welcome. Do not be afraid to speak up.'

In fact, most of the owls voiced their opinions which were, in turn, discussed with the utmost seriousness by the entire Council. Then, without exception, they were rejected as unworkable. A cloud of depression settled over the Council ring, as the realisation dawned upon everyone there that they had truly only had one shot. One chance of success. And that that attempt had failed.

Then one of the younger owls, who, feeling less sure of himself, had held back, finally found the courage to speak up. 'Perhaps we could force small birds to come to Birddom. Our need is desperate and maybe desperate measures are called for!'

'May time teach you the folly of those words!' responded Tomar, angrily. 'Yours is an inauspicious start as a member of our Council, if you propose violence against your fellows in the bird world. Would you become like the magpies?'

'Forgive me, Tomar,' answered the young owl,

taken aback by the Great Owl's anger. 'My nervousness has made my brain and my tongue clumsy. I would relinquish my position on the Council, newly gained and treasured, before I willingly harmed one of my kin. I meant only that a larger, more imposing entourage might make the attempt at persuasion more effectively. Not meaning any disrespect to our honoured guests, who tried so valiantly, in their turn.'

'Well spoken,' Tomar said. 'We may make a Council member out of you yet. I understand your thinking more clearly now and, although I personally would baulk at such an idea, we must open up the discussion to the whole Council. Perhaps the time has come for more forceful measures, if we are to safeguard the future of Birddom as somewhere . . .'

Tomar's voice trailed off in distracted fashion and every head turned in the direction of his stare. Portia was gazing into the sky and cheeping in excitement. Mickey, by her side, was jumping up and down, crying out, 'It's Swoop! It's Swoop!'

And, in confirmation, the rapidly approaching dot in the sky transformed into the fast-flying swallow, as she sped towards the clearing. The owls all held their breath, as if aware that the arrival was a portentous one. Indeed, as Swoop dropped among them, she was already calling out her news:

'They are coming!'

*   *   *

The flight south took them over the ancient site where, long ago, a natural disaster had befallen Birddom. A virulent plague brought to the shores of the land by insects. Only the wisdom and swift actions of Eamonn, then the Great Owl, had saved Birddom, by preventing the spread of the plague. Now Nature, it seemed, had taken a hand again, but this time in Wingland. Swoop had regaled the Council with stories of terrible fires, which raged, unchecked, through the countryside there. Whole habitats had been consumed by the flames.

And it seemed that Man had abandoned the rural areas almost entirely to its ferocity. Trenches had been dug and large tracts of land cleared, wherever the fire had threatened urban clusters. But no attempt had been made to quell the flames. Man had merely decided to let the fire burn itself out. And, in doing so, had condemned millions of creatures to death. Birds can fly, however, and fly they did. With the fires at their backs, they flew further north and west until, at last, no other choice remained for them but to abandon their homelands altogether.

Tomar and Portia sat together in a gnarled horse-chestnut tree and watched them come. The horizon from side to side, as far as they could see, was dark, and the cloud approached ever nearer, blotting out the sun and plunging Birddom into the preternatural gloom of evening. The owl's keen sight began to distinguish between individual birds, whilst the massive flock were still some distance away. So many! Every species imaginable. Birds that had been indigenous to Birddom flying alongside more-exotic varieties. And all coming, as if in answer to his prayers. The Great Owl smiled and turned to Portia, tears in his eyes and momentarily unable to speak through his emotion.

She nodded her comprehension. 'Birddom is whole once more, my dear friend. I only wish that Kirrick was here to see this.'

The owl and robin looked to a spot nearby, where they could see the pair of young robins, dancing around with unconfined joy, as the myriad of birds flew overhead. Tomar found his voice once more.

'Perhaps he is, Portia. Perhaps he is.'

EPILOGUE

'Dad!' shouted the young boy, in his excitement. 'I got one! I got one!'

'What's all the commotion about?' asked his father, as the boy rushed towards him, carrying something heavy. It was the body of a magpie.

'I shot it, Dad. I really did! Killed it stone dead, with just one shot. I think it's the rotten magpie who hurt Jenny. And I killed it!'

The boy held up the carcass of the dead bird for his father's inspection. In spite of the profusion of blood which coated much of the plumage, it was unmistakable as a magpie. The head lolled, limp and lifeless near the ground, as the boy held on to the bird's feet. The child's stature meant that it had been unceremoniously bumped along the ground, as he had hurried towards his father. The man took the dead magpie from his son and inspected it closely.

'No, lad. This is not the one. Look here, this one's still got both his eyes, though much good they'll do him now. That bastard only had one, remember? Never mind, though. As far as I'm

345

concerned, the only good magpie is a dead magpie. I'm sure that the world will be a better place without this one in it!'

And, so saying, the man swung his arm in an arc and tossed the inert body high into the air. The bright sunlight glinted on black, white and blue, as the bird's carcass spiralled, before falling to earth among the undergrowth.

Discarded. Unwanted. And unloved.